The Case

of the

Jewel Covered Cat Statues

Also by Cindy Vincent

The Case of the Cat Show Princess:
A Buckley and Bogey Cat Detective Caper

The Case of the Crafty Christmas Crooks:
A Buckley and Bogey Cat Detective Caper

The Mystery of the Missing Ming:
A Daisy Diamond Detective Novel

The Case of the Rising Star Ruby:
A Daisy Diamond Detective Novel

Makeover For Murder:
A Kate Bundeen Mystery

Cats Are Part of His Kingdom, Too:
33 Daily Devotions to Show God's Love

The Case
of the
Jewel Covered Cat Statues

A Buckley and Bogey
Cat Detective Caper

Cindy Vincent

Whodunit Press
Houston   Bozeman

The Case of the Jewel Covered Cat Statues

A Buckley and Bogey Cat Detective Caper

Published by Whodunit Press

A Division of Mysteries by Vincent, LLC

For information, please contact:

Whodunit Press

c/o Mysteries by Vincent

Mysteriesbyvincent.com

ISBN: 978-1-932169-28-7

Printed in the United States of America

Dedication

To my friends, the real treasures in my life.

CHAPTER 1

Holy Mackerel! There I was, sitting in our living room, when I suddenly noticed a fishpond right in the middle of the floor. Funny, but I sure didn't remember *that* being there before! I tiptoed over to the edge and saw lots of tiny fish swimming around in the water. Now my brother, Bogart, joined me and sat on the other side of the pond. Together we stuck our paws in the cool water, grabbed some fish and pulled them out.

Before long, we had a whole pile of fish, all ready for a nice lunch. Except these fish didn't exactly look like regular fish. No, they looked a whole lot like the fish-flavored cat treats we usually eat.

That's when I felt someone shaking my shoulder. "Wake up, kid. Look alive."

It was Bogart, or Bogey, as I call him. Not only are we brothers, but we're best friends and cat detectives, too.

I lifted my head and glanced around. But there wasn't a fishpond in sight. And I wasn't even in the living room. Instead, I was lying right on top of our Mom's desk, in her home office.

It turned out the whole thing had been nothing but a dream!

I sighed and laid my head back down. Then I shut my eyes really tight and tried to go back to sleep. Back to my dream. After all, how often does a guy get to see a fishpond smack dab in the middle of the living room?

"C'mon, kid," Bogey said. "Rise and shine."

I pried one eye open and saw him waving a fish-flavored cat treat right in front of my nose.

He grinned at me. "Here you go, kid. This'll get you going."

I had to say, that cat treat smelled pretty good.

Bogey dropped it next to me and helped himself to one from a foil pouch.

I opened my other eye. "I had the best dream."

Bogey took another treat and then stashed the pouch into a vase on the desk. "You can tell me all about it while we run our rounds, kid. Let's get a move on."

I rolled onto my feet. "I know, I know. We always run extra surveillance on Saturday nights. Because burglars like to stay out late on Saturday nights."

"You got it, kid," Bogey said.

He took one last glance at the computer screen where he'd been working. The glow from the screen gave off the only light in our Mom's office downstairs. The rest of the house was completely dark, while our human family slept upstairs.

Bogey tilted his ears toward the hallway and then moved over to the edge of the desk. I could tell he was ready to roll. Sometimes I was amazed at how different Bogey and I really are. Sure, we're both black cats with big, gold eyes. But he's thin and wiry, and he can run so fast that some say he can even fly.

As for me, well, I'm a Maine Coon cat. Maine Coon cats are very, very large. And I do mean large! My paws and tail are gigantic, and my fur sticks out a mile wide. Especially since I've got three layers of the stuff. I'm just two years old, so you might say I'm still a growing boy.

It seems like I barely get used to my big paws when they grow some more. No matter how hard I try, I still can't get them to go exactly where I want them to go. When I want them to go there.

But I did manage to scoop up the cat treat Bogey had dropped for me. I popped it into my mouth and glanced at the computer to see what Bogey had been looking at.

Bogey and I use the computer mostly at night, when our family is asleep. Especially since we opened the Buckley and Bogey Cat Detective Agency on the Internet not long ago.

Now the screen was filled with a news story from our town paper, *The St. Gertrude Times.* The title read, "Rare Jeweled Statues to Go On Display at St. Gertrude Museum. Items in Daunton Exhibit Nearly 150 Years Old."

Right below the title were a bunch of pictures that showed all kinds of little statues. Some looked like they were carved out of rocks, and some looked like they'd been made from gold and silver. There were dogs and birds and rabbits. There were turtles and elephants and horses. Even though the statues were all different, they had one thing in common — they were decorated with jewels. Lots and lots of jewels. And those jewels made the little statues very, very sparkly.

Holy Catnip!

I pointed to the computer screen. "Wow, Bogey, those statues are so beautiful!"

Bogey nodded. "Yup, kid, you got it. And they're going on display at our museum. The lady who owns them lives right here in St. Gertrude."

Right then, I'm sure my eyes went about as wide as my food dish. "She does?"

Bogey sat back and flexed the claws on his right paw. "Oh yeah, kid. She's related to the guy who made them. He was one of the first people who lived in St. Gertrude."

I blinked a couple of times. "So I guess he must have passed this stuff down through his family."

Bogey shook his head. "Nope, kid. He sold most of them right after he made 'em. It was part of his business."

"So how did she get all those statues?" I asked.

Bogey stood up and stretched his hind legs. "She did some detective work of her own, kid. She tracked them down and found the people who owned them. She searched all over the world and bought all the pieces she could get. It probably took her a while."

"Oh . . ." I tried to put a paw to my chin, but I ended up poking myself in the mouth instead. "So she hunted for those little statues, kind of like we hunt down the bad guys."

Bogey grinned. "Something like that, kid. But I wonder why she's letting them go on display. According to the article, she usually keeps them locked up tight."

Suddenly my heart started to pound. "Maybe we could go see them! I wonder if they let cats into the Museum."

Bogey looked past the office doors and out toward the front entryway of our really old house. "Cats probably aren't welcome there, kid. Not usually, anyway. But that shouldn't be a problem. We'll figure out a way to get in. You can bet we'll be heading to that museum before long."

I turned and stared at my brother. "We will?"

His ears tilted forward. "Yup, kid. I've got a bad feeling about all this. Something's fishy here."

I sniffed the air. "It is? I don't smell any fish."

Especially since we'd already eaten our cat treats and Bogey had put the bag away.

Bogey shook his head. "Just an expression, kid. Just an expression. It means 'something is suspicious.'"

Before I could ask more, he jumped down to the floor. "Time to put it in gear, kid. We've got a schedule with our names on it."

"Aye, aye!" I tried to salute him, but I only ended up

poking myself in the ear with my huge paw.

Luckily he'd already trotted into the hallway and didn't see me. I jumped off the desk and ran after him.

Part of our job as cat detectives is to run surveillance on our house every night. And if you don't know what the word "surveillance" means, well . . . like my brother would say . . . don't sweat it. I didn't know what it meant either. Not until I got adopted from the cat shelter and came to live here with my forever family. That's when Bogey took me under his paw and taught me everything he knows about the cat detective business. He's an expert, and he's been a cat detective ever since he got adopted from the cat shelter years ago. Bogey told me that "surveillance" is a fancy word for checking out the whole house. Just to make sure everything is okay. And to keep our family safe.

And believe me, I wanted to do everything I could to keep my family safe. After all, they gave me a home and plenty of food to eat. Not to mention, lots and lots of love. Plus, my human Mom and Dad are always happy to cuddle me. So is my human sister, twelve-year-old Gracie. So I'm happy to repay the favor and earn my keep. Especially since I'd once been out on the mean streets and didn't know where my next meal was coming from.

I caught up to Bogey in the front entryway and we took off, running side by side. Together we checked out doors and windows and all around the main floor of the house. We made sure everything was locked and secure, exactly the way it was supposed to be.

Plus we took a good "sniff" wherever we went. A cat can sure learn a lot by smelling things. Cats have a really good sense of smell, and we can also pretty much see in the dark. That's why it didn't bother us that our whole house was dark while our human family slept upstairs.

We finished our downstairs run and headed toward the staircase. Even though I've probably run surveillance a million times, it still makes me kind of nervous. A guy just never knows what he might run into. So I always keep my senses on full alert, to be ready to spring into action.

Or, at least I *try* to be ready to spring into action.

Yet somehow it didn't actually work out that way tonight. Not when we saw a white streak zip down the hallway. That same streak turned and flew straight into our Mom's office.

Holy Mackerel!

But instead of springing into action, I just sort of froze in my tracks. I could hardly breathe.

"What was that?" I whispered to my brother. "A ghost?"

In all my training as a cat detective, Bogey had never told me anything about ghosts. And, to tell you the truth, even the thought of a ghost scared me.

Beside me, Bogey just rolled his eyes and flopped onto the floor. "Dames. I can never make heads nor tails of 'em, kid."

"Dames?" I managed to squeak. "Um, Bogey . . . shouldn't we go investigate this?"

Bogey pointed toward our Mom's office. "Knock yourself out, kid."

By now I was shaking in my paws. "Aren't you coming with me?"

Bogey shook his head. "Nope, kid. I think you can handle this one on your own."

I gulped. Did Bogey really want me to investigate this by myself? Sure, I had a little experience under my belt, and I'd even helped solve a big case or two. But that didn't mean I was ready to investigate something like a ghost on my own.

I glanced at my brother again. But he just grinned and nodded toward the office.

Well, I guess that answered that. I guess it was all up to me to go check things out. So I tiptoed as quietly as I could to the open French doors of the office. All the while, I wondered if this ghost was going to jump out and yell, "Boo!" Or scream like ghosts do in movies.

Not that it mattered. My heart was pounding so loud I probably wouldn't have heard a ghost scream anyway.

I glanced inside the room, but I didn't see any white streak. Or a ghost, either. So I slowly stepped into the office, moving one paw at a time. To tell you the truth, I didn't know what I'd do if that white streak headed straight for me. I wasn't really sure how cat detectives were supposed to handle ghosts.

I moved toward my Mom's desk. Then I carefully tiptoed around the corner.

Just in time to see the white streak go straight up the tallest bookcase.

Every strand of fur on my body stood on end.

Especially when that white streak turned and stared down at me.

With big, green eyes.

It was the Princess.

Now I wasn't sure if my heart was pounding because I was scared, or because my heart always pounded when she looked at me like that.

"Hello, Buckley," she said. "Would you like to join me? The view up here is lovely."

The Princess, or Lexie, as the humans call her, was the newest cat to join our family. She was all white, and a kind of cat called a Turkish Angora. She had once been a show cat who was expected to be prim and perfect. But since she'd come to live with us, well, she acted a whole lot more free. She usually raced around the house at lightning speed. Plus she smiled a lot these days.

"Thanks, Princess," I told her. "Maybe later. Right now Bogey and I are on our rounds."

She tilted her head and slowly blinked her eyes at me. "I'm so glad you're here to protect us, Buckley."

Right about then I felt the room start to spin. For some reason I had a hard time breathing. I nodded goodbye and barely managed to get out to the hallway before I flopped onto the floor.

Bogey was right there with a cat treat in his paw. He waved it over my nose. "I told you, kid. Dames."

"Dames," I murmured.

"Here," he said. "Take this and let's get rolling."

I took a few deep breaths and munched on the cat treat. Then I wobbled onto my legs and nodded to Bogey. Seconds later I was running behind him to the staircase.

We were halfway up when it happened.

The phone rang.

Let me tell you, I've learned a lot of things since I came to live in this house. Lots and lots of things. And one of the things I've learned is that it's never good when the phone rings in the middle of the night. Humans don't exactly call each other to chat right then. No, it usually means there is some kind of an emergency.

"C'mon, kid," Bogey hollered. "I smell trouble. We've gotta check this out!"

I ran behind him as he raced up the stairs and into our Mom and Dad's room. Our Dad flipped on his bedside lamp and picked up the phone. Beside him, our Mom moaned and rolled over.

I wonder if she'd been dreaming about a fishpond, too.

"Yes, this is Mike Abernathy," our Dad said into the phone. "Uh-huh, okay." Then he suddenly sat up straight in bed. "It did?" he practically shouted.

Next he spoke six numbers into the phone. The alarm code to our Mom's store.

He combed his fingers through his blond hair while he listened for a second or two. Finally, he said, "We'll be right there, Phoebe."

I looked at my brother. "Did he say 'Phoebe?'"

Bogey nodded. "Yup, kid, he did."

Right away, Bogey and I knew who Phoebe was. Her full name is Officer Phoebe Smiley, and she works for the St. Gertrude Police Department. We'd met up with her on a couple of cases, and we liked her a lot. Though like most humans, she really had no idea that we were actually the ones who had solved the cases.

Probably because cats always switch to cat language whenever humans are around. Plus, some humans have no clue what cats are capable of.

Now our Mom woke up. "What's going on, honey?"

"It's your store," our Dad told her. "The burglar alarm went off."

Her dark eyes went wide. "Oh no!"

Our Mom owns Abigail's Antiques, the best antique store in downtown St. Gertrude. She loves her store, and she works very hard running it. Sometimes she even takes us to work with her, but only if she has time. Then she loads us up in our pet carriers, and we go spend the day at her shop. Bogey and I always enjoy our time there.

Our Dad slid out of bed. "Phoebe wants one of us to head down there and take a look. To make sure nothing was stolen."

Our Mom jumped up and stretched. "Better let me go."

Our Dad frowned. "I don't want you alone out there if burglars are running around." His blue eyes were full of worry.

"I'll be fine," she told him. "Phoebe and the police will be there. Plus I'm the only one who'll know if anything is missing."

"Well . . ." our Dad started to say.

Our Mom kissed him on the cheek. "We can't both go. One of us has to stay here with Gracie."

"Okay," he agreed. "But call me as soon as you know anything. And why don't you take my truck instead of your car? In case you want to cart anything back home."

"I will," our Mom said before she pulled her long dark hair into a ponytail. Then she ran to get dressed.

A few seconds later, the alarm company called, too.

While our Dad took the call, Bogey glanced at the door.

"Our Dad doesn't need to worry about our Mom, kid," he said.

I turned to my brother. "He doesn't?"

Bogey shook his head. "Nope, kid. Because we'll be going with her."

Now *my* eyes went wide. Really wide. "We will?"

He motioned toward the door. "Yup, kid. We've got to investigate."

Before I could ask more, Bogey turned and raced out of the room. I tried to keep up with him.

My paws felt a little wobbly. "B-b-but, our Mom will never take us to her store in the middle of the night."

"Don't sweat it, kid," Bogey yelled over his shoulder. "I've got it covered."

He did? But how? Bogey and I sure couldn't run all the way downtown. Plus, well, we weren't really supposed to go outside. Especially since we were supposed to be housecats.

So how in the world did he plan to get us to her store?

What did Bogey have up his paw?

Holy Mackerel!

CHAPTER 2

Holy Catnip! I chased after Bogey as he raced down the upstairs hallway. I was just dying to know how we were going to get to our Mom's antique store! I finally caught up with him when he came to a screeching halt at the top of the stairs.

That's where we ran into Lil Bits, another former shelter cat who lives at our house. But when I say we ran into her, well, I don't mean we *actually* ran into her. Lil is a kind of cat called a British Shorthair. She is white with black spots and she looks sort of like a linebacker. Even though I'm a big guy, I wouldn't want to run into her. And I wouldn't want to get tackled by her, either.

She nodded to us. "Good evening, Detectives Bogart and Buckley. I heard the telephone ring. I suspect there is trouble."

Lil always talked to us like that. She called me "Detective Buckley," and she treated me with a lot of respect. It's been said that she used to be one of the best cat detectives in St. Gertrude. But she retired mysteriously one day, and no one knows why. She only recently came back to the business, to help Bogey and me when we needed her. Even so, she spends most of her nights in Gracie's room, watching over her.

Bogey glanced back at our Mom and Dad's bedroom. "I'm afraid so, Lil. The alarm went off at our Mom's store. Our Mom is about to go down there and meet Officer Phoebe."

Lil looked from Bogey to me. "Sounds like it needs to be investigated by cat detectives, too. Are you headed there now?"

"Yup," Bogey told her. "We're on our way."

We were?

My breath caught in my throat for a moment. I really wanted to ask Bogey more questions, but I didn't want to look like a big baby in front of Lil. After all, I was the junior detective in the bunch. I didn't exactly want to advertise it.

"Good call," Lil told him. "I would be happy to help, Detective Bogart."

Bogey grinned. "That'd be great, Lil. Our Mom is taking our Dad's truck."

"Very good," Lil nodded. "I assume you'll be hitching a ride with her. I'll hold the door to the garage open long enough for you to get through. Then you can take it from there. But it wouldn't be good if you boys got slammed in the truck door."

Boy, she could say that again! I shuddered at the thought.

"Thanks, Lil," Bogey told her. "And don't worry, we can zoom right into the truck. She won't even know we're there."

Now he turned to me. "Right, kid?"

My mouth fell open wide. I still wasn't sure what Bogey had in mind. But he and Lil seemed to know exactly what the other one was talking about. Unfortunately, I was the only one who seemed to be in the dark. Maybe it was because Bogey and Lil both had a lot of experience as cat detectives. And I was barely more than a rookie.

So I just said, "Aye, aye."

I tried to salute Bogey and Lil, but I only ended up poking myself in the nose. Lucky for me, they'd already turned and headed down the stairs.

I raced after them. Once we hit the hardwood floor of the main level, we zoomed into the kitchen. We didn't stop until we got to the door that led to the garage. Then we all hid behind the wall across from the door.

"Okay, kid," Bogey whispered. "This is going to go quick."

My paws started to shake. "But . . . um . . . our Mom won't have time to get our pet carriers out and load us into the truck . . ."

"We've gotta make a run for it, kid," Bogey told me.

"You mean . . .?" I gulped.

"Yup, kid," Bogey nodded. "We're going to zoom out when our Mom opens the door. Lil will hold it open as long as she can. That'll give us a few more seconds to get through. Then we'll fly into the truck when our Mom opens the driver's side door."

My heart pounded in my throat. "Um . . . we will?"

Bogey glanced back into the kitchen. "That's right, kid. She's so tired, she won't even know we're there."

"B-b-but . . . shouldn't we talk about this first?" I glanced around our house. I sure did like our house. I sure would have liked to stay in our house for the rest of the night. Especially since there might be burglars running around outside.

Bogey put a paw on my shoulder. "No time for dilly-dallying, kid. Timing is everything. When I say 'go,' you've got to go. No stalling."

Now Lil turned to me. "You can do this, Detective Buckley. Just give it all you've got. Don't hold back."

"Um . . . okay," I managed to squeak out.

Suddenly I felt like I had a whole bunch of butterflies inside my stomach. And they all seemed to be fluttering at once. I was about to suggest that maybe I should stay home and keep a lookout here. But I didn't get a chance. Not when we heard our Mom's footsteps headed our way.

"Okay, everyone, this is it!" Bogey whispered.

I barely had time to breathe before our Mom got to the door. She grabbed the doorknob and pulled that door open wide. She stepped through and Lil jumped into place. Lil pushed her wide body against the door and planted her stout paws on the hardwood. Even so, she was no match for the heavy wooden door. It started to close slowly anyway, pushing her ahead.

"Run, kid! Now!" Bogey hollered.

Let me tell you, right then and there, I wanted to turn around and run the other way. I wanted to stay in my nice warm house where I was safe and sound.

Bogey sprinted through the opening, just inches from our Mom's feet. In a split second, he'd made it to the truck and was ready to jump in.

But all I could see was that solid wood door, starting to close right in front of my eyes.

"Go, go, go, kid!" Bogey hollered.

"Leap of faith, Detective," Lil managed to sputter as she worked hard to keep that door from slamming shut.

I don't know how I gathered the courage, but somehow I did. I took a deep breath and scampered through what little opening was left. Lil couldn't hold it any longer, and she had to jump out of the way. The edge of the door caught a few hairs on the tip of my tail as it slammed shut.

But I didn't let that stop me. By now our Mom was pulling the door to the truck open. I flew straight through the garage. Then I leaped inside the truck and onto the front floor. Bogey was on my tail. He barely made it up into the truck before our Mom put her foot inside.

"Into the backseat, kid!" Bogey whispered.

So we both jumped in the back and hid down on the floorboard.

Only seconds before our Mom got in and pulled her door shut with a loud *whump*! Then she pushed the garage door opener and the big, outer door roared to life.

It went up and our Mom started the engine.

I glanced across at my brother and he grinned back at me.

"Good job, kid," he said. "You got into the truck faster than I did. You're really getting the hang of this business."

I was?

Sometimes I felt like I knew what I was doing. And other times it seemed like I didn't have a clue. But one day I hoped to be as good a cat detective as Bogey. And Lil.

Bogey found a bag of cat treats hidden under the front seat. He passed one to me and then took one for himself.

I was so nervous I could hardly even eat. There we were, headed to our Mom's store. Just to check out the alarm that had gone off. And our Mom didn't even know we were along for the ride.

"Okay, kid," Bogey said. "Here's the drill. We've gotta do this all over again."

"We do?" I hung on as our Mom made a turn onto another street. I noticed she didn't take the turn as fast as she usually did.

Bogey just rolled with the curve. "That's right, kid. When she opens the truck door, we zoom out. And when she opens the door to her store . . ."

"We run in," I nodded to Bogey.

Bogey gave me a paw bump. "You got it, kid. You got it."

I glanced up and out the window. Above me, I could see streetlights passing by. Only those streetlights weren't shining as brightly as they normally did. Instead they looked kind of hazy and funny. That's when I realized it was foggy out. And though cats can see in the dark, they can't see in the fog so well.

To tell you the truth, I never really liked the fog very much. It always seemed sort of frightening and creepy to me.

And tonight that fog seemed extra creepy. Especially since we were out investigating in the middle of the night. Who knew what we might find at our Mom's store?

Holy Mackerel!

All of a sudden, I really missed my house.

I gulped and tried not to act as scared on the outside as I was on the inside.

"How are we going to get home?" I asked Bogey.

He passed me another treat. "After we look around, kid, we'll let our Mom know we're there. Then she'll take us home with her."

I had to say, I sure liked that idea. I didn't want to get stuck at her store for the rest of the night. Even though she had everything set up in the back room for us. We had cat beds and a food and water dish. We had toys and cat treats and everything a cat could want. Plus the people who worked for her were really nice to us.

Even so, something had set that burglar alarm off. And if it was a real burglar, I sure didn't want to be around if they tried to break in again.

After all, we'd had some experience with burglars on our last case. And let me tell you, I wouldn't mind if I never came across another burglar again!

I glanced at my brother. He looked like he was almost enjoying himself.

Our Mom took another turn. The fog had grown thicker, and she slowed the truck way down. Seconds later, we could see hazy red and blue lights flashing all around us.

"We must be in the alley, kid," Bogey whispered. "I'm guessing there is more than one police car here. So look alive. Follow my lead and stay on my tail. This is gonna go fast. We'll go right out under our Mom's feet when she starts to get out of the truck."

Our Mom hit the brakes a little harder than she usually does, and Bogey and I both fell forward. But we dug our claws into the carpet so we didn't hit the seats in front of us.

Now Bogey motioned for me to crouch down, ready to spring into action. And I did just that. After all, we only had a few seconds to get outside after our Mom opened her truck door!

Our Mom put the truck in park and turned off the key. She unlocked her door and started to push it open.

Bogey signaled to me. Our Mom had barely leaned over in her seat and put one foot outside. That's when Bogey smoothly slid onto the seat and then to the floorboard. He slipped out the opening before her foot even touched the ground. I was right behind him, moving just like he'd told me to.

"Over here, kid," Bogey whispered. "Follow me."

Together we ran and hid behind one of the truck's tires, seconds before our Mom slammed the truck door shut.

"Keep your eyes peeled, kid," he said.

That wasn't going to be easy on a night like tonight. Not when we could barely see ten feet in front of us.

We peeked around the tire and saw our Mom join Officer Phoebe.

"Some night," our Mom said. "What do they call weather like this? A pea-souper?"

Officer Phoebe nodded. "I think so. It's the kind of weather every crook dreams about. They can break in without anyone seeing them."

Our Mom shook her head. "My goodness, Phoebe. In all the years I've owned this store, we've never had a break-in."

Officer Phoebe glanced at her police notebook. "It's the second one we had tonight. Another store down the street got hit, too. That's why we were in the area. And that's why we got here so fast."

Our Mom's eyes went wide. "Oh, so it wasn't just someone who bumped into the door and accidentally set off the alarm? Someone who was out too late on a Saturday night? Or, I guess I should say, Sunday morning?"

Officer Phoebe shook her head. "I'm afraid not, Abby. This was a real break-in."

Our Mom glanced toward the back door of her store. "I can't even tell that someone got in."

"It's really hard to see," Officer Phoebe said. "But let me show you. We've already gone inside and checked out the whole building. Whoever broke in is gone. And I turned off the alarm after your husband gave me the code over the phone."

The two women walked toward the door.

Officer Phoebe shined her flashlight on the doorknob and the doorjamb. "See those scratches, Abby? Whoever broke in did a pretty crude job. And it doesn't even look like they tried to disable the alarm in any way. So I think our burglar got spooked when it went off. Or they just planned to get in and get out in a hurry."

Our Mom put her hand to her cheek. "Well, if they didn't plan to stay long, I guess they didn't plan to steal much either."

"It's very odd," Officer Phoebe said. "Because they seemed to have a real purpose to what they were doing. Maybe they had something special they were after. But we'll find out for sure when we go inside and you take a look around. To see if anything's been stolen."

Our Mom shivered. "I sure hope not. I've got some pretty valuable antiques in there. Though the burglar wouldn't have had time to take anything too large. Like furniture. And I lock up all the money and the jewelry in the safe every night."

"Hmmm . . . that's interesting," Officer Phoebe said. "Most crooks case out a place before they break in. That adds to my theory that our crook had something specific in mind."

"I wonder what?" our Mom kind of murmured.

Officer Phoebe reached up and pulled the door open from the top edge. "Me, too. It's a strange one, all right. We already checked for prints and we didn't find anything. The door and knob were clean."

Beside me, Bogey whispered, "That means the burglar wiped them off, kid. Or, they wore gloves."

"Oh, okay," I whispered back. "I guess that was pretty smart. So they wouldn't leave fingerprints."

Bogey glanced around. "Probably, kid. Probably. Or maybe their hands were cold. Now, get ready to zoom. I think they're going in."

I followed Bogey's lead and got into a crouched position.

Our Mom and Officer Phoebe had just pulled the door open all the way when Bogey gave the signal.

A half a second later, we flew from under that truck and straight into our Mom's shop.

Officer Phoebe froze. "Did you hear that?"

"I didn't hear anything," our Mom answered.

"There was a noise," Office Phoebe said. "And I felt something. Like a little breeze going past my legs."

She shined her big, bright flashlight around.

And straight into our eyes.

We were caught in the act!

Holy Mackerel!

CHAPTER 3

Holy Catnip! I could hardly believe it! There we were, sneaking into our Mom's store, and Officer Phoebe had just spotted us.

Bogey and I both blinked in the bright beam of her flashlight. I turned to see our shadows on the wall behind us in the small back room. And wouldn't you know it, but our shadows came out giant-sized! They made us look as big as panthers.

Not exactly the kind of thing a couple of cat detectives wanted when they were trying to be stealthy.

"Isn't that . . .?" Officer Phoebe started to say.

"Buckley and Bogey?" our Mom gasped. "How in the world?"

Officer Phoebe laughed. "You brought your cats with you tonight?"

Our Mom's mouth fell open and she looked like she was trying to speak. Then she just sort of sputtered, "Uh, uh, uh . . ."

In the meantime, Bogey grinned up at the women while I tried to hide behind him. It wasn't an easy thing to do, considering I'm twice his size.

Finally, our Mom said, "I *guess* I must have brought

them. But I had no idea they were with me."

She shook her head and wobbled over to the wall to turn on the light switches. First the back room lit up. Then one by one, rows of lights in the main part of the store blazed on. We could see it all through the open entrance to the huge front room.

Officer Phoebe clicked her flashlight off and reached down to pet us. "Looks like the boys must have hitched a ride. You bring them to the store a lot, don't you?"

Our Mom nodded. "Yes, but in their pet carriers. I hardly ever let them travel out in the open like that."

Officer Phoebe crinkled her forehead. "You know, it's strange, but it seems like they show up to a lot of crime scenes. Almost like they're . . ."

"Investigating?" our Mom finished.

Our Mom and Officer Phoebe both stared at us for a few seconds. Then they spoke at the same time and said, "Nooooo . . ."

Officer Phoebe shook her head. "It's not possible."

"It couldn't be," our Mom added.

But Bogey and I just sat up straight and looked right at them. It was funny how humans never understood what good crime solvers cats could be.

"We'd better take a look around, Abby," Officer Phoebe said. "And make sure nothing's missing." She stepped into the main part of the store.

Our Mom started to follow. But then she stopped and turned back to us. "Okay, boys, I'm not sure how you got here. But no more sneaking out tonight. I want you to go to your cat beds now. You'll be going straight home with me when we're finished here."

Bogey and I made a beeline for her and rubbed around her legs. Then Bogey headed to one cat bed and I trotted over to the other. We quickly flopped onto our comfy beds and curled into place. We looked up at our Mom and purred.

"That's better." She moved from Bogey's bed to mine, and petted us both softly on the head. "Your Dad and Gracie and I would be pretty upset if anything ever happened to you two. You're an important part of the family, you know."

As a matter of fact, we did know. We knew exactly what she was talking about. Because Bogey and I would be pretty upset if anything ever happened to *her* and the rest of our family, too. It was the reason we ran surveillance on our house every night. And it was the reason we sneaked out and came with her to her store tonight. As cat detectives, we wanted to make sure that she was safe. And that our whole family was safe.

Bogey grinned at our Mom and I meowed up to her. And then I meowed a few more times. Just so I knew my message came across loud and clear.

"Okay, boys," she said with a laugh. "You're forgiven. I'll be back to pick you up when I'm ready to go."

We started purring again and kept on purring as we watched her walk out. Then Bogey grabbed a bag of cat treats he had hidden behind his bed.

He pulled the bag open and passed me a treat. "Let's sit tight for a minute, kid. To give our Mom and Officer Phoebe a chance to get to work. Then we'll go out and look around ourselves."

I took the fish-flavored treat from him. "But what if our Mom sees us? Won't she make us come back to our beds?"

Bogey grabbed a treat for himself. "We'll stay out of sight, kid. Our Mom will never even know we're out running around the store. But we've gotta be back here before they're finished."

"Aye, aye," I told him. I ate my cat treat in a hurry.

Bogey pulled out a few more treats for us both and then stashed the bag back in its hiding place. "Let's get a move on, kid. We don't have much time."

With those words, he stood up and loped toward the opening to the front room. I jumped up and joined him. Seconds later, we were zooming along the hardwood floor and into the main part of the store. Bogey took the lead and I tried to keep up. I scrunched down just as low as I could go to the floor. So I wouldn't be so noticeable.

Though I had to say, a giant fuzzy black cat running by wasn't exactly invisible. No matter how low I scrunched!

Holy Mackerel!

As we flew out of the entryway, I spotted our Mom and Officer Phoebe in the far corner of the gigantic room. Thankfully, our Mom had a big inventory book with her and she was checking things off as they went. That meant we had a little bit of time to do our job.

And that was just what we planned to do.

Bogey and I ran around to the other side of the store so we wouldn't be seen.

Normally, I loved being in our Mom's store. It was such a fun place for a cat to explore. There were antiques of all different shapes and colors stacked and displayed everywhere. Shelves and old dressers and couches and wardrobes sort of defined the rows. Plus there were wooden chairs and tables and bed frames. On top of the furniture sat pictures and pretty dishes and dolls. Glass cabinets in the front displayed jewelry and old coins and silverware. Our Mom's store had almost anything you could imagine when it came to antiques. And lots of the stuff was over a hundred years old.

Plus, the place was loaded with interesting smells! Old smells and new smells. All topped off with the scent of lemon oil.

But tonight, Bogey and I didn't take time to enjoy it all. Instead we ran to a row of old wooden furniture where we knew there'd be plenty of hiding places.

In case we needed to hide.

We paused under a desk with feet that had been carved into the shape of eagles' claws.

"All right, kid," Bogey said. "Keep your eyes peeled for anything that's missing."

"Missing?" I repeated.

"Yup, kid," Bogey nodded. "Something that used to be here but isn't any more. After all, nobody knows all the stuff in this store better than we do."

Well, I had to say, he sure had that right. Us cats spent so much time exploring our Mom's store, that we knew every item in every spot there. And we also knew when our Mom sold stuff.

Bogey stood up, ready to run again. "And keep an eye out for any clues, kid."

"You mean . . . clues that might help us figure out who broke in here?" I asked my brother.

Bogey grinned and gave me a paw bump. "You got it, kid! You got it. You're getting better at this job every day."

"I am? Um, thanks," I told him.

It felt so good to hear Bogey say that. And it made me want to try even harder to do a good job. I wanted to prove to Bogey that I could do my part and share the load.

Now Bogey jumped up and headed toward a cluster of old bookcases and small tables with cabinets.

"Something's fishy here, kid," he told me.

Okay, Bogey had already explained this expression to me. And now, as a good cat detective, I was supposed to read between the lines. I had to figure out *what* it was that Bogey thought was "fishy," or suspicious.

I thought back to some of the other cases we'd been on. To the moments when we'd found important clues. And I remembered the kinds of clues that had helped us crack the case.

"So . . ." I started. "Does that mean you found a disturbance in the dust? Or maybe there's a piece of paper with someone's initials? Or . . . wait . . . I know! Did you see a footprint?" I couldn't keep the excitement out of my voice.

Bogey shook his head. "Nope, sorry, kid. Nice try though. This time I really do smell fish. Probably just a leftover smell in one of the old cabinets here."

"Oh," I said and stared at the floor.

Then I put my nose to work and started sniffing around, to check out what Bogey had been talking about. For a moment, I thought I picked up the smell of fish, too.

I glanced around the area. "But I don't see anything missing. All the stuff our Mom had here before is still here."

Bogey nodded. "Yup, kid. I noticed that. We'd better keep looking."

And so we did. We zoomed past row after row of antiques. We ran past shelves filled with glasses and bowls and pretty pottery.

Finally, we finished up on the other side of the room. But we hadn't found a single thing that was missing. And we hadn't found a single clue either.

Bogey paced the floor. "I don't get it, kid. Someone broke in here for a reason. Someone was after something."

I crinkled my brow. "But nothing is gone. So I guess the people who broke in didn't get what they were after."

Bogey shook his head. "That's how it looks, kid. But it doesn't add up. A burglar had time to break in, take what they wanted and get out. And they would've disappeared into the fog before the police got here. So why didn't they take anything?"

I sat down on my haunches and slid my front legs forward. "I don't know. It all seems kind of backwards."

I sure wished I could help figure out what was going on. Especially since we didn't have much time to figure things out. I could hear our Mom and Officer Phoebe working their way to the other side of the store. The side where we had started. It wouldn't be long before they were finished. That meant Bogey and I would have to head back to our cat beds.

And soon!

Suddenly Bogey turned his head and stared at me.

"Wait a minute, kid. What did you just say?"

I turned my ears toward him. "Um . . . I guess I said, 'I don't know.'"

Bogey jumped to his feet. "No, kid. After that."

I looked up at the ceiling and tried to remember. "Um . . . I think I said something about everything being kind of backwards."

Now Bogey began to bounce around the room. He acted like I'd just told him he'd won a lifetime supply of cat treats!

He grinned bigger than I've ever seen him grin. "That's it, kid! You're brilliant!"

Holy Catnip!

My jaw practically dropped to the floor. "I am? Me? Are you sure?"

Bogey started to trot back into the row nearest to us. "I'm sure, kid. C'mon. We've gotta hurry!"

He took off running.

I jumped up and raced after him. "We do? What did I say?"

"Backwards, kid! You said it was backwards," he hollered over his shoulder. "You were right. We were looking at this all backwards."

We were? We'd gone up and down all the aisles and looked at everything. I couldn't think of any other way we could have looked at it.

"I don't get it," I told him.

Bogey whipped around a corner at lightning speed, digging his claws in for better traction. "We were looking for something that was missing, kid. Maybe we should've been looking for something that was added."

Suddenly I wondered if Bogey had been eating too many cat treats.

"But we looked for clues, too," I said as I zoomed to keep up with him.

Bogey shook his head. "Not the same thing, kid. We were looking for smells and footprints. That sort'a stuff. Not the kind of stuff our Mom would put in her store for sale."

"Oh," I murmured.   Though I still wasn't exactly sure what he was getting at.

Bogey picked up speed as we raced past rows and rows of antiques.   "We don't have much time, kid.   We've gotta narrow down our search."

Holy Mackerel!   How in the world were we going to do that?

Bogey slowed to a trot and let me catch up to him. "Let's go back to the place where we smelled the fishy smell, kid.   I have a feeling about that.   The smell was new to us.   Maybe there's something else new there, too."

It sounded like a good idea to me.

So together Bogey and I made a beeline to that exact spot.   We put on the brakes when we got to the same bunch of bookcases and little end tables with cabinets.

Then Bogey looked in one direction and I looked in the other.   We looked under things and on top of things and around things.   But we didn't see anything new that someone had put there.

We could hear our Mom and Officer Phoebe talking and getting closer.

"Just one more row, Phoebe," our Mom said.   "And then we're done."

"I'm glad nothing's missing so far," Officer Phoebe replied.

"Let's hope nothing's been stolen from this last row, too," our Mom sort of sighed.   "Then we can all go home."

Beside me, Bogey urged us on.   "We've gotta hurry, kid.   They'll be finished in a few minutes.   Where else can we look?"

That's when I pointed to the little end tables with cabinets.   "Something could be hidden in one of those."

"Good call, kid," Bogey said.   "Let's start pulling the doors open."

Well, Bogey sure didn't have to tell me twice!   There were seven of those little tables, all sitting in kind of a half circle. They were built from different kinds of wood, in different shapes and heights. But they each had a flat tabletop and a little cabinet with a door right below that. Some had handles on the doors, and some didn't.

As for getting those doors open, well, let me tell you, it wasn't exactly easy. Because they were really, really old, most of the doors stuck in place a little bit. And no matter how hard Bogey tried, he couldn't even get one open. But because my paws are so huge and my arms are really strong, I was able to hook a claw in and pull the first three doors open wide.

For once, it paid to have oversized paws!

Still, there was nothing inside those first three cabinets. So I took a deep breath and moved on to the next one. After a little tugging, it opened up, too. But again, there was nothing inside. Then I stepped over to the fifth cabinet. I hooked my claw into the door and pulled. For once, the door opened up pretty easily. Unfortunately, it was empty just like the others.

Now I started to wonder if this had been a good idea at all. Maybe if something had been added to our Mom's store, it had been added in a different spot.

Or maybe nothing had been added at all. Maybe the person who broke in hadn't taken anything or left anything either. Maybe someone was just playing tricks on us.

Bogey glanced in the direction where our Mom and Officer Phoebe were still working. "Hurry, kid! Don't give up now!"

So I didn't. Because, even if we didn't find anything, at least Bogey would know how hard I'd tried. That's why I raced to the sixth cabinet and gathered up all my strength. Then I tried to pull that door open as quick as I could. There was only one problem. The door to the cabinet was stuck.

And I do mean stuck!

I hooked my claw in a little deeper and pulled for all I was worth. I leaned back and put every ounce of my weight into it.

But no matter what I did, that cabinet door would not budge.

Beside me, Bogey said, "Let it go, kid. Move on to the next one."

I turned to my brother and stared. "But . . ."

To tell you the truth, it was hard to leave that sixth cabinet alone. Especially since I figured that door might be stuck for a reason. Maybe that cabinet was the hiding place of the very thing we were looking for. Maybe someone had put something in there and fixed the door so it would stick.

Bogey touched me on the shoulder. I gave the door one last tug, but it still wouldn't open. It took all the willpower I had to leave that cabinet alone.

"C'mon, kid," Bogey said. "We can come back to it another day. Time to move on."

I let out a big sigh and did what Bogey told me to. I scooted over to the seventh cabinet. I hooked my claw into that door and yanked the thing right open.

If Bogey thought he'd smelled something fishy before, well, it didn't compare to what we smelled now. Because the odor of fish hit us right in the face.

Just before we looked inside that cabinet.

And that's when we saw it.

There, right in front of us, was a little package about the size of one of our Mom's shoes. It was wrapped in brown paper and tied up with string.

Holy Catnip!

CHAPTER 4

Holy Mackerel!

My chin practically hit the floor the moment I saw that package. Bogey and I both just stood there, frozen, and stared at it. But we only stared for a couple of seconds!

That's because we heard our Mom talking to Officer Phoebe from not too far away.

"It's such a relief," our Mom said. "I'm so glad everything is here."

"Me, too," Officer Phoebe agreed. "It's always nice when a case turns out like this. With no one harmed and nothing stolen."

"Let's lock up and get out of here." Our Mom sounded very, very tired. "Would you please help me put the boys inside my truck?"

Officer Phoebe chuckled. "Sure, I'd be happy to. Anything to keep those two out of mischief."

Bogey and I turned and stared at each other.

Did we have time to run back to our cat beds in the back room? Before our Mom and Officer Phoebe discovered we were gone?

"Hurry, kid," Bogey told me. "Grab that package!

Let's hide it in the place where I stash the cat treats."

The string on the package had been wrapped around both the middle and the length. Then it had been tied in the center with a big knot. So I clutched the knot in my teeth and lifted up the whole bundle. It weighed a lot more than I thought it would. I struggled a little bit to pull it out of the cabinet and set it on the floor. Beside me, Bogey quickly closed all the cabinet doors to all the little tables.

"Gotta cover our tracks, kid," he told me.

I touched the package with my paw. "Wow, I wonder what's in there. It sure is heavy."

Bogey ran a few steps forward and peeked around a dresser. "Yup, kid, it looks like it's taking some real muscle. But let's talk about that later. First, we've gotta get back to our beds. And hide that package."

I gulped. "B-b-but we'll never make it. Our Mom and Officer Phoebe will see us when we run in."

Bogey jumped to the top of the dresser. "Don't sweat it, kid. I'll create a distraction. Then you run in with the package when they're looking the other way. Stash it and run to your own bed."

"But what about you?" I glanced at my brother. "You'll never make it if you distract them for me."

Bogey grinned. "Haven't you heard, kid? I can fly. I'll be there before you know it."

"Um, okay," I told him.

Bogey looked down at me. "It's teamwork, kid. I'm not strong enough to carry that package, but you are. And with you carrying that heavy load, you won't be fast enough to make it in under the wire. So I'm the one who makes them look away while you run in. You'll see. Together we'll make this work."

Boy, I sure hoped Bogey was right. Because one thing was for sure — by ourselves, we'd never get that bundle back without being spotted.

Holy Catnip!

But we might pull it off as a team.

Sometimes it sure was nice to have friends.

"Okay," I hollered up to Bogey before I picked up the package again.

Bogey pointed in the direction of the opening to the back room. "Shake a leg, kid. I've got a path all picked out for you. Zoom straight ahead as fast as you can!"

"Aye, aye," I tried to say as I held on to the knot with my teeth. I was going to salute him, but it was hard enough just to stand up and carry that package at the same time. So instead I started moving in the direction that Bogey had pointed.

"Wait when you get to the end of the row, kid." His voice came from above me. "Stop there until you see our Mom and Officer Phoebe take off. Then run on in."

Until I saw them take off? Where were they supposed to be going?

To tell you the truth, I had no idea what Bogey was talking about. But it was too late to ask questions now. Besides, I figured Bogey had something up his paw. The last I saw him, he was standing on the dresser, next to a group of metal kitchen canisters. And it didn't look like those canisters were going to stay on that dresser for very long. Not with the way Bogey was scooting them over.

Maybe that was the thing about teamwork. Everyone focused on the job they had to do. Then they counted on the other part of the team to do their job, too. So I decided not to worry about Bogey's part and just focus on my part of things. I picked up the pace and worked as hard as I could to carry that heavy package toward the back room. And let me tell you, it was a *lot* of work. Even for a big guy like me!

What in the world was wrapped up in that package?

I was almost out of breath when I finally paused at the end of the row. Just like Bogey had told me to. Now there was nothing but open space in front of me. That meant I had no place to hide when I ran across the floor. If our Mom and Officer Phoebe were there, they'd spot me in a heartbeat.

Kind of like the way I spotted them.

Holy Catnip!

I had barely stopped and looked up, and there they were. Heading for the back room themselves. Probably ready to get Bogey and me and go home.

I quickly set my bundle on the floor and scrunched down behind a loveseat.

"So you said another store was broken into tonight?" our Mom asked Officer Phoebe.

"Another antique store," she nodded. "Abascal's Antiquities."

Our Mom shook her head. "That's a shame. Abe Abascal just moved back to St. Gertrude and opened his store a few months ago. I know he grew up here, but he's been in Turkey or Greece or somewhere like that for the past few decades. I hope this doesn't give him a bad opinion of his hometown."

"I hope not, too. Especially since St. Gertrude doesn't normally have much crime," Officer Phoebe responded. "But do you mind having another antique store in town? He is, after all, your competition."

Our Mom smiled. "We may both sell antiques, but we sell very different things. Most of the things he sells comes in from overseas. I stick with things that I buy in our part of the country."

"That's interesting," Officer Phoebe said. "Funny, but before tonight, I guess I'd never been inside his store. And tonight I wasn't in there for long. Abe was so sweet when we called him down. He apologized for bothering us and insisted that everything was fine at his store. Especially since the place was all locked up and there was no sign of a break-in. Except for the alarm going off. But he said we didn't need to look things over. He told me I probably had more important things on my plate. Then he shooed me out of there."

Now our Mom stepped right in front of the opening to the back room. "You know, I'll try to stop in and say hello to him one day soon. He really must be shy, because I never see him around town."

"That would be nice," Officer Phoebe said. "Just to welcome him back to St. Gertrude. Though watch out. He's got a parrot in there who squawks and talks and carries on. I was glad to get out of the place."

Our Mom laughed and took one more glance around her store. "Speaking of getting out of a place . . . Let's go wake up the boys and get out of here."

I took a deep breath and tried not to be upset. Any second now, our Mom would walk into the back room and find out we weren't there. Then we would be in trouble.

That's when it hit me. If our Mom and Officer Phoebe saw us with our package, they might take it away from us. Then we would never find out what was in it.

For all I knew, it was an important clue.

Suddenly my heart started to pound really hard. If this package was a clue, did that mean we were on an official case? Another mystery for the Buckley and Bogey Cat Detective Agency to solve?

Holy Mackerel!

That must have been why Bogey wanted me to hide it. So we could look at it first. And find out what was wrapped up in all that brown paper.

Tingles ran straight up my spine and back down again. I knew beyond a doubt that I had to get that package into the back room. Without anyone seeing me. And I had to hide it so no one would find it.

But how?

I didn't even have a moment to think about it. Because somewhere behind me, I heard a very loud *Kerrr-rrrash!*

I knew it was Bogey. And I knew this was the distraction he'd been talking about!

Our Mom and Officer Phoebe took off running.

But I didn't wait to see where they went. Instead I just grabbed the bundle at my feet. I raced across that open floor as fast as I could. The package jiggled in my mouth and the string sort of burned my gums.

Finally, I made it into the back room! I made a beeline for Bogey's bed and the spot where he hid his cat treats. Then I scooted his bed over a little. I dropped my package behind it, right next to a curtain against the wall. I hooked a claw into the curtain and pulled it over my bundle. Then I scooted the cat bed back into place, on top of it all.

Without looking back, I ran straight to my own bed.

Just as I did, Bogey came flying in. Or at least, I thought it was Bogey. All I really saw was a black streak. I wasn't sure his feet even touched the ground.

He flopped down on his bed and grinned at me. "Got it hidden, kid?"

"Got it," I nodded. "What was that noise out there?"

His grin went even wider. "Kitchen canisters, kid. Made a huge racket when they hit the ground."

I don't know why, but I kind of chuckled.

"Okay, kid, act like you're sound asleep," he told me.

I curled into my own bed. "But Bogey, when are we going to see what's in that package?"

Bogey sighed. "It'll have to wait, kid. Until we can get back here."

Not exactly what I wanted to hear. But I didn't get a chance to say more.

Because right that minute, our Mom and Officer Phoebe walked in.

"I guess I must have left those canisters too close to the edge," our Mom said.

"Sometimes these old buildings have drafts," Officer Phoebe told her. "But we know that no one else is in here. We already checked the place out completely before you came down."

Our Mom shook her head. "Well, in any case, it's time to get out of here. Would you mind taking Bogey? I'll get Buckley."

With those words, Officer Phoebe reached down and picked up Bogey. He rested his front legs up on her shoulder. Then our Mom leaned over and I climbed into her arms. I gave her a kiss on the nose. Just because I loved her.

She laughed and hugged me tight. "Okay, boys. We're going straight home. No more sneaking out for you two."

Our Mom punched the alarm code into the alarm keypad by the back door. Then Officer Phoebe opened the door and we all went outside.

Straight into the thickest fog I've ever seen.

Holy Catnip.

Our Mom opened the door to the truck and that's when we heard it.

Baaaaaaaa-room! Baaaaaaaa-room!

I glanced back at Bogey. "What was that?" I meowed.

Like I said, cats always switch back to cat language when humans are around.

Before Bogey could answer, our Mom asked, "Is that a foghorn?"

Officer Phoebe squinted and looked into the fog. "It sure sounds like it. But that's weird. Last I knew, St. Gertrude didn't have any foghorns. We're nowhere near the ocean."

Then we heard it again. *Baaaaaaaa-room! Baaaaaaaa-room!*

All of a sudden I shivered. If our town didn't have any foghorns, then why were we hearing a foghorn now? Somebody was making that foghorn go.

"Where in the world is that coming from?" our Mom asked. I thought her voice sounded a little nervous.

Officer Phoebe put Bogey in the truck and grabbed her radio mic on her other shoulder. "I don't know. Let me call it in."

But before she could make the call, her radio started squawking instead. First we heard a woman's voice saying something, then a couple of men's voices responded. All I could understand was something about the St. Gertrude Museum.

I looked over to Bogey. He had his ears pointed straight at Officer Phoebe. He listened intently as the message was repeated. In case you didn't know it, police talk in numbered codes over their radios. And Bogey knew those codes well.

Officer Phoebe answered her mic and turned from us.

"What is it?" I asked Bogey.

He frowned. "It's the Museum, kid. The burglar alarm went off there, too. About fifteen minutes ago. Someone tried to break in."

"The Museum?" I meowed as our Mom put me in the truck, too. "Isn't that where those jeweled statues went on display?"

Bogey kept his eyes on Officer Phoebe. "Yup, kid. You've got it. And I'll bet all this stuff is connected somehow."

I looked at him. "It is?"

Bogey nodded. "I don't know how yet, kid. But we're gonna find out."

"We are?" I gulped.

"Oh yeah, kid," Bogey nodded as our Mom got in and shut the door. "And we've got to get to that museum and find out."

"But how?" I glanced out into the thick fog.

Let me tell you, I *sure* didn't want to go anywhere else tonight. Not in that scary fog. Right now all I wanted to do was go home.

And stay home.

But somehow I had the feeling my brother might have other ideas. Especially when he turned to me and grinned.

"I've got a plan," he told me.

I flopped down on the seat and closed my eyes.

Holy Catnip!

CHAPTER 5

Holy Mackerel! I could hardly believe that Bogey had another plan already! Especially since we were barely on our way home from investigating at our Mom's store.

I opened my eyes and looked at my brother. "Are we going to the Museum tonight?"

Bogey shook his head. "Nope, kid. But I can swing it so we can go tomorrow."

I'm sure my eyes would have gone really wide right about then. If they hadn't felt so heavy all of a sudden. "You can?"

He glanced at the fog outside the window. "Yup, kid. If I play my cards right."

At that moment, I wasn't sure what playing cards had to do with anything. And to tell you the truth, as cats, we didn't exactly play a lot of cards.

I wanted to ask more, but for some reason, my mouth just wouldn't work. I couldn't seem to form any words, even though I wanted to learn all about Bogey's plan. And I wanted to ask him about the package we'd just found at our Mom's store. As well as the foghorn and the other stuff we'd heard about tonight.

I glanced up at our Mom. She was driving very, very slowly since it was hard to see in the fog. Fuzzy light filled the car every time we passed under a streetlamp. And the air smelled sort of damp and wet. I settled back into the seat and tried to keep my eyes open. To help her watch the road.

Plus, I figured a good cat detective would keep their eyes and ears open. In case we came across any clues along the way.

After all, Bogey was completely alert. *His* eyes were wide open as he watched outside the window.

"We're almost home, boys," our Mom said in a soft voice.

And that was the last I heard. I barely remembered driving into the garage and our Mom carrying me into our house. I cuddled up to her nice and tight and didn't want to let go. She felt so warm and snuggly.

I must have slept in my cat bed for hours after that. The next thing I knew, it was noon and our Dad and Gracie were getting home from church. Our Mom had slept in since she'd been out so late the night before. She had barely taken a shower and gotten dressed.

I dragged my big, fuzzy body into the kitchen and flopped down on the floor. Our Dad was making ham sandwiches and our Mom was cooking soup.

Our Dad leaned over and gave me a little piece of ham. "Here you go, big guy."

I meowed up to him to tell him thank you. Boy, oh boy, I sure liked ham a lot! I was about to bite into it when Gracie suddenly squealed.

I jumped up and looked at her. Was she hurt? Was she scared by a mouse or a big bug? I ran over and leaned into her legs. Just to let her know I'd be there to protect her.

I may not be the best cat detective in the world yet, but I definitely know how to take care of a bug.

"Look!" Gracie yelled and pointed to the kitchen table. "It's 'Take Your Cat to the Museum Day!' At the

St. Gertrude Museum!"

Our Mom blinked and our Dad crinkled his eyebrows.

"It's what?" they both said at the same time.

Gracie picked up a piece of paper from the table. From my spot on the floor, I could see the paper had some pretty pictures and some writing on it. Before I could take a closer look, Gracie started to dance around the room with it.

"Take Your Cat to the Museum Day!" she practically sang. "It says so right here. Oh, this will be so much fun!"

She handed the paper to our Mom and ran straight back to me. Then she picked me up and started spinning around the room. Around and around and around we went. I held on for dear life and watched our kitchen go by in a big blur.

Gracie had been going through her "spinning phase" for a while now. I only hoped this phase would be over soon.

Really soon.

She finally stopped turning and held me out so she could look directly into my face. "Did you hear that, Buckley? You're going to the Museum today."

I was?

She set me down and I tried to walk forward. The only problem was, the room still seemed to be going in circles. I wasn't even sure which direction *was* forward.

Now Bogey came and sat beside me. I could barely focus my eyes enough to see his paw reaching up under the cabinets. He snagged a bag of cat treats he had hidden there and pulled it out.

"Did you hear what Gracie told me?" I asked. "I'm going to the Museum today. Doesn't that sound like fun? I've always wanted to go to the Museum. Maybe you can come, too."

Somewhere in the back of my mind, I remembered Bogey saying something last night about going to the Museum. To investigate. Maybe this "Take Your Cat to the Museum Day" would be the perfect way for us to get there! I planned to give it some more thought, just as soon as my dizziness went away and I *could* think again.

Bogey handed me a cat treat. "Here you go, kid. This'll get you straightened out."

"Thanks," I managed to mumble.

I took the treat in my huge paw and tried to put it in my mouth. I missed the first time, but got a direct hit the second time.

I blinked my eyes and looked up at our Mom and Dad. They both stood in the middle of the room, reading the piece of paper together.

"Where did this flyer come from?" our Dad asked.

Our Mom rubbed her forehead. "I don't know. I don't remember seeing it before."

Our Dad laughed. "I've never heard of 'Take Your Cat to the Museum Day.' Must be some new kind of marketing plan."

Our Mom pointed to a section on the paper. "I guess so. It says it's limited to two cats per family. And there's free admission if you bring a cat. But this part is strange. It says black cats are preferred. Especially boy cats. No pet carriers. Collars only."

Our Dad shook his head. "Wow. All those cats, around all those artifacts . . . Since when did the Museum start doing something like this?"

I turned to my brother. "Our Mom and Dad seem kind of surprised. Have you ever heard of this before?"

Bogey grinned. "Yup, kid. I have."

Was there anything Bogey didn't know about?

"Oh," I said. "I'm sure glad Gracie got this flyer. Because I'd really like to go. How many years have they been having this?"

"This is the first year, kid," Bogey said. "It's brand new."

I crinkled my brow. "Then how did you know about it?"

"Because I made the whole thing up, kid," he said.

"Last night. When we got back from our Mom's store."

Holy Catnip! Did I hear him right?

My chin practically hit the floor. "You made this up?"

He grabbed a cat treat for himself and then passed one to me. "You got it, kid. So we could get to the Museum. I told you I had a plan. I made up that flyer and printed it off on the computer. Then I put it on the kitchen table where Gracie would see it right after church."

I choked on my cat treat. "But . . . but . . . won't someone notice when we're the only cats going to 'Take Your Cat to the Museum Day?' Won't someone figure out that it's not really real?"

Bogey grinned and glanced up at our Mom and Dad. "Don't sweat it, kid. I've got it covered. I invited some other cats. And their Moms."

Right about then, I'm sure my eyes went pretty wide. "You did?"

Bogey nodded. "Yup, kid. I emailed Ranger. And I emailed Amelia. They're in on the whole thing. I sent each of them flyers, too. They're putting them on their kitchen tables at their houses. They'll make sure their Moms see them, too."

For a few seconds, I couldn't say a word. I just kind of sputtered, "Uh . . . uh . . . uh . . ."

Ranger and Amelia were friends of ours. We'd met them when we were on another case at a cat show. And they'd both helped us out just when we needed it. We'd stayed friends with them ever since.

"Wow . . ." I finally managed to say. "Is anyone else invited?"

"'Fraid so, kid," Bogey told me. "I had to invite . . ."

But before he could say another word, the phone rang. We listened as our Mom talked to the caller. I could tell she was still pretty tired by the way she kind of slurred her words. And when she said the name, Cassandra, we knew exactly who she was talking to. It was our neighbor who lives across the street and down a few doors. A neighbor who has a Siamese cat.

A Siamese cat who was a really big blabbermouth.

Hector.

I rolled my eyes while Bogey grinned.

Not only is Hector a blabbermouth, but he's very, very nosy. If you've got a secret that you don't want anyone else to know about, well, don't tell Hector. Because he loves to find out any juicy gossip about anyone. And whenever Hector gets any juicy gossip on *anyone*, he quickly passes that on to *everyone*.

Our Mom frowned. "Yes, it seems strange to us, too, Cassandra. But if you got one and we got one, well . . . I guess it must be for real."

Now Gracie moved over to our Mom and hugged her around the waist. "Please, Mom. We *have* to go. It'll be so much fun. Buckley and Bogey can see the Museum."

Our Mom nodded to Gracie and put her arm around her shoulders.

Then she spoke into the phone. "Sure, I guess we're going. It looks like we have to bring our flyers. We have to present them at the door to get in. Would you and Hector like to ride with us?"

Now Gracie started to jump around the room again. Our Mom talked on the phone a few more minutes while our Dad set lunch out on the table.

When our Mom finished talking on the phone, she turned to our Dad. "I'll take Gracie and two of the cats. We won't stay long though. Gracie's got to practice for her piano recital."

"Which two cats?" our Dad asked.

"It has to be Buckley and Bogey," Gracie announced. "It says black cats and boy cats. The other cats probably wouldn't like it, anyway."

Our Dad shook his head. "Wow, this is really, really strange."

Our Mom shrugged. "Well, I guess that's who's going then. Cassandra and her cat are going to ride with us."

Now I turned back to Bogey. "Hector? Hector's coming with us?"

Bogey put his paw on my shoulder. "Sorry, kid. It had to be done. I sent a flyer to Hector's Mom over the Internet. He's so nosy I knew he'd see it before she did. Then I knew he'd find a way to bug her about going. A guy like him couldn't resist."

I lay down on the floor, and covered my head with my huge paws. "But why Hector?"

"We need him, kid," Bogey said. "He's going to be a distraction for the real distraction I've got set up. With Ranger."

I peeked out at Bogey. "More distractions?"

"Yup, kid," he told me. "So we can sneak away and investigate. Hector will distract everyone with his non-stop chatter. Then Ranger can do his thing. Amelia's going to help, too. They'll keep people busy for a long time. It's all going down in the Dinosaur Room."

The Dinosaur Room?

There were dinosaurs at the Museum?

Suddenly "Take Your Cat to the Museum Day" didn't sound all that fun.

I gulped. "Are they real . . .?"

Bogey nodded. "That's what I've heard, kid."

Holy Mackerel!

Weren't dinosaurs supposed to be dangerous? And couldn't they eat us?

My heart started to pound really hard and I started to shake. Nobody told me there were dinosaurs at the Museum!

I never dreamed our trip to the Museum was going to be so scary. But the funny thing was, Bogey didn't act like he was afraid at all. In fact, I was the only one who was scared.

And I sure didn't want to act scared when the Princess and Lil showed up. We all gathered around our food dishes and had a bite of lunch.

The Princess blinked her big, green eyes at me. And my heart just went right on pounding like it was going to bounce out of my chest. I sort of remembered that I wanted to ask Bogey some questions about his plan. But for the life of me, at that moment, I couldn't remember what those questions were.

"I want to hear all about the Museum when you get back, Buckley," she said. "Especially about the statues in the Daunton Exhibit. I've heard they're all so pretty."

Lil nodded to me. "Detective Bogart has filled me in on your activities last night. Sounds like you've got another case for the Buckley and Bogey Cat Detective Agency. And the plan for today sounds excellent. Inviting Hector was a nice touch."

About a half hour later, I sure wished Bogey hadn't invited Hector. That's because I was stuck in the back of our Mom's car with him. And the guy hadn't stopped talking since the second we picked him up. While Gracie held on to me, Bogey sat in the front passenger seat as our Mom drove. Hector's Mom sat beside Gracie and held on to him.

As much as Hector annoyed me, I have to say, I sure liked Hector's Mom a lot. She had brown hair that she always kept in a ponytail, and she worked as a nurse. She was always nice to us cats, and to people, too. Plus, she took really good care of Hector. She even seemed like the kind of cat Mom who had enough love for more than one cat. The only problem was, it would be pretty hard for another cat to put up with Hector.

Just like I was having a hard time putting up with him now. Because he talked and talked and talked and talked. He talked so much, I couldn't even hear myself think.

"And did you hear where the Nelsons went on vacation?" Hector rambled on. "They even took little Bella, their black cat, when they went to Florida. They took her to the beach and she said it was the biggest litter box she had ever seen. And she had such a great time chasing all the bugs . . ."

It was about that time when I snuggled my head

right under Gracie's chin. I ducked in as far under her hair as I could go and tried to cover my ears. I still had lots of questions for Bogey about his plan to investigate at the Museum. And the distraction he had set up with Ranger. But I couldn't ask him a thing, since we both knew better than to talk in front of Hector. If Hector heard about our plan, he'd have it broadcast all over St. Gertrude in a matter of minutes.

Then it would never work. And I figured we already had enough trouble, since we might have to deal with dinosaurs at the Museum.

I squeezed my eyes shut tight and tried not to think about those dinosaurs! When I became a cat detective, I never knew that running around with dinosaurs would be part of the job. And I still couldn't believe that Bogey didn't seem bothered by it at all. Then again, he was a really good cat detective. One of the best. Maybe good cat detectives like him weren't scared of things like dinosaurs.

But our Mom and Gracie weren't cat detectives. And they didn't seem to be scared either.

Why was I the only one who was scared?

Holy Catnip!

CHAPTER 6

Holy Mackerel! The closer we got to the Museum, the more I thought about those dinosaurs. And the more nervous I got. I even started to shake all over again.

Gracie held me nice and tight. "Don't be afraid, Buckley," she whispered to me. "You're going to like the Museum a whole bunch."

I sure hoped she was right.

When we arrived, she kept her arms wrapped around me as she got out of the car. Then she headed for the entrance of the Museum. I peeked around her hair to see our Mom and Hector's Mom walking right behind us. Our Mom carried Bogey over her shoulder, and Hector's Mom carried him like a baby. Gracie had put Bogey's royal blue collar on him and my red collar on me. I had to say, we both looked pretty spiffy.

Unfortunately for Hector, his Mom had put a leopard-print collar on him. It had tons of dangling ribbons with beads attached to them. It kind of made him look like a circus cat.

If only it would have made him be quiet.

But it didn't. Instead he talked the whole way to the

front door.

That's when we ran into our friends. First I spotted Amelia, cuddled in her Mom's arms. Amelia is a beautiful, long-haired calico cat with orange, brown, tan, black, and white fur. But let me tell you, she's as sweet on the inside as she is pretty on the outside. I waved at her and she waved back. She was my good friend and Bogey's . . . well . . . Let's just say that he was staring at her with his eyes kind of glazed over.

Funny, but the only time I ever saw Bogey act like that when he was around Amelia. And he *always* acted that way around her, since the first time he'd met her at the cat show. I wanted to give him a cat treat, just like he would've given me. To help him snap out of it. But since I didn't have any cat treats, I just whispered, "Dames." Like he would have done.

He nodded back. "You got that right, kid. Dames. That Amelia's a one-in-a-million gal."

"Hello," Amelia meowed to us when we got closer.

We said hello back, and then we saw our old pal, Ranger. Ranger is a kind of a cat called a Tonkinese. He has mostly light beige fur and blue eyes. But the interesting thing is, he has dark brown hair on his face and tail and ears.

He waved the second he saw us. "Good to see you guys again! Things have been pretty boring lately, so I was happy to get your email. Quite a plan you've got going here. Reminds me of the time I climbed a redwood tree in the Sequoias. Such great fun! The humans were pretty upset though."

I have to say, I always liked to hear Ranger's stories. And believe me, he had lots of stories to tell! That's because he is a grand adventurer who has gone kayaking in a wild river, rubbed noses with an elk, and all kinds of things. Obviously *he* didn't seem too worried about any dinosaurs! Ranger is a pretty muscular guy, and his skinny blonde Mom was having a hard time hanging on to him.

"Thanks for lending us a paw," Bogey meowed to

Ranger and Amelia. "Without friends like you, we wouldn't be able to pull this off."

Amelia smiled and glanced at each of us. "Anything to help. I'm so happy to have friends like all of you, too."

With those words, Bogey looked right at Amelia, and his face sort of hazed over again.

I reached over and waved my paw in front of his eyes to bring him back.

In the meantime, the humans talked among themselves as they carried us into the Museum.

"I'd never heard of 'Take Your Cat to the Museum Day' before today," our Mom told the other Moms.

Ranger's Mom shifted him around in her arms. "It was a big surprise to me, too. Especially since it was such short notice. I just got the flyer before lunch."

Amelia's Mom kissed Amelia's head. "Me, too. Though my little Amelia doesn't mind getting out. She enjoys seeing the other cats. Especially since she's an only cat."

The next thing I knew, we had arrived at the ticket counter. Then the Moms all reached into their purses and took out their "Take Your Cat to the Museum Day" flyers. Together they handed them to the scrawny young man who worked behind the counter.

He brushed his messy orange hair out of his eyes. He looked at a flyer and his bushy eyebrows shot up his forehead. Kind of like a couple of caterpillars.

"What is this?" he asked. "I've never heard of this."

"We all got the same flyer," our Mom told him.

"Are you kidding me?" the young man sneered. "'Take Your Cat to the Museum Day?' That's ridiculous. Why would anyone want a bunch of cats around?"

Suddenly I felt Gracie stiffen up as she held me. "We love our cats and you're being very rude. You shouldn't talk to your customers like that. And you shouldn't make fun of our cats."

The young man laughed at her. "I'll have to call my

manager about this cat thing."

"Good!" Gracie spoke without blinking. "Because I'd like to talk to your manager, too!"

Our Mom touched Gracie's shoulder. "Don't worry, honey. I know you want the boys to see the Museum. We'll get this all straightened out."

And that's when it suddenly hit me. What if Bogey's plan didn't work? What if we weren't allowed into the Museum? Then how would we investigate? Much as I was worried about running into dinosaurs, I knew we still had a job to do.

The young man called his manager on a microphone and his voice went out over a loudspeaker. That meant everyone in the entire Museum probably heard it.

I had to say, that made me even more nervous. Since we were trying to sneak into the Museum, we didn't exactly want it broadcast to the whole world!

I looked over at my brother. But he didn't seem shook up at all. Instead, he just grinned and dug a claw into the pocket of our Mom's jacket. He fished around for a few seconds and came up with a bag of cat treats.

Our Mom laughed. "I don't remember putting those in my pocket, Bogey. Come to think of it, I can never find any of the bags of treats I bring home from the store."

"Bags of cat treats disappear at our house, too," Ranger's Mom added.

They both shook their heads while our Mom passed out treats to all of us cats. She made sure everyone got two, before she put the bag back in her pocket.

By now I felt like I had a whole bunch of butterflies flapping around in my stomach. So I could only manage to eat one of my treats. I kept the second one in my paw to save for later. All the while, I kept waiting and waiting for that manager to show up. And I kept glancing around to see if there were any dinosaurs sneaking up on us. What if some of them had escaped their room? Then again, how did the Museum even manage to keep dinosaurs in just one room?

Finally, the manager stomped in. Her long, silver hair shook behind her. And her yellow-green eyes looked as cold and mean as pictures I had seen of real dinosaurs' eyes. For a moment, I wondered if she might even be related to some dinosaurs. I figured she was almost as scary.

"What's the problem, Murwood?" she demanded of the young man.

"Did you hear about this?" he pointed right at me.

I gulped.

Murwood crossed his arms. "These people brought their cats for 'Take Your Cat to the Museum Day.'"

"Huh . . . what?" the manager sputtered. "That's the weirdest thing I've ever heard of."

The young man handed her the flyers.

She read them quickly and kind of let out a little scream. "Why wasn't I informed of this?" She glared at Murwood.

He shrugged his skinny shoulders. "Beats me. Nobody told me about it either. I thought it was kind of stupid . . ."

The manager's silver eyebrows plunged down into a "V" across her forehead. "I can't believe this!"

Uh-oh. I ducked my head under Gracie's chin and peeked out.

"Uuuuuugh!" the manager shrieked. The sound reminded me of the steam that came out of our Mom's teakettle.

I noticed she had a nametag that read, "Evaline Esterbrook."

"Chill," Murwood told her. "Don't have a conniption."

But those words seemed to make her even madder. That's when I figured it would only be a few minutes before we were all kicked out. I glanced at the door. Maybe if we made a run for it, we could still get away before this lady started yelling at *us*.

She stomped her foot. "I can't believe he did that."

"Who did what?" Murwood asked.

"Byron," she screamed. "Since he got to be curator, he keeps me in the dark about everything. It makes me so mad. Especially since he owes me. Now here he is, trying to make me look bad."

Murwood gasped. "You know, I think he might be trying to make me look bad, too. He sure keeps me in the dark about everything."

Now Evaline started to tap her foot. "First, he wouldn't tell me anything about the break-in last night! I got here right after he did, not long after the alarm went off. And he told me to go home. He wouldn't even let me stay while he talked to the police."

Ranger's Mom's eyes went wide. "Oh no! I hope nothing was stolen."

"Not a thing," said Evaline. "Whoever tried to break in didn't even get inside. But that's not the point."

"My antique store was broken into last night, too," our Mom added.

"Not my problem," Evaline snapped at our Mom. "My problem is Byron B. Bygones! Museum Curator! But I'll show him!"

"Me, too!" Murwood jumped in.

Evaline stomped her foot again. "If he thinks he can get away with this . . . and if he thinks he can keep us in the dark about his new programs, well . . . he's got another think coming."

"Yeah," said Murwood. "That's right. What she said. That's what he's got."

Then all of a sudden, Evaline grabbed the flyers and pointed to the main part of the Museum. "Go in! Now! Just don't go into the Daunton Exhibit. We were lucky to convince that lady to let us put it on display in the first place. I don't want to ruin things by having a bunch of cats running around!"

The Daunton Exhibit? That was the very exhibit Bogey wanted us to investigate! I guess it was a good thing he had our distraction all set up. Because obviously we were going to need it.

The only problem was, I hadn't had a chance to ask him any more about it. I didn't even know exactly what he had planned for this big distraction.

"I expect you to be on your best behavior," Evaline said. "Because I will be alerting the media, to make sure they know about 'Take Your Cat to the Museum Day.' You can expect to see some pictures in tomorrow's paper. That'll show Byron. He thought he could keep me in the dark about this. In his dreams maybe!"

Our Mom looked at the other Moms. Ranger's Mom kind of giggled and Amelia's Mom shook her head. Then the Moms and Gracie all turned and carried us into the main part of the museum.

"My goodness," said Hector's Mom. "Usually they're so nice here at the Museum. I wonder when that all changed."

"I know," our Mom agreed. "Usually they are. But I've never seen those two before. I think they're pretty new. And I know the curator is new, too."

Amelia's Mom shook her head. "I miss the people who used to work here. I wish they'd come back."

"Me, too," Ranger's Mom agreed. "Or maybe they could simply hire some people who *actually* care about the Museum. Instead of caring only about themselves."

As they talked, Gracie whispered in my ear. "Did you hear that, Buckley? You're going to be in the newspaper."

I gave Gracie a kiss on the nose. To tell you the truth, I didn't really care about getting my picture in the paper.

But I had to say, as it turned out, I sure did like the Museum. A lot.

Holy Catnip!

We went past displays that showed the history of the town of St. Gertrude. We saw all kinds of old artifacts in glass cases. Things that belonged to the first families of St. Gertrude, over a hundred years ago. Gracie paused along the way and explained everything to me.

"Do you see that, Buckley?" she said softly as she pointed into one of the cabinets. "Those are some really old books. And that's an old violin. Back in the old days, they didn't have TVs or computers. Instead they sang songs and played music and read books at night."

That sounded like a lot of fun to me.

We moved past more and more displays. All the Moms carried their cats and Gracie carried me. As we went, she kept on explaining things to me and telling me things she'd learned in school. I was so proud of her. She knew lots and lots of stuff, and I really liked listening to her. I gave her a kiss on the nose, just to tell her thank you.

She giggled and hugged me tight.

Along the way, people sort of stared and gasped when they saw us. They would glance at our Moms, then at us, and finally they'd walk by with funny looks on their faces.

One lady even asked, "Why do you have cats with you? I didn't know animals were allowed in the Museum."

But Gracie piped right up and said, "It's 'Take Your Cat to the Museum Day.'"

Another woman said, "I didn't know about this. Or I would have brought my little Georgie Pie."

"Maybe next year," our Mom told her with a smile.

Once we'd finished looking at the History section, our little group moved on to some Science exhibits. That's where we learned lots of things about rocks and minerals. We saw pretty stones in all kinds of crystal formations. Those rocks were in every color you could imagine. Red, green, gold, yellow, blue, pink and purple. I couldn't stop staring at them, since they were so beautiful.

Next we moved on to a display about the moon and stars and planets. I really enjoyed this section since I always like looking at the stars at night. It was nice to learn more about stuff that was in outer space.

Amelia leaned over in her Mom's arms and touched

Bogey on the paw. "Isn't that a pretty moon?" she asked him.

But instead of answering, Bogey's mouth just kind of fell open and he sort of gurgled.

It was a good thing I'd saved a cat treat. I reached over Gracie's shoulder and handed it to him.

"Here," I told him. "This'll get you going."

He took the treat from me and munched away. "Thanks, kid. I needed that."

Of course, Hector talked as loud as he could the whole way. He talked and talked and talked. He talked about the neighbors and something he found out about somebody. Pretty soon I couldn't keep track of who he was talking about.

But his Mom didn't seem to mind all the noise coming from him. She hugged him in her arms and cooed to him like he was a little baby.

Hector was so noisy that I could barely hear Bogey when he meowed over to me.

"Okay, kid," he said. "Are you ready? We're about to go into the Dinosaur Room."

The Dinosaur Room? All of a sudden, I froze. And to think, up until now, I'd been enjoying the Museum so much. Now all of a sudden, it didn't seem like such a great place.

I swallowed hard. "Um . . . okay. I guess I'm ready."

Bogey glanced at the entryway in front of us. "This is gonna go quick when we walk in, kid. When I tell you to 'go,' slide out of Gracie's arms. I'll slide out of our Mom's arms, too. We'll hit the ground running."

I'm sure my eyes went really wide right about then. "Won't they notice? Won't they come after us?"

Bogey grinned. "Not when they see my distraction, kid."

"Your distraction?" I squeaked out.

"Yup, kid," Bogey said. "You're gonna love it."

He waved to Ranger. "Are you ready?"

Ranger gave us a little salute. "You bet I am, you

guys.   This'll be fun.   First time I ever wrangled a dinosaur."

"I'm ready, too," Amelia joined in. "I've never played with a dinosaur before either."

Now my heart started to pound really, really hard. Wrangle a dinosaur? Play with a dinosaur? What was going on?   Were our friends about to do something dangerous? Was this a good idea? I sure didn't want them to get hurt! Just so we could investigate!

"Okay, everyone," Bogey nodded. "Be ready when I give the signal."

"But-but-but . . ." I started to say.

Then I noticed Hector looking over at us. "What are you cats up to? Are you going to do something fun? If you're going to do something fun, then I want to do something fun, too."

And he went on and on and on like that. He got louder and louder. Let me tell you, no matter how hard I tried, I couldn't get a word in edgewise.

I turned and cuddled in close to Gracie again.   I knew I was supposed to be a big, brave cat detective. But the truth was, I was scared! For me and my friends and my family.

Gracie held me nice and snug. "Get ready, Buckley. We're going into the Grand Hall. The Dinosaur Hall. Wait till you see this."

But I didn't want to see anything.   I really just wanted to go home. I started to shake like I've never shook before.

Holy Catnip!

CHAPTER 7

Holy Mackerel! I could hardly believe it. There we were, about to go into the Dinosaur Hall. Let me tell you, I've done some pretty scary things as a cat detective. But none of them were even half as scary as running around with some dinosaurs. I sure hoped this wouldn't be the end for us. Because I really didn't want to get eaten by a dinosaur.

I turned to see a sign on the door that said "Paleontology Exhibit, Grand Hall," just as our whole group moved into the next room. To tell you the truth, I had no idea what "Paleontology" was. And I didn't really want to know. Instead, I closed my eyes as tight as I could.

But then I realized I'd probably better keep them wide open. So I'd be ready in case a dinosaur came after us.

Funny, but the first thing I noticed once we entered the Grand Hall was the ceiling. It was kind of rounded at the top and it went up about three stories. It was painted with pictures and decorated with gold. I had to say, it was really, really pretty.

The second thing I noticed was that Hector's voice

sounded ten times louder than normal. With the tall rounded ceiling, his meows echoed all over the place. It was so loud in there I could hardly even think straight.

But even with all that, there was one thing I noticed more than anything else. Because, right there in front of me, was a gigantic dinosaur. Or rather, the *skeleton* of a dinosaur. It was so huge that it reached almost all the way up to the ceiling. The whole thing was held up with wires and poles and screws.

Holy Catnip!

So this was what Bogey had been talking about? This dinosaur wasn't alive at all! And it sure wasn't going to come and get me. Or my friends. Or any of the Moms and Gracie!

It turned out I'd been scared for nothing!

Still, until right now, I had no idea how big dinosaurs really were! Not until I saw that skeleton. And let me tell you, they were big! Sure, I always thought I was a big guy, but I was nothing compared to this dinosaur.

I looked around the room and that's when I noticed some other, smaller dinosaurs. But these were made out of rubber and wood and stuff. So I figured I was safe from them, too.

That was, until Bogey meowed over to me. "Time for our distraction, kid. Ready?"

I gulped. "Um . . . ready."

Now Bogey looked at Ranger. "Ready, Ranger?"

Ranger put his paw to his forehead, like he was tipping a hat. "At your service. I'll stay until I see you guys come back."

"Go any time you like, Ranger," Bogey said. "And then wait for my order, kid," he said to me.

"Aye, aye," I told him.

By now I was dying to find out what distraction Bogey had planned. In the meantime, Hector's meows just kept echoing and echoing all over the place.

I watched while Ranger's Mom walked closer to the gigantic dinosaur skeleton.

And that's when Ranger made his move.

He pushed out of his Mom's arms and made a flying leap right onto one of the rib bones of that enormous skeleton. Then he dug his sharp claws in and climbed straight up to the backbone. Next he started making his way up the backbones, called vertebrae, like a mountain climber scaling a mountain. He went up one vertebra at a time, clear to the top of that skeleton's head.

All around us, people screamed. Ranger's Mom shrieked and started to jump up and down. Hector got excited and turned up the volume on his meowing. Everything echoed off the ceiling and the room grew louder and louder.

There was so much commotion going on in that Grand Hall that my head started to spin. People gasped and yelled and shouted. Little kids giggled and squealed. Everyone was looking up at Ranger, who was sitting way, way up on the top of that gigantic dinosaur skeleton!

All the while, Ranger's Mom danced around at the bottom of the skeleton and waved her arms. She hollered and hollered for Ranger to come down.

But he just kind of smiled and ignored everyone as he sat on that dinosaur skull. He yawned, stretched out and licked his paw. I had to say, he sure looked right at home up there! You would have thought he climbed enormous dinosaur skeletons every day of his life.

Now more people came running into the Grand Hall, probably to see what all the fuss was about. The new people saw everyone else looking up, so they looked up, too. Pretty soon, Ranger had a huge crowd all staring up at him. Some of these people even seemed pretty upset. To tell you the truth, I thought they were making an awfully big fuss about a bunch of old bones.

Finally, the newspaper people showed up, too, with their cameras. They started taking pictures, and the bright flash of those cameras bounced all around the room. Now, not only was it hard to hear, but it was hard to see, too.

Gracie kept pointing at Ranger, and she kind of jumped from one foot to the other. But I latched my claws into her sweater and held on for all I was worth. That was, until I saw a black paw waving in front of my eyes.

It was my brother.

Bogey nodded to me. "Ready, kid?"

I nodded back at him.

Then I caught another movement out of the corner of my eye. Amelia had leaped out of her Mom's arms and started to climb up one of the smaller dinosaurs. This one was about twenty feet high. Amelia kept climbing until she reached the back, and then sat up nice and tall and pretty. She sort of looked like she was riding a horse. Only this horse was more like a gigantic lizard. One made out of rubber.

Cameras flashed all around, taking her picture.

Amelia's Mom put her hands to her cheeks and gasped. Then she waved her arms and tried to get Amelia to come down.

Bogey nodded toward a hallway. "Let's get a move on, kid."

I guess that was my cue to go!

Bogey slid out of our Mom's arms and I quietly slid out of Gracie's arms, too. Neither one of them even noticed. They were so busy with all the noise and hubbub, they didn't even realize we had slipped away.

But once we touched the floor, we didn't waste any time at all. Bogey made a beeline to the back of the crowd, right at everyone's feet. I followed him. He pointed to a sign that read "Daunton Exhibit."

And that was exactly where we headed.

Just as we left the Grand Hall, I glanced back at Ranger sitting high atop that dinosaur skull. He gave us both a "paws up" and a huge grin. All the while, cameras flashed and Hector talked and everyone else made noise, too.

Bogey ran on and I was about to chase after him.

But suddenly Hector jumped onto the same skeleton that Ranger had just climbed. I could barely hear him meowing, "If you guys are going to have fun, then I am, too!"

The last I saw of Hector, he had made it onto the back of that huge dinosaur. The funny thing was, his voice sounded even louder up there.

Holy Catnip! This was the biggest distraction I'd ever seen!

But I didn't have time to watch any more. Instead, I turned and raced after my brother. Or at least, I *tried* to race after my brother. Unfortunately, the floor was covered in black and white marble tiles in a checkerboard pattern. The black marble tiles also went up a few feet on the bottom of the walls. And even though marble tiles are really pretty, they're also very slippery.

So when I tried to zoom after Bogey, it seemed like I was just running and running and getting nowhere. I couldn't dig my claws in and get any traction on the floor no matter how hard I struggled! It kind of reminded me of cars that got stuck on our street in the snow. Their wheels would spin, but they wouldn't go anywhere!

That's when I realized I was going to have to do something different. After all, Bogey wasn't having any trouble running. He was so far ahead of me that he was almost out of sight. So I tried jumping from one paw to the other, landing on the pads of my feet only. That worked pretty well, so I tried it going forward. I started out slowly at first and then I picked up speed. Pretty soon I got used to it and I finally started to zoom pretty fast.

Thankfully, the hallway was empty and I didn't come across any people as I raced along. I figured they must have all gone into the Grand Hall when the commotion had started.

By the time I caught up to my brother, he had

reached a "Y" in the hallway. He paused and waited for me to join him. But I was so happy I had figured out how to run on that floor, that I forgot all about stopping. So I came flying in at full speed. And then I put on the brakes — my claws.

But instead of coming to a stop, I went sliding, sliding, sliding. I skidded clear across that floor, until I ran smack dab into the wall!

Then I stopped completely.

Holy Mackerel!

At least I didn't get hurt.

Even so, it wasn't exactly the kind of thing a guy wants to do when he's trying to be a really good cat detective!

Bogey grinned at me. "Like a skating rink out here, isn't it, kid?"

I wobbled on over to him. "You can say that again."

Though to tell you the truth, I hadn't actually been on a skating rink before. And well, I wasn't completely sure what Bogey was talking about. But I guessed he just meant it was slippery.

Bogey pointed up to another Daunton Exhibit sign on the left. "Looks like it's this way, kid."

And we took off running once more. A few seconds later, we saw the entrance to the exhibit. The only problem was, there was a security guard sitting directly in front of it! He had the back of his chair against the wall, and his feet stuck out into the hallway. All the while, he sat staring at the floor in front of him.

How would we ever get past him without being spotted?

Bogey swerved over to the side wall and scrunched down low. I followed him, but this time I slowed *way* down before I wanted to stop. I slid in right beside him and then sat just as low as I could go.

I'm sure my eyes were pretty big when I turned to Bogey. "Now what do we do?" I asked very, very quietly. "That guard won't let us in. And Evaline said we weren't supposed to go in here."

Bogey grinned at me. "Follow my lead, kid. Stay glued to the side," he said in a whisper. "We'll blend in with the black tile and sneak in at the back of his chair. Right behind his feet. He won't even know we're there."

"Aye, aye," I whispered back.

And we did just that. We hugged the side wall, and tiptoed silently toward his chair. When we were just inches away, Bogey zoomed in behind the chair and flew into the exhibit.

I was just about to do the exact same thing. That was, until the security guard shifted in his seat and moved his feet under the chair. Now his feet were directly in front of me!

I almost skidded right into them. But thankfully, I was able to stop just a whisker or two away. I stared at the back of his heels, and at his big, black boots. With rubber soles. Funny, but I hadn't realized how huge his feet were until I came face to foot with them.

Now how was I going to get in? There wasn't much room between his boots and the wall. And there wasn't much room in front of his feet either. And in case you haven't figured it out — a big cat, big boots, and small spaces don't exactly go together!

Holy Catnip!

Bogey peeked out from behind a cabinet in the exhibit room and shrugged. I looked at him and shook my head. I knew he couldn't talk to me and give me any advice. If he did, he'd get the attention of the guard and he'd get kicked out. So until I could figure out what to do, I had to stay scrunched next to the wall and wait until I could get through.

That's when I heard more footsteps coming from inside the Daunton Exhibit. Bogey jumped behind a display case and I pushed right up against the wall.

Seconds later, another pair of shoes appeared in front of the security guard's shoes. This pair of shoes looked nice and shiny. A lot like the kind of shoes my Dad wears when he goes to work.

A deep voice echoed above me. "There isn't anyone in the exhibit right now, André! What's going on?"

"Sorry, Mr. Bygones, but I guess there's some kind of incident in the Grand Hall," the security guard said.

Mr. Bygones? *Byron* Bygones? Wasn't that the name of the Museum Curator? The person who ran the whole place?

"An incident?" Mr. Bygones repeated. "Ah, yes, I shouldn't be surprised," he said, with a smile in his voice. "After all, I am expecting some people to show up. And they would most likely create a distraction. So they would have access to the exhibit. Alone."

Wait a minute . . . Did he just say he was expecting some "people" to show up and create a distraction? But the distraction had been caused by us cats. Either he had us confused with people, or he was actually talking about some humans. But then I had to wonder, why would he be "expecting" some humans to cause a distraction anyway? I crinkled my brow and tried to figure it out. It sure was confusing.

The security guard leaned his body forward and his feet moved a little closer to the wall. I backed up a few inches.

"Well, Mr. Bygones, I would hope you'd be expecting some people," the guard said. "After all, isn't that why we put up an exhibit anyway?"

Mr. Bygones laughed. "Not just any people, André. But people who couldn't resist the Daunton Exhibit. People who would be drawn to it like flies to honey."

"It's a very nice display, Mr. Bygones," the guard said. "I think anyone would be drawn to it."

Mr. Bygones' laugh became deeper. And I have to say, sort of creepier.

"You wouldn't understand, André," he said. "But the people I'm looking for are the very people who might know something. Like the location of the lost pieces. There are people who have been chasing them since they disappeared almost a hundred and fifty years ago. Those are the people I'm looking for."

"Well, if you give me their names and descriptions, I'll notify you when they arrive," the security guard said.

This brought even more laughter from Byron. "If I knew that, I wouldn't have to set this bait for them, now would I? Besides, they might be in disguise."

"They might? You set out bait?" the guard asked.

And to tell you the truth, I was wondering the exact same things. Because I sure was having a hard time following this conversation. It sounded like the security guard couldn't figure out what Byron Bygones was saying either.

"Yes, you nit," Byron said. "The exhibit is the bait. But I certainly wouldn't expect you to know that. Being the simple man that you are."

Okay, now this Byron guy was just being rude. Funny, but I hadn't even set eyes on him and I didn't like him already.

"Yes, Mr. Bygones," the guard said in a sad voice.

I would have been sad, too, if somebody had talked to me like that!

Byron's shoes started clapping down the hallway. "Don't worry," he called back over his shoulder. "I'll know when they arrive. And I assure you, it won't be long now."

I got a glimpse of the back of Byron Bygones as he strode away. He was tall and thin and had dark brown hair slicked back on his head.

Lucky for me, the guard stood up. I figured he was probably saluting his boss. That's when I ran under the chair and straight into the Daunton Exhibit.

Bogey popped out from behind a display case.

I glanced around the room and then looked at my brother. "Bogey, did you hear that? Did you hear what Byron Bygones said to the security guard?"

Bogey nodded. "Oh yeah, kid. I heard it all right."

I felt my heart start to race. "What do you think it means?"

Bogey looked up at the cabinets and displays all

around us. "I'm not sure yet, kid. But I think we've found another clue. A really big one."

We had?

Holy Catnip.

CHAPTER 8

Holy Mackerel! Did Bogey say "a big clue?" By now my heart was pounding so loud that I was afraid the security guard might hear it.

I stared at my brother. "Um . . . I don't understand. Exactly what part of what Byron said is the 'big clue?'"

"All of it, kid," Bogey told me. "Especially the part about using the Daunton Exhibit for bait."

I crinkled my brow. "Bait? What does that mean?"

"It's like fishing, kid," Bogey explained. "When humans go fishing, they use bait to lure in a fish. Then they can hook it and reel it in."

I tilted my head. "O-o-o-h . . . You mean they don't just use their claws? Like we do?"

Bogey shook his head. "Nope, kid. They do it the hard way."

I tilted my head to the other side. "Um, okay. So I guess we could say that 'something's fishy here.'"

Bogey grinned at me. "You got it, kid. Just like all the other strange things going on around town. You can bet they're connected somehow. But we won't know *how* until we've got all the pieces to this puzzle. Then we can put it together."

Well, I had to say, it would be pretty hard to put a puzzle together if you didn't have all the pieces.

"So . . . tell me, what pieces do we have again?" I asked him.

You know, just to make sure I was on the same page as my brother.

Bogey squinted up at a display case. "Too many suspicious things happening at once, kid. It's a pretty long list. Starting with the Daunton Exhibit going on display, which Byron is using as bait. Plus our Mom's store is broken into and someone leaves a mysterious package. And, someone breaks into the Museum and another store. They didn't take anything from the Museum, but we don't know about the other store."

"Wow," I sighed. "That's a lot of stuff in a short time. Stuff like that doesn't usually happen in St. Gertrude."

Bogey nodded his head. "That's right, kid. You got it. Too much stuff to be happening by chance. This has got to be our most bizarre case yet."

I sighed. "Boy, you can say that again. I sure hope we can figure it all out."

"Me, too, kid," Bogey said. "Especially since our family might be in danger."

I'm sure my eyes went as wide as my food dish. "Danger?"

"'Fraid so, kid." Bogey flexed his back legs, like he was getting ready to jump. "Whoever left that package at our Mom's store might come back for it. Or they might be hiding it from someone else. And that 'someone else' might want it and figure out where it is."

I gulped. "And you think those people could be dangerous?"

Bogey squinted his eyes. "That would be my guess, kid. Only shady characters operate this way."

I started to shiver just a little bit. "What do you think is in that package?"

"Wish I knew, kid," Bogey said. "Must be something pretty valuable if someone went to so much trouble to hide it like that."

I glanced around. "I sure wish we could have opened it when we found it."

Bogey nodded. "Me, too, kid. But we'll get our Mom to take us to work with her in the morning. Then we can check it out. Right now, we'd better get a move on and investigate here."

"And get back to our Mom and Gracie," I said.

Bogey nodded. "You got it, kid. We'd better hurry. Let's find out what's so important about all this Daunton stuff."

With those words, Bogey jumped up onto the wooden counter around a glass display case.

I followed him. Once I was up on the counter, I took a good look around the room. It was about half as big as the front room of our Mom's store. And it was filled with a whole bunch of glass display cases on top of wooden stands. Around each display case was a wooden counter for people to lean on. Or, in our case, cats to sit on.

The displays were about ten feet apart, probably so people had plenty of room to walk around. And, probably so the place wouldn't get too crowded if lots of people came in at once.

Bogey nodded toward the case in front of us. "Take a look at this, kid."

So I glanced inside. And that's when I sort of gasped. Because there, with the lights beaming down, were three little statues. They sparkled and shined so brightly that I couldn't help but blink a couple of times. The statues were the same ones I'd seen in the pictures on the Internet, only they looked a *whole* lot prettier up close and personal. And well, for a few seconds, I couldn't stop staring at them.

Each one was about seven inches tall. There was a bluebird, a mallard, and a cardinal. The card that went along with the display said they'd been carved out of three different colors of marble. The bluebird was decorated with small sapphires, the mallard was decorated with small emeralds, and the cardinal had little rubies on it. They were so stunning I could barely take my eyes off them.

Holy Catnip!

"Wow, Bogey . . ." I sort of breathed. "I've never seen anything so . . ."

"I know, kid," he said before I could finish. "But don't get too dazzled. We've gotta keep going."

So we did. We jumped down and ran to the next display. Then we quickly leaped up onto the wooden counter and looked inside this glass case, too. This time we saw a dog and a rabbit and a squirrel. The display card said they were made out of a kind of stone called agate. And they were decorated with lots of small gems, just like the other statues.

Let me tell you, those little statues glowed and shined and sparkled. Almost like they had a light coming right out of the middle of them. It seemed like the more I looked at them, the more I was in a daze. I tried to speak, but for some reason, I couldn't say a word. Instead, I just followed Bogey as we went from case to case. We saw lots more statues. Some were made out of gold and silver, as well as different kinds of metals and stones. And they were all decorated with gems. Lots and lots of gems. It seemed like each statue looked more beautiful than the last.

Once we reached the middle of the room, we came across a big sign that told the story of Mr. Daunton. Bogey and I read it just as quickly as we could. That's when we learned that Mr. Danby Daunton was one of the people who helped found the town of St. Gertrude. About 150 years ago. He was a jeweler and an artist, too, and he really liked to make those little statues. He was so good at it that he became famous for them. And he sold them to aristocrats and nobility, and politicians and famous people all around the world. When he retired, he moved to St. Gertrude and used some of the money he'd made to help get the town started. He passed away about fifteen years later, and that's when his stuff became even more famous than ever.

Then, about ten years ago, Mr. Daunton's great-great-great-granddaughter, Mrs. Vera Glitter, wanted his work to be back in the family. So she decided to collect as many of those pieces as she could find. She went to lots of auctions and stores and searched all over to buy those statues. And this was the first time she'd ever loaned it all to a museum to be put on display.

Well, I had to say, I sure was glad she'd done just that. Because even though we were investigating, I was really glad I got to see all those statues. I'd never seen anything like them before.

I turned to my brother after we finished reading the sign. "Wow, Vera was kind of like a detective, too. She had to do a lot of investigating to find all this stuff."

Bogey glanced around the room. "She sure did, kid."

For some reason I smiled just thinking of how Vera tracked down all those pretty pieces. She must have gone to a lot of work to find them all.

Bogey paused and pointed at the statue of a turtle. "Do you see that, kid?"

"Uh-huh," I nodded. "The display card says 'It's a figurine made out of bronze and decorated with emeralds from Colombia.'"

Bogey pointed again. "Take a look at the foot, kid."

I scooted in closer until my nose was pressed up against the glass. That's when I spotted a tiny marking outlined in the bronze. It looked like a sun with four pointy rays peeking out from a behind a cloud.

"I see it," I told my brother. "I wonder why he carved that into the metal."

"I was wondering the same thing, kid," Bogey murmured.

Then he pointed at the bear in the middle of the set. "Check out the foot on this one, kid. It's got the same symbol."

I looked where Bogey pointed, and sure enough, there was a little sun peeking out from behind a cloud.

So I turned to the third statue in the case, a little owl. I stared right at the base, and after a few seconds, I spotted another symbol. But instead of a sun, this one was a flower with four petals.

I pointed to the owl. "Look, Bogey! Here's another one. But it's not the same as the first one."

Bogey squinted his eyes. "Good job, kid. I wonder why it's different."

For some reason, chills suddenly ran up and down my spine. "Do you think Mr. Daunton put symbols on *all* his statues?"

"Good question, kid," Bogey murmured. "Let's split up and find out. You take one side of the room and I'll take the other. Search for symbols on every piece."

"Even the ones we've already looked at?" I asked him.

"Yup, kid," he said just before he jumped down. "We've got to check 'em all. And we'd better put it in gear!"

Well, he didn't have to tell me twice. I knew our Mom and Gracie might be looking for us by now. So I bounced to the floor and backtracked to the display cases we'd already seen. I quickly inspected each statue in each case before zooming on to the next display. Across the room, Bogey was doing the same. He flew from display to display in a black blur.

So far every one of the statues I'd seen had symbols on them. Funny, but I wondered why I hadn't spotted them in the first place. After all, that was one of the jobs of a cat detective — to see things that others might miss. And well, I'd done a very good job missing the things I was supposed to see.

But why?

It was something I'd have to think about later. Because right now, I had a job to do.

By the time I finished checking my side, I'd counted four different symbols. There was the sun peeking behind the cloud, the flower, a pine tree, and a moon peeking out from a mountain.

I was headed over to Bogey just when he hollered to me. "Come take a look at this, kid."

I raced over and jumped up to join him by another glass case. I looked down into the display.

But there weren't any statues there.

Suddenly my heart started to pound really hard.

"Bogey," I barely squeaked out. "What happened to the statues in here?"

"They're missing, kid," he said quietly. "Been missing for almost a hundred and fifty years."

"Huh?" I'm sure my eyes went pretty wide right about then. "What happened to them?"

Bogey pointed to a painting inside the case. "Here's what they looked like, kid. They were Daunton's best and most expensive work. The card here says they would be priceless if somebody located them today. Take a look."

I glanced at the painting that showed two cat statues completely covered in jewels. Both of the cats were made from platinum. One was covered from head to tail in white diamonds and the other with Kashmir sapphires. And when I say they were covered, well, I do mean covered!

Holy Mackerel! There sure were a lot of jewels on those cat statues!

The cats were sitting up and they each had their tails entwined around the other. That way they fit together as a set. One cat without the other probably would have looked sort of funny. Both cats had big almond-shaped emeralds for eyes, and square rubies for noses.

I looked down to read the small sign beneath the picture. It said the statues were called "Best Friends." Mr. Daunton designed them after his own two cats. One was a white Turkish Angora, just like our Princess at home. And the other was a kind of cat called a Russian

Blue. The sign also said the cat statues mysteriously disappeared, shortly after Mr. Daunton had made them.

I had barely finished reading about the missing cat statues when we heard footsteps. They were coming from the entrance to the exhibit. Then we heard a woman talking to the security guard. Seconds later, the flowery scent of perfume filled the air.

Strong perfume.

Strong enough to make my eyes water.

Then all of a sudden, I felt a little tickle in the back of my throat. Then in my nose.

Before I knew it, those tickles weren't so little any more. My nose started to scrunch up and I knew exactly what was going to come next — a very big sneeze!

And if a big guy like me sneezed, well, it would give us away for sure.

Holy Catnip!

CHAPTER 9

Holy Mackerel! There I was, just seconds away from the biggest sneeze of my life. And I knew the sound would probably echo around the whole room. Then the guard would probably come running in and find us.

Somehow I had to figure out how to stop that sneeze! And fast!

So I ducked my head down, closed my eyes, and tried to hold my breath. But it was no use. I could feel the explosion coming at any moment.

Then I felt a furry arm wrap around my face and press right up against my nose. It pushed in tight. Really tight.

And that was that. No sneeze.

I waited a few more seconds, and still no sneeze!

All at once I kind of wanted to laugh. I opened my eyes to see Bogey grinning at me.

"Thanks," I said to my brother. "I needed that!"

"Don't sweat it, kid," he said as he pulled his arm away. "Now let's go hide behind that corner display. I think we've got company."

Together, we quietly hopped down to the floor. We crept over to the front corner of the room and slid in between the wall and the wooden base of a corner display. It was the perfect hiding place. Yet we could still peer around the corner to see what was going on.

And we could also hear what the security guard and the woman were talking about.

"I do declare," we heard her say in a smooth voice. "There is the most *awful* commotion going on in that gi-gan-tic room with those b-i-i-i-i-g dinosaurs. They're trying to bring in some h-u-u-u-g-e machinery with a lifting device. It looks like a whole bunch of giant crisscrosses." She drawled out her words to make them extra long.

"They are?" the security guard said.

"Oh my, yes," she answered. "And they're asking for all the big, strong, handsome men like you to go and help."

"I don't know," the guard answered. "I'm not supposed to leave my post."

"Oh, but they need you," the woman practically sobbed. "My, oh my, if you don't go and help, all manner of madness may rain down on them!"

"I'm supposed to protect the exhibit," he protested.

"Oh my. That is a shame." Now she sounded like she was having a hard time catching her breath. "But surely there is more to the security for this room than a mere guard. Surely you must have cameras and weight sensors and alarms . . ."

Suddenly the guard sounded kind of eager. "Oh yes, ma'am. We most certainly do. We've got all those things."

"And more guards are probably watching it all on cameras in a control room," she said.

"Oh no, ma'am, we don't have that. Mr. Bygones fired them all," the guard answered her.

"Well, he probably knew they weren't necessary. Not with all the high-tech equipment you have around here. My, but a lady like me could hardly understand such things . . . That's why a big, handsome man like you needs to run off and save the day. You need to go to the hall and help. And don't worry about little, old me. I'll just take a peek around here until you return. Then I'll be here to welcome back a hero such as yourself. My, oh my, what broad shoulders you have!"

The next thing we knew, heavy footsteps echoed down the hallway. Going away from the exhibit. Then we heard the tap-tap-tapping sound of a woman's high heels coming right into the room.

We peeked out and saw a lady in a blue dress stroll in. She had hair the color of the brass doorknobs at our house. And she was wearing a big black hat and long black gloves.

And let me tell you, if I thought her perfume smelled strong before, well, it was nothing compared to how strong it smelled now. This lady must have used the whole bottle.

She started humming as she looked at all the statues in the display cases. But then, to my surprise, she quit looking at the statues. Instead, she glanced up at the ceiling above her, and then at the corners of the room.

That's when she quit humming. She pulled a little flashlight from her purse and shined it into one of the glass cases. Then she got down on her knees and looked at the base of the display.

All of a sudden, my heart started to pound really loud. I sure hoped she wasn't going to look at the base of the corner display case. The one we were hiding behind!

Holy Catnip!

I'm sure my eyes were pretty wide when I glanced at my brother. But he just held up his paw and shook his head. I guessed that meant I wasn't supposed to sweat it, like he always said.

Now we heard loud footsteps pounding up the hallway and coming toward the entrance to the exhibit. They sounded like they probably belonged to a man.

The woman stood up and put her flashlight back

into her purse.

Just as Byron Bygones flew into the room.

He stared at the woman and she stared back. He had kind of a funny expression on his face. I couldn't tell if he was mad or surprised or just trying to look really, really bossy. Or maybe he was kind of happy. But he didn't even blink. He just kept staring with his dark eyes while his dark brown hair shined in the lights.

I wondered how long they would stand there staring at each other like that.

Finally, a sly smile slid across the woman's face and she flipped her hair behind her shoulders.

"It's been a long time, Delilah," Byron said in a deep voice.

"Why, yes, it has," she answered smoothly. "When did we run into each other last? Was it in London? Paris? Or Istanbul?"

"I don't remember the place," came his booming answer. "I only remember you. And your perfume."

Well, I had to say, I knew exactly what he meant by that. Because it was going to be a long time before I got the smell of that perfume out of my nose! I would be remembering her perfume for a long time. Whether I wanted to or not!

Now Delilah sort of sashayed over to another display case. "Lovely exhibit you've got here. You must have done a lot of sweet-talking to arrange for all this to go on display. Especially since the security doesn't look very tight for such a valuable collection."

Byron smiled. "Don't be fooled, Delilah. Someone tried to break in last night and didn't succeed. The security only looks loose. But you, of all people, should know that looks can be deceiving."

"My, my," she said with a smile. "But I fear your manners have suffered since I've seen you last."

He took a step closer to her. "You've come a long way to see this exhibit. Is that all you came to see?"

She let out a little, tinkling laugh. "Don't flatter yourself, Byron. I was merely in the neighborhood."

Byron laughed, a lot like the way people laugh in scary movies. "Oh, sure you were. There are some things you simply can't resist, aren't there?"

Delilah turned her back to Byron. "And you're not one of them!"

I turned to Bogey. "Dames?" I whispered.

He nodded. "Yup, kid. Dames."

Byron circled around until he was back in her line of sight. "If you're here, then you must be looking for them. Unless you're looking for something else."

Them? I wondered who "them" might be.

The woman looked down at a display case. "We're all looking for something, aren't we? And judging by that empty case you've got there, I'd say you are looking for something, too."

"I heard they were found. I intend to get my hands on them." For once, Byron actually sounded kind of excited.

She wiggled her fingers. "Things can change hands very quickly, you know. There can only be one winner."

Byron kept his eyes on her. "That's not true, Delilah. There can be two winners. I'd be willing to share."

Well, I had to say, the more these two talked in circles, the more my head started to spin. For the life of me, I couldn't make heads nor tails of what they were really saying.

"What are they talking about?" I whispered to Bogey.

"They're fishing, kid. Fishing for information. But they don't want the other to know it," he whispered back.

I was about to say that "something was fishy here" when Bogey held his paw against his lips. Letting me know to be quiet and just listen.

"Why don't we talk about this in my office," he told her. "I've got a fresh brewed pot of coffee."

"Vienna coffee?" she smiled.

"Of course," he answered back. "Just like I always

make."

With those words, she glanced at the entrance to the exhibit. "I didn't come here for coffee, Byron. But you may escort me out. Since you don't have what I'm really after."

Then Bryon scowled and bent his left arm at the elbow. She put her hand on his arm and he walked her out of the room.

I looked at my brother cross-eyed.

"Later, kid," he said. "We'll talk about it later. Right now we'd better make a run for it."

And so we did.

We went flying out of the Daunton Exhibit and passed by the empty chair where the security guard had been sitting before. Then we ran straight down the hallway and turned the corner. This time we didn't stop. Instead we made a beeline for the Grand Hall.

The closer we got, the louder it got.

Outside the Grand Hall, there were people looking in and looking up. So we ducked around their ankles. They were so busy staring up that they didn't even see us.

We kept on going until we got inside the Grand Hall. Then we dodged around the feet of a whole crowd of people. But again, they didn't even notice us since they were all looking up in the air. Finally, we stopped for a second. Just in time to see a scissor lift slowly stretching up toward the skull of the gigantic dinosaur skeleton.

And our friend Ranger was still sitting on top. He yawned and flexed a front paw. All the while, he completely ignored the man operating the scissor lift. Even though it kept moving up and up and up toward him.

Below the man on the scissor lift, we saw another man on a big ladder. He had climbed up to reach Hector. But for some reason, this seemed to really annoy Hector. He yowled and hissed at the man. Then Hector turned his back to the man and latched his claws deep into a dinosaur bone.

Of course, Hector kept on talking the whole time. Even when the man grabbed him and tugged. Finally, Hector let go and let the man carry him down the ladder. Hector's Mom stood at the bottom and reached her arms up, ready to take Hector the second he was down.

Beside me, Bogey stood on his back legs and let out a high-pitched yowl. Then he waved at Ranger.

"We're back!" Bogey yelled to our friend.

Ranger's ears immediately perked up. He turned in our direction and grinned. Then he gave us a "paws up."

Just as the man on the scissor lift was almost high enough to reach Ranger, our friend started to make his way down that gigantic skeleton. He went headfirst, and bounced from one vertebra to the next. He kept going until he reached the part of the dinosaur's back just above the rib cage. Then he leaped down to the floor and ran right over to his Mom.

She grabbed him and hugged him tight while the man in the scissor lift slowly returned back to the ground.

That's when Bogey and I started looking for our own Mom and Gracie. We spotted them right away. Bogey ran straight for our Mom and put his front paws on her leg. Without even looking at him, she picked him up and cradled him in her arms. All the while, she kept watching the scene in front of us.

I found Gracie and stretched my front legs up her side. She picked me up, too, and cuddled me in her arms. I gave her a kiss on the nose before I turned my head to look for Amelia.

I saw her still sitting on top of the same rubber dinosaur that she'd been on when we left. She waved, tilted her head, and smiled to the people below. A man on a ladder was just climbing up to her, and she let him gently pick her up. Then he carried her down and placed her in her Mom's arms. Amelia wrapped her own arms around her Mom's neck and her Mom kissed the top of her head.

Right about then, everyone in the whole room started to clap and cheer. Cameras flashed and people laughed and shouted. Our Mom kissed Bogey's head, and Gracie started spinning around with me. Around and around and around we went. I threw my arms around her neck and held on for dear life.

A few minutes later, people began to file out of the Grand Hall.

The cat Moms and Gracie all huddled together with us cats. Our Moms began to talk right away.

"I don't know what got into him," Ranger's Mom shouted excitedly. "He's never done anything like this before. Ever, ever! Well . . . except for the time we camped in the Northern Rockies . . . and well, then there was this other time . . ."

Amelia's Mom leaned her head on top of Amelia's head. "I think Amelia did it as a cry for attention. I don't think she likes being an only cat. Maybe it's time I started looking for a little cat brother or sister for her."

Meanwhile, Hector's Mom crinkled her eyebrows. "I have no idea why Hector acted like this. Maybe he needs another cat in the house, too. Though to tell you the truth, Hector's enough of a handful, that I never even thought about adopting a second one."

Gracie smiled while she held me. "Maybe that's why Buckley and Bogey were so good. They have each other."

Us cats all looked at each other and grinned. If only the humans really knew what had happened!

Ranger nodded to us. "Did you find some good clues?"

"Yup, thanks to all of you," Bogey said. "We sure appreciate your help. We couldn't have done it without you."

"Happy to help," Ranger said with a nod. "The view up there was fantastic. As an adventurer, now I can say

I've even climbed a dinosaur skeleton. That should make for some great tales around a campfire."

Bogey touched his head like he was tipping a hat. "I'll bet it will. You did a great job up there!"

"Let me know if I can ever help out again," Ranger told us. "What a great life you lead, being cat detectives. I always enjoy getting in on your cases."

"Glad to hear it," Bogey grinned.

Then he turned to Amelia and sort of got this goofy-eyed look on his face. I could tell he was trying to talk, but for some reason, the words wouldn't come out. That's when I figured I'd better jump in.

"You did a great job, too, Amelia," I told her. "You jumped right up on that dinosaur and everybody wanted to take your picture."

Amelia smiled. "It was fun! I've never done anything like that before. Maybe I can help with another case sometime, too."

"We'd love it," I said with a smile.

And I knew Bogey would especially love it, though he wasn't able to say so right at the moment.

"I had fun, too," Hector edged into the conversation. "Did I help out, too, Buckley and Bogey? But hey, what did you guys need help with anyway? Did you plan all this out? Were we supposed to jump on those dinosaurs? Why didn't you tell me? I didn't like being up there. I couldn't hear what people were saying . . ." And he went on and on and on.

"Thanks, Hector," Bogey tried to say. But it was clear that Hector wasn't listening.

Us cats stopped talking when our Moms turned and started carrying us out of the Museum.

Along the way, we passed Evaline and Murwood gabbing in a corner.

"We are never, ever, ever having 'Take Your Cat to the Museum Day' again!" Evaline shrieked.

Murwood rolled his eyes. "Boy, you can say that again."

"But the good news is," Evaline went on. "Byron will be blamed for this whole mess. Maybe he'll even get fired!"

Murwood sat up straight. "And you'll be the curator."

Now Evaline smiled. "That's right."

Suddenly Murwood's eyes went wide. "Be sure to give me a raise, okay?"

Evaline crossed her arms. "We'll see . . ."

And that was the last we heard of them while our Moms and Gracie carried us outside and into the sunshine. They had just about taken us all the way to our cars when we heard it.

A foghorn. Coming from somewhere in the distance.

Bogey and I looked at each other. Then we both glanced around the parking lot and to the small hills around the Museum. Just before our Mom and Gracie put us into our car. Hector's Mom sat inside with him, too. And with him talking nonstop, we couldn't hear another thing that was going on outside.

So where in the world had that foghorn sound come from?

Holy Catnip!

CHAPTER 10

Holy Mackerel! The whole way home, I kept thinking about those little statues, decorated with all those pretty gems. And I also remembered the way I kept staring and staring at them. Like I was in a trance or something. They were so bright and beautiful that I forgot about everything else.

Including the job I was supposed to be doing.

Which was probably why I didn't notice those tiny symbols at the bottom of the statues. And for all I knew, those symbols might be the most important clues in our case!

But a good cat detective wasn't supposed to get distracted like I did. Especially when I should already know lots about distractions anyway. After all, we'd been setting up plenty of distractions ourselves on this case. So I should have had my eyes open for things like that. It was pretty sloppy for me to be the one who got distracted.

No, a good cat detective would have spotted those symbols right away. Like Bogey did.

I closed my eyes and snuggled up to Gracie. Hector and his Mom sat in the backseat with us. As usual,

Hector just kept on talking the whole time.

Talk about distractions! It was hard to even think with him gabbing like that!

Gracie hugged me a little tighter. "Didn't you love the Museum, Buckley?" she whispered in my ear. "Wasn't it a great place to visit?"

Boy she sure had that right. It *was* a great place. I started to purr and pushed my head in under her hair. She giggled and rested her head on top of mine.

Minutes later, we dropped off Hector and his Mom. Then we drove to our house. For once, it was quiet inside the car. But the funny thing was, my ears were still kind of ringing.

Our Dad was waiting for us when we pulled into the garage. He helped us all get out of the car. He took me from Gracie and leaned me over his shoulder.

He kissed our Mom hello and put his arm around Gracie's shoulders. Our Mom carried Bogey and we all went into the house.

"How was it?" our Dad asked as he set me down on the floor.

Our Mom flopped onto an antique kitchen chair and sort of laughed. "Let's just say, dinosaur exhibits and cats don't exactly go together."

Our Dad's mouth fell open. "Don't tell me . . ."

"Oh yes," our Mom said. "Some of the cats climbed those skeletons like they were cat towers."

"But Buckley and Bogey were good!" Gracie informed him. "They were the only cats who didn't climb the dinosaurs."

Gracie smiled down at us. We rubbed around her legs and she petted us on our heads.

"Now, Buckley and Bogey, it's time for me to go practice the piano," she told us. "I sure wish all you cats could come to my recital."

I sure wished we could, too. I loved when Gracie played the piano. The music was so wonderful. It would be fun to see her perform on the stage.

I purred with pride for her as I watched her walk out

of the kitchen.

Then our Mom got up to leave, too. "I don't think we'll see another 'Take Your Cat to the Museum Day' any time soon," she said to our Dad.

He sort of chuckled as he followed her out. "I still wonder whose idea it was in the first place . . ."

I glanced at my brother and he grinned back at me. I was proud of him, too.

"It's too bad no one will ever know that 'Take Your Cat to the Museum Day' was your idea," I told him.

He flexed his front paw. "Doesn't matter, kid. It's all in a day's work." He pulled out a bag of cat treats he had stashed beneath a cabinet.

"We sure learned a lot at the Museum," I said to him.

Bogey passed me a cat treat. "You got that right, kid. Just a few more pieces to this puzzle."

I took the treat and started to munch on it. "It looked like Byron and that lady, Delilah, knew each other."

Bogey took a treat for himself. "From a long time ago, I would say, kid."

I shook my head. "Boy, it was hard to tell if they liked each other or not."

Bogey passed me a second treat and took another one, too. "I hear you, kid. I'm guessing they were friends once. But I don't think they're friends any more."

"That's kind of sad." I popped the next treat into my mouth and munched away.

Bogey nodded. "You can say that again, kid. Hard to imagine not being friends with your friends any more."

Holy Catnip. I remembered what my life had been like before I had Bogey for my best friend and my brother. Or before I had Lil or the Princess or any of the rest of my family. To tell you the truth, it was pretty lonely. I was on my own. And the world seemed like a big, scary place.

And well, it *still* seemed like a big, scary place sometimes. But having my brother and my family and friends made the world seem a whole lot less scary.

Just then, we heard piano music coming from the living room. It was the song that Gracie was practicing for her recital on Saturday at church. She'd been practicing a bunch. She told us the name of the song she was going to play was called "Rondo Espressivo." That was quite a name, if you asked me. She said it was written a long time ago by a guy named Carl Phillipp Emanuel Bach. Well, I'll bet it sounded just as pretty then as it did now.

Bogey stashed the treats in his hiding place and nodded to me. I knew exactly what he meant and we made a beeline for the living room. Us cats always gathered around while Gracie played the piano. It was like having a concert right there in our own house.

Lil and the Princess were already there when we trotted in. They waved hello, and we joined them to make kind of a semi-circle around the back of the shiny black, baby grand piano.

"Did you see the Daunton statues, Buckley?" the Princess whispered.

"Uh-huh," I whispered back. "They were really beautiful and sparkly."

Lil glanced from me to Bogey. "We'll want to hear all about the Museum when you get a chance."

"You got it," Bogey said in a low voice. "I'll fill you in when we're done here."

After that, we all kept quiet and just listened to Gracie's song. I slid down onto the floor and closed my eyes. Gracie played on and on, and I just sort of floated away. I could feel a smile slide right across my face.

Then Gracie hit two wrong keys and stopped playing. That's when I kind of woke up. Just in time to see our Mom walk in.

She smiled at Gracie. "How's it going?"

Gracie shook her head. "Not very good. This is an

awfully hard piece to play. Way too hard for me."

Our Mom slid her arm around Gracie's shoulders. "It sounded to me like you were playing it pretty well."

Gracie sighed. "But then I make mistakes. I always make mistakes."

Our Mom picked up the sheet music that was sitting up on the music-holder shelf of the piano. "Nobody does anything perfect at first. But the more we practice, the better we get at something. It just takes a little time."

A tear rolled down Gracie's cheek. "It doesn't seem like I'm getting any better."

Well, let me tell you, I knew exactly what that felt like! I kept trying and trying to be a good cat detective, and sometimes it didn't seem like I was getting any better either. To tell you the truth, lots of days I felt like I was barely more than a rookie. I really wanted to be a great cat detective just like Bogey. But so far, well, I wasn't even half as good as he was. And I still made lots of mistakes.

Even so, when I looked back, I had to say, I really had learned lots of things. There was a time when I didn't even know how to run surveillance. And I didn't know anything about creating a distraction, either. And well, I'd never helped to solve a case before. But now I'd done all those things. So, I guess when I thought about it, maybe I was getting to be a better cat detective.

Maybe better than I thought.

Just like Gracie was getting to be a better piano player. After all, the first time she played this piece of music, she couldn't even make it all the way through. Now she played most of it really well, with only a few mistakes. And she made fewer mistakes every time she played it.

I smiled up at her. Somehow I had to let her know that she was going to get better at playing her song. Just like I was probably going to get better at being a cat detective.

So I jumped up on the piano bench right beside her.

Then I reached up and gave her a kiss on the nose.

I guess it must have cheered her up, because she started to giggle. And I figured if one kiss was good, two kisses were probably even better. So I gave her a second kiss. That's when she wrapped her arms around me and held me tight.

Now Bogey got in on the action. He jumped up on the piano, on the ledge right above the keyboard. Then he reached his paws down and hit a few piano keys. Like he was trying to get her to start playing again.

Our Mom laughed. "It looks like Buckley and Bogey like your piano playing!"

Lil and the Princess sat up nice and tall. Lil meowed and the Princess started to purr.

Our Mom petted everyone on the head. "And the rest of the cats seem to like it, too!"

"I wish they could come to my recital," Gracie said. "Then it wouldn't be so scary."

Our Mom put the sheet music back on the piano. "Much as we love them, I think they'd better stay home."

Gracie kissed me on top of my head. "But they'll be going to church anyway on Friday. For the Blessing of the Animals."

The Blessing of the Animals? I leaned back and looked at Gracie's face.

She smiled down at me. "That's right, Buckley. You and Bogey and Lexie are all going. Lil and Miss Mokie have already gone before. So now it's your turn. You're going to be blessed by the minister."

I was? As far as I was concerned, I was really blessed already. I had my brother and my family and my home and plenty of food to eat.

I gave Gracie another kiss on the nose. She giggled again and put me on the seat beside her.

Then she took a deep breath. "Mom, I don't think I can do this. I think this music is too hard for me."

Our Mom stood right next to the piano. "Are you sure, honey? Your teacher seems to think you can play it."

I leaned against Gracie and purred. I thought she could play it, too.

Gracie shook her head. "I've never played anything this hard before. It'll be really scary to play this in front of a bunch of people."

"I see," our Mom said softly. "You know, sometimes it's good to stretch ourselves a little. Having a challenge can make us do bigger and better things. Sometimes we don't even know what we're capable of until we try."

"Do you really think so?" Gracie murmured.

Our Mom nodded. "I do. If we never try to do something difficult, we never grow and improve ourselves."

"Maybe . . ." Gracie sort of sighed.

But I knew our Mom was right. I'd learned the same thing as a cat detective. Bogey knew I could do lots of stuff that I never dreamed I could do. And long before I actually did it. That was how I *did* get to be a better cat detective.

Our Mom touched Gracie's shoulder. "Why don't you try practicing some more? Maybe that's all you need."

"Okay, Mom," Gracie said. Then she started to play again.

I jumped down and rubbed our Mom around her legs. I had to say, she sure gave Gracie some great advice. And now I wondered if I needed some great advice, too. To become an even better cat detective. Maybe I could start by figuring out why I got so distracted by those sparkly statues today. And why I didn't see the little symbols on the bottom of them.

I knew just the place to go to get the kind of advice I needed.

The only problem was, I was scared to go there.

The Wise One.

Actually, she wasn't a "place" at all. Instead, she was a very, very, very old cat. Her real name was Miss Mokie, and she was so old you could even say she was ancient. It was said she'd been to lots of different places and seen lots of different things in her lifetime. Some said she'd even flown on an airplane once. Bogey told me she'd lived in five different states and two different countries.

Apparently, that's the way it goes when you add more candles to your birthday cake. Because the older you get, the more places you've been and the more you've learned in life. So by the time you get to be as old as Miss Mokie, you have all kinds of wisdom. And let me tell you, that old cat in the sunroom was known for her wisdom. That's why everyone just called her "The Wise One." She was absolutely revered among us cats.

Yet even though she'd become very wise, her joints were kind of stiff and achy. That meant she had a hard time getting around the house. So she mostly just stayed in the sunroom where she could feel the warmth of the sun. The heat made her aching joints feel a whole lot better.

I didn't usually see much of the Wise One. Except during our surveillance runs at night. Mostly I just stayed away from her. To tell you the truth, I was really kind of scared of the Wise One. It was said she once ruled our household with an iron paw. Besides that, every time I talked to her, I felt like she was reading my mind or something.

Even so, whenever us cats needed advice, she always seemed to have the answer.

And this was one time when I needed some answers.

So I took a deep breath and trotted up the stairs to the second floor. I kept on moving until I reached the door of the sunroom. That's when I froze in my tracks and started to shake in my paws just a little bit.

For some reason, I couldn't make myself go inside that sunroom. I even started to wonder if I really needed her advice as much as I thought I did. Come to think of it, maybe I should have asked Bogey instead. And well, I sure didn't want to bother Miss Mokie if she was taking a nap or something.

Still, because she was so old and wise, I knew she'd have some good information for me. And I really wanted to hear what she thought about the situation.

But what would I say to her? How would I ask for advice?

It was always so hard to know how to act in the presence of one so honored as Miss Mokie. It was almost like I needed advice on how to ask for advice!

Holy Catnip!

I tried to take just one step toward the doorway. But my big paws suddenly seemed to weigh about a thousand pounds more than they did a few minutes ago. And no matter how hard I tried, I couldn't make them move.

Then I saw a white streak headed my way. It looked an awful lot like the ghost I thought I saw the other night. The ghost that really turned out to be the Princess.

Just like this time.

She came to stand right beside me. And if I thought I was having a hard time already, well, it was nothing compared to how I felt now. When the Princess stared at me with her big, green eyes.

"Hello, Buckley," she said in her sweet voice. "Are you having a little trouble?"

"Um, no," I told her. "I don't think so . . . Um, okay, maybe just a little. Okay . . . maybe a lot."

"Want me to go in with you?" she asked. "You know, for moral support? After all, Miss Mokie and I have become friends."

"Oh, okay," I told her. "That would be nice." I tried to smile, but I'm sure my lips were sort of trembling a little.

The Princess didn't have a problem smiling. "Let's go then."

And so we did. The Princess ran in front of me, and I managed to follow. Miss Mokie noticed us the second we walked in. She was a huge, gray cat with long fur. Her fur stuck out in a ruff around her neck that kind of made her look like a lion. She was lounging on her purple velvet couch with her long arms stretched out before her. And even though she was a little wobbly these days, her green eyes were still bright and full of life.

She raised a paw, letting us know that we should halt. "Please announce yourselves."

The Princess and I both bowed.

Then I cleared my throat. "Detective Buckley Bergdorf and Princess Alexandra here to see you, oh Reverent One."

She nodded to us, like a queen nodding to her subjects. "Ah, yes, young ones. Please enter and partake of a drink." She pointed a paw in the direction of her private water dish.

I let the Princess take a drink first. Then I leaned over the dish and took a sip. It would have been rude not to. And us cats always used our very best manners around Miss Mokie.

When I stood up again, Miss Mokie nodded to me. "I can see something is troubling you, young Detective. What is the purpose of your visit?"

"Well, um . . ." I started to say.

The Princess looked right at me. "You can do this, Buckley. Just tell her what's on your mind." Then she moved over to a chair, jumped up, and settled into place.

Miss Mokie waved her paw above me. "Yes, please proceed, young Detective."

"Um, okay . . ." I started. "It's kind of hard to explain. But when Bogey and I were at the Museum today, investigating our case, we saw some little statues in the Daunton Exhibit."

"Ah, yes," Miss Mokie murmured. "I've heard of such statues. I should guess you have, too, Princess Alexandra."

The Princess smiled and nodded. "I have. They're

considered some of the most prized, jeweled pieces in the world.   Especially the pair of cats that went missing."

I raised my brow. "Bogey and I saw painted pictures of those statues. I can see they were the prettiest of all. Mr. Daunton sure must have loved his cats."

"As well he should have," the Wise One said. "But tell me, young Detective, why does this pose a dilemma for you?"

I sighed. "Because those statues were so pretty and covered with jewels. And the lights were so bright and everything was so sparkly and glittery . . . and well, I kind of lost myself and I could barely think straight with everything around me shining all over the place. And, I guess you could say I got a little dazzled. And distracted."

"I see," the Wise One added. "And this created a problem for you?"

"Oh yes," I nodded my chin really fast. "Because I completely missed the important stuff. I didn't even see the tiny symbols near the bottom of each statue. And it turns out that was the stuff I should have been looking at. Instead of all the pretty sparkly stuff. Those little symbols could be the most important clues of all. And if Bogey hadn't seen them, well, I never would have spotted them."

"Ah, yes," Miss Mokic said. "Yours is an age-old problem."

Now my eyes went wide. "It is?"

"Most definitely. As I'm sure young Princess Alexandra can attest to. Jewels and things that shine and sparkle have always been coveted. Though mostly by humans, rather than cats."

"Really?" I asked.

"Yes, young one. Humans especially are easily taken in by anything that shines. Gold and silver and diamonds and rubies. To name but a few. And most certainly, there is nothing wrong with owning and collecting objects of great beauty. But, when the quest for those objects makes you do terrible things, that's when you've crossed a line."

The Princess sat up. "I knew all about that in my former life, Buckley. I saw humans do all kinds of mean things to each other. They would lie and cheat and steal. They would deceive their own friends, just so they could own some priceless jewels."

That's when I felt my chin practically drop to the floor. How could someone do something like that to a friend? I sure couldn't understand it.

Though I knew one thing for sure — I didn't want to be like those people! My friends were too important to me. Maybe that meant I'd better start watching out for shiny things right away!

My heart began to pound. "But how can I make sure it never happens again? How can I stop myself from being dazzled like that another time?"

The Wise One flexed a front paw. "Ah, yes. The answer is easy. Always look deeper. Always look past the shine and outer beauty to see what is underneath. That goes for people and cats and any objects."

"Oh . . ." I murmured. "So I shouldn't just look at the shiny part. I should look at the rest of it, too."

For once, Miss Mokie smiled. "You have learned well, Grasshopper. And now you must leave me, for I need my rest."

With those words, she closed her eyes.

"Thank you," I said quietly before I bowed again and backed out of the room.

The Princess smiled at me once more. I knew she'd be staying in the sunroom with Miss Mokie. She liked to watch over the older cat to make sure she was okay. We all appreciated the Princess doing that. Especially since having one so old and wise in our house was such a blessing for us all.

I scooted out the door and headed down the hall. I couldn't hear any more music coming from the living room, so I figured Gracie had finished her piano practice.

I started down the stairs and ran into Bogey as he was coming up.

He waved me over. "I've been looking for you, kid," he said quietly. "I filled Lil in on our museum trip. Then I went to our Mom's office. You'll never believe what I found on the Internet."

"Another piece to the puzzle?" I asked him.

He glanced down the stairs. "You got it, kid. I'll show you tonight on the computer. After we run surveillance. It's about those missing cat statues."

Suddenly I seemed to have a hard time breathing. "It is?"

He looked up the stairs. "Yup, kid. But I've got just one thing to say right now."

"What is it?" I asked.

He leaned in closer to my ear. "We've gotta go to our Mom's store in the morning, kid. No matter what."

That's when my heart practically skipped a beat.

What in the world was going on? And what did it have to do with those cat statues?

Holy Catnip!

CHAPTER 11

Holy Mackerel! It seemed like forever before we finished our first surveillance rounds that night. Thankfully, we found all the doors and windows closed and locked. And we didn't pick up on any suspicious sights or sounds coming from the outside.

When we were almost done, Bogey flew off to the home office to get the computer booted up. And I took the upstairs run by myself. The Wise One even woke up and smiled at me when I checked out the sunroom. After I finished, I bowed and backed out of the room and headed for the bedrooms. Our Mom and Dad were sound asleep when I tiptoed around their room. And Lil gave me a silent salute when I quietly checked out Gracie's room. Lil spent most of her nights on Gracie's bed, keeping watch over her.

Finally, after what felt like hours, I trotted down the stairs and joined Bogey in the office on the first floor.

He glanced up when I jumped onto our Mom's desk. "Everything check out okay, kid?"

"Everything is just fine." I tried to salute him, but I kind of missed and hit the top of my ear. I probably looked more like I was swatting a bug than saluting my brother.

But thankfully he'd already turned back to the computer and he didn't see me.

He nodded to an article that filled the screen. "Take a look at this, kid."

I glanced at the computer, and my eyes practically popped out of my head. Because, right there, bigger than life, was a photo of the same painting we had seen at the Museum. The one that had been sitting in the empty display case. It showed the two missing cat statues, the ones Mr. Daunton had titled, "Best Friends." But this time I got a better look at them. The cats in the painting probably weren't as sparkly as the real statues. But I could still tell they were really, really beautiful.

A smile slid across my face and I couldn't stop staring at them. I remembered how shiny and sparkly all the statues had been at the Museum. I could even see them in my mind's eye. It was almost like I was right there. That's when I sort of floated off for a second.

Holy Catnip!

I guess you could say I got dazzled all over again.

But then I caught myself. And I remembered what the Wise One had told me. To look deeper. And to look past the shine and the outer beauty to see what was underneath.

So I shook my head and closed my eyes for a second. Just to get those images out of my mind. Boy, it sure was easy to get taken in by those pretty, shiny statues. Even when I only looked at them in my memory!

I opened my eyes again and studied the picture a little better. And sure enough, this time I saw some tiny symbols at the bottom of the statues. They were different from all the other symbols we had seen. These looked like outlines of little cats.

I put my paw up to the computer screen. "Do you see those? The cat symbols?"

To tell you the truth, at that moment, I felt kind of proud of myself. I'd spotted those symbols before Bogey had even shown them to me!

Bogey grinned. "Good job, kid. And yup, I saw them, all right."

I scooted closer to the screen to take a better look. "I wonder why he used different symbols for these statues?"

Bogey grabbed a bag of cat treats he had hidden in a vase on the desk. "I've been wondering the same thing, kid."

I think my chin almost hit the desk. "You were? You mean, I thought of something right when you did?"

Bogey passed me a treat and took one for himself. "You got it, kid. Like I told you, you're really getting the hang of this business. Now read the article. You're gonna find it interesting."

So I did. I munched on the cat treat while I read the title, "Lost Artifacts in History." Then I moved down to read the story out loud. "To this day, many treasure hunters still search for the joint cat statues, created by Danby Daunton about a century and a half ago. The works were said to have been Mr. Daunton's crowning achievement. Not only did he use the most expensive metal — platinum — for his statues, but he also covered them in the most expensive gems he could find."

I kind of gasped and turned to my brother. "Wow," was all I could say.

Bogey nodded at the computer screen. "Keep reading, kid. There's more."

I turned back to the article again and started reading out loud. "Though the materials in the cat statues alone are worth a fortune, that's not what make them priceless. It was said that Danby Daunton truly put his heart and soul into this work. That's because he loved his two cats, Tobias and Tessa, like they were members of his own family. And his love for his cats shows in the stunning artistry of these statues."

The article continued and said, "Of course, Mr.

Daunton didn't intend to sell these statues, since he wanted to keep them for himself. But he did agree to put them on display, and a thief tried to steal them the very first night they were being shown. Yet even though Mr. Daunton caught the burglar in the act, the thief got away with Tobias, the statue covered in Kashmir sapphires. But Mr. Daunton was able to grab Tessa, the statue covered in diamonds. Sadly, the thief disappeared and so did the Tobias statue. This was especially hard on Mr. Daunton, since the statues were not meant to stand alone. The two were a pair, and they fit together. Not long after the robbery, Mr. Daunton reported the Tessa statue as missing, too. Mr. Daunton was so heartbroken that he never made another statue from that day forward."

I glanced at my brother and then kept on reading. "Throughout the years, people have claimed they've seen the Tobias statue at different places around the world. It's believed to have been sold time and again on the black market. The last known sighting was in Istanbul. As for the Tessa statue, some wonder if it ever really left the town of St. Gertrude."

I shook my head slowly. "That's some story. It sounds like Mr. Daunton was pretty sad about it all. Especially since he never made another statue again."

Bogey passed me another cat treat. "That would be my guess, too, kid."

"What do you think happened to those statues?" I put the cat treat in my mouth and munched away.

Bogey took another treat for himself. "Don't know, kid. But I do know where to start looking."

"You do?" I asked him.

Bogey nodded. "Yup, kid. Let's start by finding out what's in that package at our Mom's store."

That's when I almost fell over. "You don't think . . ."

Bogey just grinned at me. "You never know, kid. It's about the right size."

Suddenly my heart started to pound really loud.

And for some reason, I couldn't seem to say another word. Instead I just stared at my brother.

Holy Mackerel! Could it be . . .?

Now Bogey waved a paw in front of my eyes. "We'd better get some shut-eye, kid. I have a feeling it's going to be a long day tomorrow."

Somehow I had that feeling, too. But I had a feeling it was also going to be a long night. In fact, it would probably seem like an eternity before we got to open that package.

Bogey and I trotted off to our cat beds in the family room. And just like I thought, I had a really hard time falling asleep. No matter how hard I tried, I couldn't stop thinking about everything that had happened today. And I couldn't stop thinking about all those cat statues. And most of all, I kept wondering what was wrapped up in that brown paper bundle beneath Bogey's bed.

But I must have dozed off at some point. Because the next thing I knew, Bogey was shaking my shoulder.

"Wake up, kid," he said. "Look alive. Our Mom is almost finished with her breakfast."

I curled up into a ball and dug my nose into the fur on my arm. "Just five more minutes . . ."

Bogey shook me again. "No can do, kid. Today's a big day. We've gotta see what's in that package at our Mom's store."

That was enough to make my eyes fly wide open. Minutes later, I'd had a bite of breakfast, a good drink of water and I was ready to roll.

I gave Gracie a kiss goodbye before she walked out the door to catch her school bus. Then I ran to join Bogey in the kitchen. I found him sitting on the counter, right on top of our Mom's purse.

He waved at me. "Come on up and join me, kid. We can't let our Mom go to work without us."

Normally, I would have stayed right there on the floor. That's because we weren't exactly supposed to go on the kitchen counter. And I sure didn't want to get a time-out. Not today.

But like Bogey had once told me, "Desperate times call for desperate measures." And this was one of those times when I guess you might say we were sort of desperate. We had to get to our Mom's store! No matter what.

So I leaped up to join Bogey. Then I grabbed the strap of our Mom's purse and wrapped it around my arm. Our Mom couldn't leave without her purse and that purse wasn't leaving without me.

Beside me, I noticed a copy of the *St. Gertrude Times* sitting on the counter. The headline read, "First Annual 'Take Your Cat to the Museum Day' is Complete Disaster."

Below the headline was a picture of our friend Ranger. He was sitting way, way up on top of that gigantic dinosaur skeleton. Far below him was Hector, with his mouth wide open. There was another picture that showed Amelia. She looked very pretty as she posed on top of the smaller, rubber dinosaur.

Holy Catnip!

I couldn't help but smile. "Did you see our friends?" I asked my brother.

Bogey grinned. "Yup, kid. Great pictures."

Now we heard our Mom walking down the stairs to the first floor of our house.

"Okay, kid," Bogey said. "It's showtime. Look as cute as you can. Our Mom can't resist us when we look cute."

Seconds later, our Mom rushed into the kitchen, ready to grab her purse and run out the door. But she stopped dead in her tracks when she spotted us. Of course, we weren't exactly hard to spot, since we were sitting right on top of her purse.

At first she kind of gasped.

Then she laughed. "I'm guessing you boys want to go to the store with me today."

We both purred up at her, just as loud as we could.

She put a hand to her chin. "I'm not sure if I should take you, though. Not after what happened the other night. Not after you snuck to the store like you did."

That's when I knew we had to be cuter than ever before. It was our only hope of convincing her to take us with her. So I tilted my head to one side. It was a move that Lil had taught me when I had to enter a cat show once. As part of our undercover operation.

Our Mom sort of sighed and shook her head. "I don't know, boys . . . I wasn't happy when I found out you'd jumped in the truck and I didn't even know it. You could have been hurt, you know. You could have been slammed in the door."

I tilted my head to the other side. Beside me, Bogey gave her his biggest and brightest grin.

"Then again . . ." she said softly. "You two really encouraged Gracie with her piano practice."

And with those words, I knew it was time to go in for the big finish. So I reached up and gave her a kiss on the nose. Bogey stood up and leaned his body right into her shoulder.

Our Mom chuckled. "All right, boys. I give up. I can see I am no match for your charm."

A few minutes later, we were both in our pet carriers and off to her store.

It only took about fifteen minutes to get there. We saw the big "Abigail's Antiques" sign on the top of the building as we drove past and around into the alley. A few minutes later, our Mom unlocked the back door. She set our pet carriers down while she punched the alarm code onto the keypad. It turned off the alarm system while her store was open for business. At the end of the day, when the last person left the store, they would punch in the same numbers, to arm the system for the night.

Our Mom carried us in and let us out of our pet carriers in the back room. Her two employees, Millicent and Merryweather, came in the back door a few minutes later. Millicent had short, curly gray hair and dark-framed glasses that she wore on the end of her nose. Merryweather was dressed in a blue dress from the 1950s. Her dress went really well with her red hair and her pink, pointy glasses. Our Mom always called them cat-eye glasses, and Bogey and I sure liked them a lot.

Millicent picked up Bogey the second he walked out of his carrier. "You're looking very sleek and handsome today," she told him. "You do your namesake justice."

He did? To tell you the truth, I had no idea what that meant. But Bogey seemed to understand it, since he purred and meowed up to her.

"I sure wish I could find a man who was like you, Bogey," she sighed.

Beside her, Merryweather laughed. "You wouldn't want a man like Bogey. Or Buckley. They may be very charming, but they're also very sneaky." She leaned down to pet me.

That's when I decided to give her a kiss on the nose.

This made her laugh even more. "See what I mean? I have a feeling they're up to something today. I already heard you boys sneaked down to the store on Saturday night."

Millicent kissed Bogey on the top of his head. "Maybe they just wanted to protect their Mom."

Boy, she had that right. Not to mention, we also ended up with a whole new case for the Buckley and Bogey Cat Detective Agency!

Our Mom shook her head. "I don't know what they were up to the other night. Then again, I always wonder what the boys are up to. It's almost like they're . . ."

Without finishing her sentence, she just turned and looked at us.

"You were going to say 'investigating,' weren't you?" Merryweather said.

"If I didn't know better . . ." our Mom started to say.

Then the three of them laughed. They were still laughing when Millicent and Merryweather put us in our cat beds. But minutes later, they were already talking about the day as they walked through the entrance to the main part of the store. I knew they would officially open things up and get right to work.

And they would be out of our fur, you might say. For a little while anyway.

That meant we were finally free to open up our package!

Holy Mackerel!

Suddenly my heart started to go *thunk, thunk, thunk*, really hard inside my chest. At long last, we were about to see what was inside that bundle!

Now I had to wonder, would it be something rare and valuable, like Bogey thought? Or would it be nothing important? What if the thing wrapped up in that brown paper didn't turn out to be anything special? Would I be really, really disappointed?

It was funny, but we hadn't even seen the package since the night we found it. Yet we sure had been thinking and talking about it a lot. Especially after we'd learned about those missing cat statues.

Then, like a bolt of lightning, something else crossed my mind. What if our package was gone? What if someone had been in the store and taken it?

Now I started to get really dizzy. I leaned against the side of my cat bed. Sometimes finding clues and evidence and mysterious packages could sure make a guy a nervous wreck!

My brother waved at me. "You okay, kid?"

I took some really deep breaths. "Um . . . Yes . . . Well, no . . . Um, maybe."

He grinned at me. "Rookie mistake, kid. Never let the suspense get to you."

I wanted to ask him how I was supposed to do that, but I figured I'd save that for another time.

He handed me a couple of cat treats from his secret stash. "Here you go, kid. This'll get you going."

I downed my treats in a hurry and started feeling a little better.

Bogey jumped out of his bed. "You ready to get this

show on the road, kid?"

I nodded really fast. "Uh-huh."

Bogey pulled the curtain back from the wall and I got out of my own bed. I hooked the edge of his bed with one of my big paws and pulled it out of the way. And there, exactly where I'd left it, was the package wrapped in brown paper and tied with string.

Right before our very eyes.

The first thing I noticed was that it was about the same size as the little statues we had seen yesterday.

Boy, oh boy, if I thought my heart was *thunking* away before, well, it was nothing compared to what it was doing right now! Still, I tried not to let the suspense get to me, just like Bogey had told me.

"Okay, kid," Bogey said. "Let's get this thing out where we can open it."

So I grabbed the knot in my teeth, and lifted the whole package up off the floor. I carried it over to my bed and set it down. It was a lot heavier than I'd remembered.

"Can we open it now?" I whispered to my brother.

Bogey grinned. "Knock yourself out, kid."

I started to tug at the huge knot on the front that held the string together.

That was, until Bogey held up his paw. He turned his ears toward the entrance to the store and froze in place. That's when I stopped what I was doing. I stood still and just listened.

Sounds of a commotion in the main part of the store echoed back to us.

"I've got a bad feeling about this, kid," he told me. "Quick, hide the package."

I gulped. "What should we do with it?"

He pulled the front door of my soft-sided pet carrier open. "Put it in here, kid. Under the floor pad."

And I did exactly what he told me to. I stashed the package clear in the back, right under the fluffy bottom mat. Then we closed the door of the pet carrier and pushed it back against the wall.

Just seconds before I heard footsteps heading our way. And the smell of fish filled the air.

Holy Catnip!

CHAPTER 12

Holy Mackerel! And for once, I meant it for real. Because I really did smell mackerel! Or, at least, I smelled some kind of fish.

My eyes went wide and I looked at my brother. "I think something's fishy here."

Bogey nodded. "Oh yeah, kid. You can say that again."

We both turned toward the entrance to the main part of the store. From where we stood, we could hear three voices, just past the doorway. We recognized our Mom's voice and Millicent's voice right away. But we'd never heard the third voice before. It belonged to a man. And his voice sounded very gruff and kind of scratchy.

"Arrr," the man shouted. "I'm sure I left it in here the other night."

"Night?" our Mom asked. "We're not open at night."

I could tell by our Mom's voice that she was kind of suspicious.

Bogey and I scooted up to the doorway and poked our heads out. And that's when we saw a scruffy old man barreling down the aisle. He was weaving from side to side and opening all the cabinets and drawers everywhere. The smell of fish got even stronger. From the way the man looked and smelled, I figured he hadn't taken a bath in a while.

Our Mom and Millicent rushed to keep up with him. Millicent had her lips pushed together in a very thin line. And our Mom didn't take her eyes off the guy.

But the man just kept stumbling forward. He opened canisters and china cabinets and everything he could find.

Now our Mom turned to Millicent and held her fingers up to her ear. "Call Phoebe."

Of course, we knew "Phoebe" was actually Officer Phoebe. And if our Mom was calling the police, that meant something was wrong.

Millicent nodded and headed for the cash register counter.

"C'mon, kid," Bogey motioned to me. "I don't think our Mom likes the way this guy is acting. Let's make sure she's okay."

Well, let me tell you, I didn't like anyone acting bad around our Mom. Or any other member of our family, for that matter!

So Bogey and I hightailed it out of the back room and ran to where our Mom stood.

"I'm sorry, sir," she said. "But my store was searched on Saturday night. And I can assure you, we didn't find a package."

"That's because I hid it," the old man said.

I noticed he was wearing a rain slicker and a ship captain's hat. It had the name "La Paloma" written on it.

"You hid it?" our Mom asked. "Why would you do something like that?"

He shook his head. "Arrr . . . I got confused, lady. 'Twas easy to do. I'd been at sea a long time."

He practically tripped over his own feet and almost went headfirst into a mirror. He was walking like he was on a ship being bounced around in the waves.

Not that I'd ever actually *been* on a ship before. But

I'd watched them on TV with Gracie. I shuddered at the idea of being around all that water.

"Maybe it would be best if you sat down," our Mom suggested to the man. "You don't look like you're feeling well."

He turned and blinked at her. He swayed even when he was standing still. Then he squinted at Millicent when she came back to join us.

"Yes, that's a good idea," Millicent nodded. "Why don't you sit and we'll look around for your package. Maybe you can start by telling us what it looked like."

The man pointed right at Bogey. "Just like that."

And the next thing we knew, he reached down and tried to grab my brother. Our Mom and Millicent screamed.

Of course, Bogey was way too fast for the man. And the man probably didn't know that Bogey could fly. So when he grabbed for my brother, Bogey sprang straight up in the air. The man didn't even get a chance to stand up before Bogey landed on the guy's back.

And that's when the man dropped right to the floor, with his arms and legs sprawled out. His head was turned to the side.

Seconds later, he started to snore.

Holy Catnip!

I'm sure my eyes went about as wide as my food dish. Sure, I knew my brother was one of the best cat detectives ever. But I had no idea he could bring down a full-grown man! I glanced up at Bogey as he stood on the man's back. I had to say, I wanted to be just like my brother, now more than ever before.

After all, our Mom and Millicent had been scared of that guy. And, he had tried to go after my brother. Obviously he was not a good man. But I still wondered what he was doing in our store.

Millicent petted Bogey on the head. "You're my hero, Bogey. What a great guy you are!"

Bogey grinned up at her before he jumped down to

the floor.   Then he began walking around the snoring man.   While our Mom and Millicent talked to each other very excitedly, Bogey sniffed the man's face.   Especially his mouth.   Then he sniffed the man's jacket.

"Over here, kid," he meowed to me.   "I need you to cover me.   I'm going in."

He was?   Exactly what was he "going in" to?   To tell you the truth, I had no idea what Bogey was talking about.   But I sure understood the words "cover me."

Especially since a big, long-haired cat like me can really provide a lot of cover.   So I bounded over to help him.

"I need to check his pockets, kid," Bogey meowed in a whisper.   "Don't let the people see what I'm doing."

"Aye, aye," I whispered back.

So I stood on all fours between Bogey and our Mom and Millicent.   I made kind of a big, fuzzy wall right next to my brother.   Not that it mattered.   Our Mom and Millicent were still talking really fast, and now they'd called Merryweather over, too.   I don't think they even noticed Bogey and me.

Especially when Officer Phoebe walked in.

That's when Bogey pulled a small, folded piece of paper from the man's pocket.   He slid it between the middle toes on my front left paw.   Only seconds before Officer Phoebe told everyone to give her some room.

"Take this to your cat bed, kid," Bogey whispered. "Don't lose it.   I'll keep an eye out here."

So I did.   While Officer Phoebe checked the man's breathing and his pulse, I clinched that paper in my toes.   Then I slowly backed away.

And let me tell you, *slowly* was the word!   It wasn't easy turning and walking with that paper stuck between my toes.   The paper was folded into fours and it stuck up about an inch and a half above my foot.   It also stuck out about an inch in front of me.   So I had to walk very, very slowly, or else that paper would've fallen out.

But I couldn't let that happen, because I'd never get it back between my toes again.   And I sure couldn't carry it in my mouth. Especially since it looked like it had writing on it. If I carried it in my mouth, I might get it wet and the ink might run.

So instead, I just inched along carefully in the direction of the back room.

In the meantime, I could hear a siren wailing in the distance. I wondered why.

But I didn't stop to look. I just kept on moving. One little step at a time. Step after step. Outside, the siren sounded louder and louder. I could hear more footsteps and people coming in and talking all at once.

But I just kept on going, until I got to the opening to the back room. Then I took off at a run. Of course, the paper fell right out of my toes. And that's when I batted it, just like it was one of our mouse toys. I kept hitting that thing until I'd gotten it clear over to my cat bed. After that, I scooped it up with one paw and . . . *whap!* The next thing I knew, it was on my bed. Then I pulled up the blanket and hid that folded paper right underneath.

Mission accomplished!

Or, well, at least part of the mission was accomplished, anyway.

Now it was time for me to get back to Bogey.

I raced into the main room, and suddenly, the siren sounded really, really loud. Blaring, you might even say. For a moment, I wondered if we should all be running out of the store. But then the siren quit when an ambulance pulled up outside. I figured Officer Phoebe must have called for it.

Seconds later, the ambulance workers pushed a big stretcher into our Mom's store and straight up the middle aisle. Millicent and Merryweather rushed over to help and quickly moved stuff out of the way. Then the ambulance people rolled that big stretcher right to the spot where our Mom and Officer Phoebe were kneeling by the man. His ship captain's hat had fallen off his head, showing his scraggly white hair. He was snoring even louder now.

Lots of other people walked into the store and gathered around. Just to watch, as near as I could tell.

The ambulance workers loaded the man onto a stretcher. He didn't even open his eyes. They put his hat back on his head and strapped him onto that stretcher.

I ran to sit beside my brother. "Wow, Bogey. You really knocked that man out."

Bogey shook his head. "Wasn't me, kid. Something else knocked him out. Did you smell his breath?"

"Um, no . . . did you?" I asked him.

Bogey nodded. "Yup, kid. Someone gave that man something that made him go to sleep. Probably sleeping pills. I smelled the same thing on a case I worked a long time ago. Near as I can tell, they probably gave him a pretty hefty dose."

We watched the ambulance people wheel the man out on the stretcher. They rolled it carefully past the front door and out onto the sidewalk.

"Maybe he took it himself," I suggested.

Bogey shook his head. "I don't think so, kid. I'll bet someone slipped it to him in a drink or some food. Because that guy was in our Mom's store to find *something* important. He was on a mission. You can bet he wouldn't dose himself with anything that would put him out like a light."

I glanced at the crowd of people who were still inside the store. Nobody seemed to be leaving. In fact, all of a sudden, people just started buying stuff. Millicent and Merryweather were working at the cash register, and they sure had their hands full.

I turned back to my brother. "But why would someone want to make that man go to sleep?"

"Beats me, kid," Bogey said. "And we probably won't find out anytime soon. That guy had to go to the hospital. And I'll bet he doesn't get out for a while."

I sniffed at the floor. It still smelled kind of fishy.

"I wonder who he is?" I asked Bogey.

"Sea captain, kid," Bogey told me. "Officer Phoebe looked in his wallet. He owns a ship called the La Paloma. Or, in English, it's called The Dove. He had some papers on him that said he'd just sailed over from Turkey."

I blinked a couple of times. "You mean The Dove sailed from Turkey?"

Bogey grinned. "You got it, kid."

That seemed like an awful lot of birds to me.

I crinkled my forehead. "But we're not even close to the ocean."

Bogey flexed a front paw. "Don't I know it, kid. That guy traveled a long way after he docked his boat. What he's doing here is a mystery. One we've gotta solve."

"I wonder what he was looking for in our Mom's store," I sort of murmured. And just as soon as I'd said it, I was pretty sure I knew the answer.

Bogey gave me a grin. "Bet it was our package, kid. The one we'll be unwrapping tonight. Right after we get it home. And right after our family goes to sleep."

All of a sudden, my heart kind of skipped a beat. "Do you think the package belongs to him?"

Bogey glanced at the people lined up at the cash register. "I doubt it, kid. If it was his, it doesn't make sense that he would break in here and hide it at night. But maybe we'll know more after we unwrap it. And, after we figure out what's in it."

By now people were starting to file out of our store, shopping bags in hand. We could hear lots and lots of talking coming from just outside the door to the back room.

Bogey nodded toward the front of the store. "We'd better check this out, kid. I have a funny feeling about all this."

I followed Bogey as we ran all the way around one side of the huge room and made our way to the front. Then we jumped into the huge picture-window display that faced the street. We hopped up on a tall buffet to get a better view.

But there were so many people out on the sidewalk and street that it was hard to see much at all. The ambulance workers had just finished loading up the sea captain and hooking him up with some tubes and things. The crowd of people had barely left the ambulance workers any room to get through and work.

Holy Mackerel! I don't think I'd ever seen such a crowd in front of the store before! For some reason, I shivered. I sure was glad we were inside the store and not out on the sidewalk.

More than anything, I really wanted to go back to my cat bed and curl up. Where I'd be nice and safe.

Beside me, Bogey didn't seem fazed one bit. He just kept scanning the crowd over and over again.

Finally, he nodded a little to the right. "See anyone familiar out there, kid?"

To tell you the truth, I could hardly see just one person. Instead, all I could see were a whole bunch of people, sort of packed together. But I took a closer look, and tried make out people one by one.

First I noticed the people who worked next door. Then I saw a lady in a floppy hat. Beside her was a little boy who kept tugging at the lady's arm. Beside him was a lady who came in our store every year for Christmas presents. And right next to her was . . .

I sort of gasped. "Is that . . .?"

Bogey nodded. "Sure is, kid. It's Byron Bygones. Curator of the St. Gertrude Museum. Now look on the other side of the ambulance. About ten people down. Who do you see?"

I glanced first at the ambulance and then started counting. One . . . two . . . three . . . Until I got to ten.

This time I gasped really, really loud. For standing there, looking furious, was Delilah. The same lady we had seen at the Museum yesterday.

"Bogey, what are they doing here?" I sort of whispered.

Bogey shook his head slowly, from side to side. "I dunno, kid. But this looks really suspicious to me."

Well, I had to say, it looked pretty suspicious to me, too!

I glanced back outside. "Now what should we do?"

Bogey stood up and stepped to the edge of the buffet. "I think we'd better go to the back room, kid. We'd better make sure our package is hidden really well."

I felt my heart start to pound. "Um, okay. Do you think someone might try to steal it?"

Bogey squinted his eyes and looked outside one more time. "Yup, kid. That would be my guess. I have a hunch that sea captain won't be the only one looking for it."

I gulped and followed Bogey after he jumped from the buffet. Just as the ambulance pulled away from the curb and drove off. Then together Bogey and I ran toward the back of the store.

"One other thing, kid," Bogey said. "We'd better check out that paper I found in the sea captain's pocket. I've got a hunch it's another clue."

Another clue?

I could hardly believe it. How many more clues and things were we going to run across? And to think, we hadn't even opened our package yet. Right at that moment, I had no idea how to even start putting all the pieces of this puzzle together.

Though one thing I did know for sure — this was definitely our most complicated case ever!

Holy Catnip!

CHAPTER 13

Holy Mackerel! Bogey and I raced as fast as we could to the back room of our Mom's store. More than anything, I wanted to see our package again. I just wanted to make sure it was okay. And I wanted to make sure no one had stolen it!

Along the way, we ran past our Mom, Millicent, and Merryweather. And a bunch of other people who were still inside the store talking. Our Mom looked a little bit upset, so I backtracked over to her. I took a second to rub around her legs. Just so she knew I loved her.

She leaned over and rubbed my back. "Thanks, Buckley. I needed that. I love you, too."

Then I zoomed on to catch up to Bogey. He was already in the back room when I got there. He'd pulled the door to my pet carrier open and he was halfway inside.

"The package is fine, kid," he hollered out to me. "I've got it hidden under the mat and the blanket. Someone would have to do a lot of digging to find it."

I let out a really big sigh. "Good. Boy, I sure wish we could open it now."

"I know, kid," Bogey agreed. "But we'd better wait

till we get it home.   I think it'll be safer that way.
Especially since we can't wrap it back up again if we
need to."

I nodded very slowly. "I know. It's just really hard
to wait. I wish we could take a peek."

Bogey grinned at me. "Patience, kid."

Well, to tell you the truth, I was pretty tired of being
patient.   I'd already been waiting a long time.   Being
patient had to be one of the hardest parts about being a
cat detective.   It was just another thing that Bogey was
really good at.   And one more thing that I needed to
work on.

Let me tell you, it sure was a lot of work trying to
become good at something.

I flopped over onto my cat bed.   Sometimes I
wondered if all the hard work was worth it.   After all,
lots of cats spent their days lounging around the house.
They would take time out from a nap to nibble on some
food, or maybe play with a few toys.   What if I lived a
"life of leisure" like that, as humans say?

Well, I guess I knew the answer to that one right
away.   If I lived a life of leisure, I would have missed the
fun and the adventures I'd had being a cat detective.
And I wouldn't have made so many new friends.   And I
wouldn't have felt good about myself, every time I helped
solve a case.   Or every time I helped someone that
needed our help.

But then I thought, maybe it wasn't so important
that I become a *great* cat detective.   Maybe it would be
all right if I was just a *so-so* cat detective.   What if I only
did an "okay" job when it came to trying to solve cases?

I glanced at my brother, and I guess I already knew
the answer to that one, too.   No, it sure wouldn't be all
right to only be "okay."   After all, I admired my brother.
He was one of the best cat detectives in the business.
And I wanted to be just like him.   That's when I
understood what our Mom had said to Gracie.   About
how stretching ourselves and taking a challenge can

make us do bigger and better things. And how we don't even know what we're capable of until we try.

I scooted around on my cat bed. Below my blanket, I felt the piece of paper that I'd hidden earlier. Funny, but I'd forgotten all about our new clue!

I jumped up and grabbed it from under my blanket. Bogey moved over to the side of my cat bed. Almost like he'd read my mind.

I pulled the paper out and put it on the floor. Then Bogey used his claws and together we unfolded that paper.

There was writing on the front. But unfortunately, it looked like the paper had gotten wet and the ink had run.

"I don't understand it," I said. "I didn't put it in my mouth. I was careful not to get it wet."

Bogey put his paw on my shoulder. "I know, kid. Looks like it got wet a while ago. But it's dry now. Let's see what letters we can make out."

So we did. We saw a capital "A" and a little "b." Then there was a lot of smeary stuff. After that, we could make out a lower case "a" and "l." Next there was a space and we could read part of what looked like the word "Antiques." Even though the last few letters had run. Below that, we read a very smeary number three, then a smeary number eight. This was followed by the numbers two, four, five and seven.

I rubbed my forehead. "What do you think this means?"

Bogey stared at the paper for a few more minutes. "It looks like the name of our Mom's store, kid. Followed by some numbers."

"Abigail's Antiques. And six numbers . . ." I said under my breath. "It can't be a phone number."

Bogey's ears perked up. "And it couldn't be a zip code. Or a date."

I crinkled my forehead. "It doesn't make any sense to me."

Bogey flexed his front paw. "Right now, kid."

I pointed my ears toward my brother. "Huh?"

I guess nothing was making any sense to me at the moment. Including what my brother had just said to me.

He grinned. "It doesn't make any sense *right now*, kid. But that doesn't mean it won't make sense *later*. I'll bet it's another piece to the puzzle."

Well, I had to say, Bogey had a point. There were lots of things that didn't make sense the first time we saw them. Or read them or looked at them. But they sure made sense later. I only hoped this one of those things.

I was about to say more when we smelled it.

Perfume. Very strong perfume.

Holy Mackerel. We sure had a lot of smells on this case!

Seconds later, I recognized that perfume. It was the same scent we'd smelled at the Museum. The perfume that Delilah had been wearing.

Bogey glanced at me. "Look alive, kid. I think we've got company. Let's go see what she's doing here."

"Aye, aye," I told my brother. I tried to salute him, but I accidentally hit myself in the mouth instead.

Thankfully Bogey didn't see me. Because he was already headed for the entrance to the main part of the store. I followed him and together we followed the scent.

Then sure enough, we found Delilah right smack dab in the middle of the store. She was perched on a green velvet couch with a curvy wooden back. Her brass-colored hair looked sort of greenish, too.

Today she had on a pink dress and a pink hat with a veil. She had on long white gloves and lots of glitzy bracelets. Her bracelets even sort of reminded me of the little statues we'd seen at the Museum. That's how glitzy they were!

Delilah was crying and dabbing at her eyes with an old lace handkerchief. Our Mom spotted her and then sat on the couch beside her. Bogey and I trotted over and planted ourselves on the floor just across from Delilah. To tell you the truth, it was the first time we'd come face to face with her.

"Hello," our Mom said in a very soft voice. "I'm Abigail Abernathy. What's your name?"

"I'm Miss Wunderfully," Delilah told her. Then she started crying even harder.

Our Mom patted Delilah's hand. "There, there, now. What's got you so upset?"

"It's my sister," Delilah sniffled. "She traveled here a few days ago. She was with a very horrible man. I think they were going to get married."

She drawled out her words to make them extra long. Just like when we saw her at the Museum.

Our Mom's eyebrows went up. "Uh-oh. I'm guessing you didn't want her to marry this man."

Delilah *thunked* her hand to her chest. "My goodness, no. Especially since they needed money to get married. They stole one of my dear, beloved great-auntie's most favorite belongings. They planned to sell it so they'd have some money."

"Have you reported the theft to the police?" our Mom asked.

For a second, Delilah's long eyelashes flickered up and she stopped crying. She seemed to have trouble breathing for a moment, but then she recovered really fast. She started sniffling and dabbing at her eyes some more.

"Oh my, no," she cooed. "I certainly wouldn't call the police. No need to bring them in . . . on a family matter."

"Well, then how can I help you?" our Mom asked gently.

Delilah touched our Mom's hand. "I wondered if she'd stopped in here. If maybe she'd tried to sell you something. Or if she'd left something in your store."

"Do you have a description . . ." our Mom started to ask.

Suddenly Delilah sort of perked up. "Oh yes," she

said. "A package wrapped in brown paper. About this high." She held her hand up from the seat of the couch.

Our Mom smiled a little. "No, I was asking if you had a description of your sister. And the man she was with."

"Oh, that," Delilah said. "No, I'm afraid I can't give you that."

Our Mom's mouth fell open. "You can't give us a description of your sister? I don't understand. Don't you know what she looks like?"

Delilah coughed into her hankie. "Well . . . she was in disguise . . . Yes, that's it. The last I saw her she was wearing a disguise. And you know how disguises go. They can change every day."

Holy Mackerel! Talk about something being fishy! I sure didn't believe a thing this lady was saying.

I stole a glance at my brother. He looked at me out of the corner of his eye and nodded. I could tell he thought her story sounded pretty fishy, too.

Now Delilah started to cry really hard again. "Maybe you could check and see if anyone's tried to sell you something in the last few days. Or if someone left something here."

"Okay, I'll check," our Mom told her. "But I don't think they have. And it's kind of strange . . . you're the second person who's been in here today, talking about a brown paper package."

Delilah gasped. But then she quickly started crying again.

Our Mom patted her hand once more. "I'll have Merryweather double-check our records. You wait here. I'll get you a cup of coffee while she's looking."

"Oh, thank you so very much," Delilah said in kind of a breathy voice. "I would be so very grateful."

Our Mom stood up. "Anything to help you find your sister."

"Who?" Delilah asked. But then she blinked a couple of times and finally smiled. "Oh right, my sister.

Yes, anything to help find her."

With those words, our Mom left and headed for the cash register counter. Delilah suddenly stopped crying and pulled a pointy nail file from her purse. She started to file her fingernails, and a smile slid across her face.

That was, until she spotted us. "My, my, but look at the two of you. Where I come from, cats aren't allowed inside. They're supposed to stay outside with the rest of the trash."

Right at the moment, I felt my chin practically drop to the floor. Had I heard her right? What a mean thing to say to anybody. Especially a cat!

And strangely enough, I also noticed she didn't seem to have her accent any more!

Bogey glared at her with squinty eyes. He started pacing across the floor, back and forth. He didn't take his eyes off her.

"Then again, I may have been too hasty," Delilah laughed. "I know exactly what you little varmints would be good for . . ."

She pointed right at Bogey. "You would be perfect on my gray coat. Oh yes, you're so nice and sleek, your shiny fur would look stunning as a collar."

"And you!" She pointed at me. "You'd make a nice fuzzy hat. Oh yes, your fur would keep me perfectly warm in the winter."

I crinkled my brow. But I needed my fur. It kept *me* warm in the winter.

"Don't let her get to you, kid," Bogey meowed to me.

I scooted back toward a desk. "But how would she get our fur?" I meowed back. "She'd have to . . ."

"Not gonna happen, kid," Bogey told me.

"Why don't you come over here, little kitty?" she said to Bogey. "I'll take you right on over to a tailor. I'll have that beautiful black fur on my coat in no time."

Now Bogey jumped up on the other end of the couch. He stepped toward her really big purse. It was almost as big as some suitcases.

I started to shiver and shake. "No, Bogey! Don't go

over there! Get back!" I meowed as loud as I could.

But Bogey just kept stepping toward her purse. I could see it was open wide and some stuff was even sticking out of it.

"That's a good kitty," she said. "I'll shove you right in my handbag and take you straight out the door. Nobody will even know you're gone. I'll come back for the big one later. I'll have to bring an extra large sack for that cat."

No matter how much I warned him, Bogey kept on moving toward that purse. Then Delilah raised her arm with her pointy nail file still in her hand.

What was she going to do to Bogey? And why was he still headed for her purse? Didn't he know what was going on?

That's when I let out the loudest yowl I've ever yowled in my whole life. I leaped forward, just as she swooped her arm down.

And just as someone grabbed Delilah's wrist from above.

It was our Mom!

For a few seconds, our Mom and Delilah just stared at each other. I don't think I've ever seen our Mom's dark eyes look so mad. Merryweather came up behind her and gasped.

"Let me make something perfectly clear," our Mom said in a quiet voice.

But even though her voice was quiet, it was still very, very angry. She even sounded a little scary. She held onto Delilah's wrist really tight and took the nail file out of her hand.

"Nobody, but nobody," our Mom said, "tries to harm or threaten or kidnap my cats. I consider them to be part of my family. And just so you know, it would be a very big mistake if you ever tried to harm any member of my family. Feline or otherwise. My friend, Officer Pheobe Smiley of the St. Gertrude Police, would be more than happy to back me up."

With those words, she let go of Delilah's wrist. I barely caught sight of Bogey stuffing some kind of paper between the cushions of the couch. But I was too scared to give it much thought at the moment. I was just glad she hadn't hurt or cat-napped my brother!

Delilah stood up and straightened her dress. "That's a fine way to treat a customer! Did you find my package?"

"You are certainly no customer," our Mom told her. "Because you will be leaving my store at once. And you will not be coming back. Ever."

And the next thing I knew, our Mom had Delilah by her elbow and she was pushing her toward the door. Delilah kind of tripped along as Merryweather and Millicent followed. Bogey and I ran alongside them, all the way to the front door. Our Mom opened the door and sort of pushed Delilah out.

Delilah made a *huff* noise and stomped down the sidewalk. Bogey and I jumped on top of a buffet so we could see out the front window and watch her go.

She took about five steps before she paused and turned around. She spotted us in the window and squinted her eyes. Then she pointed at us. She clenched her jaw together so tight that veins popped out on her forehead.

"I'll get you for this," she yelled at us.

After that, she twirled around and strutted down the sidewalk.

Holy Catnip!

CHAPTER 14

Holy Catnip! For a moment or two, I could hardly breathe. I just sat there and sort of gulped in air. My eyes were glued to Delilah as Bogey and I watched her slowly walk away. She swung her hips from side to side, and it seemed like an hour passed before she was out of sight.

No matter how hard I tried, I couldn't stop shaking. "Bogey, weren't you scared? That lady was going to . . ."

But I couldn't even finish my sentence.

Bogey shook his head slowly. "I know it, kid. But I still had plenty of time to jump. Plus, I knew our Mom was on her way back."

He paused and took a deep breath. "But any way you look at it, kid, that dame is bad news."

I glanced back outside. "I'm sure glad our Mom kicked her out of the store."

Now Bogey grinned. "I knew she would, kid. Plus I noticed you jumped in to save me, too."

I tilted my head. Up until that moment, I guess I hadn't even realized it. But Bogey was right. I did jump in to save my brother. Without even thinking about it. And I *would* have saved him if our Mom hadn't shown up on time. Funny, but no matter how scared I was, I wasn't going to let someone hurt Bogey. I guess it was just one of those natural instinct kinds of things.

Bogey put his paw on my shoulder. "Only a good cat detective would jump in like that, kid."

That made me smile. Because Bogey was right. It was exactly the kind of thing he would have done. And exactly the kind of thing Lil would have done, too.

Suddenly, I felt just a little bit taller than I had before.

I grinned at my brother. "Thanks for saying that."

He pulled a bag of cat treats from a glass vase on the buffet. "Nothing you didn't earn, kid."

He passed me a treat and then took one for himself. For a second, I just sat there chewing on my treat. But then I remembered the paper that Bogey had stuffed between the cushions of the couch.

I turned to my brother, all ready to say something.

But he beat me to it. "I'll bet you're wondering about the paper, kid. I grabbed it from Delilah's purse. I only got a quick glance at it. Near as I can tell, it looked like some kind of airline schedule."

"An airline schedule?" I asked. "Does that mean she was on a plane?"

Bogey passed me another treat. "That would be my guess, kid. But we'll know more after we check it out."

I took the treat in my paw. "I didn't believe the story about her sister. Did you?"

Bogey grabbed another treat for himself. "Not one bit, kid. She was here to find that package. Pure and simple."

I munched my treat and stared outside at the sidewalk. "Wow, we had two people here in one day, both looking for that package. Who do you think that package belongs to?"

Bogey grabbed a couple more treats for us before he hid the bag back in the vase. "Don't know, kid. We won't be able to figure it out until we open it."

I sighed. More than ever before, I was just dying to

see what was in that package.

I finally felt my muscles start to relax when a thin, bald man suddenly appeared in front of the window. He waved and smiled at Bogey and me.

Holy Mackerel! I must have jumped a mile. Where in the world did that man come from?

He laughed and walked into the store. Then he headed straight over to see Bogey and me.

"Well, hello there, kitties," he said in a musical voice. "I wish I would have known you were here. Because I would have brought you some of the fish I had for lunch. You two are about the most handsome black cats I've ever seen. And I do like a handsome black cat."

I had to say, I kind of liked this man, too. He sure was nice to us cats, anyway. I scooted closer to him and started to purr. I was all ready for him to pet my head or scratch behind my ears.

But he only talked to us instead. "I'd invite you over to my store. But I'm not sure you and my parrot would get along. My Petey is a rather colorful fellow. And I do like a good colorful parrot."

A parrot? This man had a parrot? And by the way, who was this man?

I turned to my brother, to see what he thought about all this. But Bogey just sat there with his eyes half-closed. He looked kind of bored, as near as I could tell. Though I did notice his eyes never turned from the man's face.

Our Mom showed up and smiled at the man. "Hello, may I help you find something?"

The man smiled back at our Mom. "Well, hello, charming lady! Please allow me to introduce myself. I'm Abe Abascal, and I would guess you must be Abigail. I hope you'll accept my apologies for not stopping by sooner to say hello. But with moving in and getting my store set up . . . I fear the time has simply gotten away from me. But it's so lovely to meet you now. And, my, how I like a neighbor who knows her antiques."

Now our Mom's eyes went wide. "Oh hello, Abe. So nice to meet you, too. And I'm sorry I haven't stopped by to welcome you back to St. Gertrude."

Abe waved his hand in front of his face. "Nonsense. No apologies necessary, my dear lady. None at all. Though I must confess, I am here today to be sure you are all right. I saw an ambulance and a huge crowd over here. Was someone injured?"

Our Mom shook her head. "I'm not sure. We had a man pass out in our store."

Abe gasped and put his hand to his mouth. "Oh my gracious . . . how awful. Was he kind of scruffy and in dire need of a shower, perhaps? And acted sort of drowsy or dizzy?"

"Why, yes," our Mom told him. "That sounds like the man."

"He was at my store, too!" Abe practically sang out. "He said he was looking for a package of some sort."

Our Mom nodded. "That's what he was looking for here, too. In fact, we had another person looking for a package a few minutes later."

Abe glanced around the room. "My good gracious, that truly is strange. Did either of them find the item they were looking for?"

"No," our Mom said. "But there's no way any package could be in my store. I checked the whole place to make sure nothing was missing on Saturday night. After someone had broken in. I'm sure we would have noticed if we had a strange package sitting around."

Abe rubbed his forehead. "My store was broken into on Saturday, too. But nothing was taken. I'm sure it was simply some teenagers out having a little fun. Perhaps doing something on a dare."

"You're probably right," our Mom agreed. "Would you care for a cup of coffee?"

Abe smiled. "That sounds divine, dear lady. I do like a good cup of coffee. And, if you don't mind, I'll take a look around to see all your wonderful items. Sometimes I have a customer who is looking for something that I don't happen to have in my store. But perhaps you might. Then I could simply send them in your direction."

"Thank you, I'd appreciate it," our Mom said with a smile. "I'll do the same for you."

"Splendid," Abe said. "I like good store owners who cooperate with each other."

With those words, our Mom left to get some coffee for him. It was the second time today that she'd gone off to get coffee for someone. I wondered if anyone would actually drink the coffee this time.

Abe smiled at Bogey and me before he started to slowly walk around the store.

He paused in front of a beautiful black glass bowl and held it up. "Stunning! Simply stunning. I do like a nice glass bowl."

Then he walked on and looked at a big candleholder with crystals hanging from it. "Beautiful! I like a sparkly candlestick holder."

"Wow, that guy sure likes a lot of things," I whispered to my brother.

"You got that right, kid," Bogey meowed back quietly. "But we'd better get a move on. Let's check out that paper I pulled from Delilah's purse."

"Aye, aye," I told him. I tried to salute him with my huge paw, but I sort of lost my balance.

Thankfully, I caught myself before I fell off the buffet. Bogey grinned and leaped down to the hardwood floor. I followed him and then we ran back to the middle of the store. We jumped up on the green velvet couch where he'd hidden the paper.

Seconds later, Bogey had pulled that paper out and had it unfolded. Sure enough, it looked like an airline schedule.

I pointed to the name at the top. "But this is for someone named Deborah Willowby. Not Delilah Wunderfully."

Bogey nodded. "Good eye, kid. What do you want

to bet that Delilah has an alias?"

I crinkled my forehead. "An alias? What does that mean?"

Bogey pointed to the name. "It means Delilah may not always use her real name, kid. It means she might use another name — or names — at different times."

I stared at the sheet. "But why would she want to do that?"

I couldn't imagine using any name but my own. I liked the name Buckley. It was my name. It was who I was. And for that matter, I couldn't imagine Bogey using any other name besides his name either.

"To hide her real name, kid," Bogey told me. "It's something criminals do a lot. If they don't want to get caught, they don't let people know their real name."

"Oh, okay," I said. "So which name do you think is her real name? Delilah or Deborah?"

Bogey shook his head. "Good question, kid. It's hard to tell. All we do know is that she flew out of Istanbul five days ago. On flight 1494. And she arrived in St. Gertrude on Friday night."

I felt my eyes go wide. "Wow, that sounds like a long trip."

Bogey turned his ears toward the back of the store. "You got that right, kid. Now we have to wonder why she made such a long trip. And why she came to St. Gertrude."

In the background, I could hear Abe and our Mom talking.

"Why don't you come back and meet the rest of my staff?" our Mom said to Abe.

"I would be most honored," he told her as they walked together. "As I understand it, we both attended the same high school. I like a good high school. However, I would suspect you attended many years later than I did. Probably about twenty or so."

Our Mom laughed. "Yes, I think that's about right."

"My, but we have so much in common," Abe went on. "I am so pleased I stopped by today, dear lady."

Seconds later, we heard our Mom introduce Abe to Millicent and Merryweather.   Then they all started talking and laughing.

Bogey nodded in the direction of the back room. "Okay, kid, here's our chance.   Let's stash this paper in my pet carrier this time.   Yours is probably getting a little heavy."

By now, I knew the drill.   Since I was so much bigger, it would be my job to carry the paper.   Though I had to say, I sure liked the times when my size came in handy.   And since this paper didn't have ink on it that could run, I could carry it in my mouth.   That made it a whole lot easier.

Still, it kind of bounced and flapped in front of my eyes when I ran along behind Bogey.   He led the way, finding a path for us to get to the back room.   Without being spotted.

Minutes later, I had Delilah's airline schedule stashed in Bogey's pet carrier.   And just for good measure, I grabbed the other paper clue we'd found earlier.   The one that Bogey had gotten from the sea captain's pocket.   Then I hid it in Bogey's pet carrier, too.

I came back out and saw Bogey flex his front paw. "Wait a minute, kid.   Didn't Abe say the sea captain was in his store, too?"

I nodded my head. "Uh-huh. He did."

Bogey glanced at the entrance to the front room again. "I wonder if there's a connection, kid.   Between our Mom's store and Abe's store.   They were both broken into on the same night.   Maybe we need to investigate Abe's store, too."

That's when I felt the room start to spin a little bit. We'd been finding clues and running across suspicious characters since the second we got here this morning. What I really wanted was a nap!   And maybe a little lunch.

And now we were going to sneak outside our store

and go to another store?

Holy Catnip!

I flopped over on my cat bed. For a second or two, I thought about closing my eyes and going to sleep.

But I knew a good cat detective wouldn't do that. A good cat detective would be like Bogey. Ready to go.

Even when he was tired.

And since I wanted to be a good cat detective, well, I jumped up and followed Bogey out into the main part of the store.

We found our Mom and Abe talking near the front.

"Yes, yes," Abe was saying. "There was a woman at my store this morning. Nasty bit of work, that one. Rather a bit dramatic. Went by the name of Delilah, I believe. Though I do like a mysterious woman."

"He's leaving, kid," Bogey whispered to me. "We'll run out when he opens the door. Just hug the wall until you get to the door. Then zoom out and stay close to the side of the building.

"Bogey . . ." I started to say. "Do you really think this is a . . .?"

But I didn't even get a chance to finish my question. Or ask any other questions, for that matter. Questions like, how were we going to get back? Or would our Mom be mad because we took off?

No, I didn't get a chance to say another word. That's because everything happened so fast. Abe opened the door and held it open for almost a whole minute. Our Mom was busy talking to him and shook his hand. Neither one of them noticed us when we slipped out. And they sure didn't notice us when we flattened ourselves right up against the brick wall outside.

Then Abe walked out and we followed closely behind him till we got to his store. Just a few stores away. We were only a few feet from his front door when I glanced back. That's when I saw some people going into our Mom's store down the street.

Evaline Esterbrook. The manager at the St. Gertrude Museum. And Murwood was with her.

I wanted to say something to my brother. But I knew I couldn't. If I made so much as a peep, Abe would look down and spot us.

So I kept my mouth shut.

And when Abe opened the door to his store, Bogey and I zoomed inside. We were so fast he didn't even see us.

But someone else did. We had barely gotten inside when a voice started screeching at us.

"Traitors! Traitors! Traitors! Arrest them! Arrest them!"

Holy Catnip!

CHAPTER 15

Holy Mackerel! I heard it again. That screechy voice kept on yelling, "Traitors! Traitors! Traitors! Arrest them! Arrest them!"

Bogey and I dove behind a display case, but the screeching didn't stop. My heart started to pound so loud I thought it would drown out the sound of that voice.

Unfortunately, it didn't. I could still hear it just as plain as day.

All the while I wondered, had Bogey and I been spotted? We'd barely slipped into the store and someone was already yelling about having us arrested.

But what exactly did they plan to arrest us for? As far as I knew, we hadn't committed any crimes. Sure, we'd snuck out of our Mom's store and then into Abe's store. But that hardly seemed like a crime to me. I didn't think it was something a cat could be arrested for. And for that matter, did cats actually get arrested? Would we be taken to the "big house" as Bogey called it and have our mug shots taken?

I glanced at my brother and he shrugged his shoulders.

Then I heard Abe laugh. "Now, now, Pete, my fowl friend. What's got your feathers in a bunch?"

Pete? Did he say Pete? Suddenly Bogey grinned.

That's when it dawned on me. Didn't Abe say he had a parrot named Pete? And didn't parrots talk sometimes? But surely this parrot couldn't have us arrested.

Beside me, Bogey made a flapping motion with his front arms. And I knew exactly what he was trying to tell me. He was letting me know that Pete really *was* a parrot.

Right about then, I sure hoped my family never adopted a parrot. Because that was one bird who would not be quiet. Holy Catnip! If I thought Hector was a blabbermouth, well, he was nothing compared to Pete! I tried to imagine the two of them together in the same room. Nobody else would get a word in edgewise!

Now Bogey and I peeked out from our hiding place. On the other side of the room, we saw a huge cage on a stand. Inside was a big bird perched on a little wooden swing. He had a bright yellow head and green feathers on the rest of his body. Except for a few red feathers at the top of his wings.

I figured that must be Pete. And sure, he was a big bird, all right. But it seemed like his voice was about four times bigger than he was.

Abe had the cage door open and was feeding Pete some food by hand. That bird just kept on talking between bites. But at least he wasn't yelling out "Traitors" any more. Instead he was screeching things like, "Pretty diamonds! Pretty jewels! So shiny!"

Bogey motioned for me to follow him. Then together we turned and headed to the back of Abe's store. The place was kind of dark and musty smelling. It wasn't nearly as big as our Mom's store, and it didn't have as much stuff in it. And most of the things looked like they'd been carved in stone or made with wood. There were stone statues that stood as tall as a chair and wooden faces that kind of looked like masks. We saw some faded pottery with a sign in front of it that read, "Ming Dynasty." To tell you the truth, I thought the stuff that Gracie made at school was a whole lot prettier. Though we did see a few nice statues decorated with blue stones and shiny gold. These had a sign in front of them that read, "Straight from Ancient Egypt."

I had to say, I didn't know why anyone would want to buy something from ancient Egypt.

I turned away from those statues and followed my brother as we wove around all the things on the floor. We were very careful to stay out of sight while we looked for anything unusual. But as near as I could tell, there wasn't a clue in sight. Nothing stood out to us at all.

Now we could hear Abe singing in the front of the store. Pete sang along with him sometimes, too. At least Pete's singing sounded a whole lot better than his talking!

"I think we're done here, kid," Bogey whispered to me. "Now we'll just wait for someone to come in so we can run out. Let's make our way to the front door."

I nodded, and together we ran between all the stuff that Abe had on the floor. So far, no customers had come in the store while we'd been there. But I sure hoped someone would open the front door and walk in soon. Because I really wanted to get back to our Mom's store.

We were almost to the front door when we heard it open up. Someone was coming in. I glanced at Bogey and he looked at me. Did we have time to make it to the door before it closed?

He motioned for me to run. He took one bounding leap and I was about to race after him. Then something stopped us dead in our tracks.

Actually, that "something" was more like a smell.

Perfume.

Delilah's perfume. It came floating through the door before she even walked in.

Holy Catnip!

A cold chill ran up and down my spine and my fur stood on end. No matter what, we couldn't let Delilah know we were there. If she found out, she might try to hurt Bogey again. Plus she might try to take us for our fur!

Bogey and I both shrank back and flattened ourselves against a stone statue. Then Bogey nodded toward the same display case that we'd hidden behind when we first sneaked into Abe's store. So we carefully padded over to the case and then zoomed in behind it.

Now more than ever, I wished we were back at our Mom's store. We knew our Mom would protect us from Delilah. And Delilah was a woman us cats needed to be protected from!

But we were a long way from our Mom. To make things worse, she didn't even know where we were!

I shivered and scooted closer to the back of the display case. I really wished I was home and cuddled up in my Mom's arms. I wanted to close my eyes and drift off to sleep.

Bogey tapped me on the shoulder and pointed to the edge of the display case. I knew he wanted me to peek around the side with him. So we could keep an eye on Delilah. Funny, but Bogey didn't seem like he was scared at all.

I guess that was the difference between a good cat detective and a guy like me. If only I could be as brave as he was one day!

Pete the parrot started shrieking at the top of his lungs again. "Danger! Danger! Run for cover!"

For once, I had to agree with that bird.

"Lousy dame!" he screeched. "Lousy dame. Run for cover!"

"My, my," Delilah drawled. "But I do believe your bird would make a lovely feather hat."

I felt my eyes go wide. Now Delilah wanted to make a hat out of Pete? How many birds and animals had she threatened around St. Gertrude in one day? I wished we'd found an airline schedule that showed she was leaving town. Instead of just getting here.

"Come, come, Delilah," Abe said. "You, no doubt, have plenty of feather hats already. What is it I can help you with today?"

"I'm sure you know," Delilah said sweetly. "I'm looking for a couple of cats."

I gulped and almost started choking. Luckily, Bogey *thunked* me on the back. Had Delilah followed us to the store? Did she know we were there?

"I'm afraid I can't help you," Abe told her. "I haven't seen any cats. Is there anything else you might be in the market for? A nice tribal mask? Or perhaps a statue from Egypt?"

"No," she answered smoothly. "But I do have a foghorn I'd like to sell. It doesn't seem to be working."

I swung my head around and looked right at my brother. He stared back at me. Had we heard her right? Did she say a "foghorn?"

Abe laughed. "I'm afraid I can't help you there either, Delilah. I'm not in the market for a foghorn. Especially one that isn't even working. But that's a moot point, anyway, wouldn't you say? Since I suspect the condition of your foghorn isn't your true problem. I would imagine you don't actually have a foghorn, but rather a very good recording of one. Though I must say, I do like the sound of a good foghorn."

Before they could say anything else, the front door flew wide open. I nearly jumped to the top of the ceiling. My heart was still pounding by the time I remembered we were supposed to run out that door.

I was all set to zoom when Bogey grabbed my shoulder and held me back. I looked up to see two people walk by.

Evaline and Murwood.

What were they doing here? And what in the world was going on?

Now I couldn't help but peek out from behind that display case. I was dying to know why Evaline and

Murwood were here. I'd seen them go into our Mom's store right before we ran into Abe's store. What were they shopping for?

Beside me, Bogey peeked his head out, too. Just in time to see the sparks fly.

Okay, maybe we didn't *actually* see any sparks go flying. But well, if eyes could make sparks, let me tell you, we would have seen a bunch. Because Delilah looked right at Evaline and Evaline looked right back. Evaline clenched her teeth and her green dinosaur eyes looked so angry, I thought she was going to attack Delilah. And Delilah squinted her eyes and focused them right on Evaline. Kind of like a couple of laser beams. I wondered if Evaline might go up in smoke at any minute.

Holy Mackerel! That was the most scared I'd been all day. I sure hoped those two didn't spot Bogey and me!

"Big trouble! Lousy Dame!" Pete suddenly shrieked. "Run and hide! Run and hide!"

But Evaline and Delilah didn't seem to notice the parrot at all.

"It's you," Evaline seethed at Delilah.

Delilah continued to stare while a slow smile slid across her face. "You will have to excuse me, Abraham, but I've suddenly taken ill. Perhaps it's the horrible odor that just entered the room. I'm afraid I must leave, to save my genteel nature."

With those words, Delilah strutted past Evaline. She smacked her on the shoulder with her own shoulder when she strode past.

I'm sure my eyes went pretty wide right about then.

"Hello, Abe," Evaline said in an icy voice. "Long time no see."

Abe gave Evaline a slight smile. "How may I assist you?"

"I was wondering if you've had any recent shipments," Evaline said.

Abe shook his head. "I'm afraid not. Nothing new in quite some time."

Now Evaline kind of sneered at Abe. "Then I guess you'll probably tell me you haven't seen a couple of cats either."

Bogey and I turned and stared at each other. Was Evaline looking for us, too? But why?

Abe chuckled. "I should think, Evaline, that after the article I read in this morning's newspaper, you wouldn't be interested in any cats. Though I do like a good disaster."

Evaline put her hand on her hip. "'Take Your Cat to the Museum Day' was Byron's idea. Not mine."

"Yes, of course," Abe smiled. "Always Byron's fault, isn't it? And it's your belief that Byron always owes you something of some sort. Am I correct?"

Murwood bounced from one foot to the other. "Let's get out of here. I'm bored."

Seconds later, with barely a goodbye, Evaline and Murwood left Abe's store.

Right about then, I flopped over onto the floor. What in the world was going on?

I could hardly wait to talk about it all with my brother. Just as soon as we got out of there and back to our Mom's store. Bogey peeked around the corner of the display case and I did the same. If only we could see another customer coming into Abe's store.

Unfortunately, what we saw wasn't a customer. Instead, we saw Pete staring right at us. Apparently, Abe had let his bird out.

"Traitors! Traitors! Traitors!" he screeched. "Arrest them! Arrest them!"

"My goodness gracious, Pete, old chum. What has got you in such a tizzy this time?" Abe asked.

Seconds later, Abe himself leaned over the display case and spotted us.

My heart skipped a beat. What would Abe do now? What would happen to Bogey and me? Would we be in big trouble?

Abe laughed loudly. "Well, good afternoon, gentlemen. So lovely to see you both again. I suspect you must have followed me over from Abigail's store. Apparently we've become fast friends. So much so that you decided to pay me an unexpected visit. Though I wish I had known you were here, so I could have provided proper hospitality. Even so, I do like having feline visitors."

Bogey nudged me. "Go into your cute routine, kid."

And I did just that. Even though I had started to shake, I tilted my head to one side. Then I tilted it to the other.

"Well, my fine furry friends," Abe said. "Perhaps it's best that I take you back to your Mother's store. She might be worried about you by now."

Well, I had to say, that sounded like a good idea to me.

Minutes later, Abe put us both into a box. He kept the top open and carried us out of his store. I wanted to give him a kiss on the nose to thank him.

But I forgot all about it when we reached our Mom's store.

That's because Byron Bygones was walking out just as Abe was walking in. Byron held the door open wide and kept it open while Abe put the box on the ground. He let us jump out and into our Mom's store.

"Hello, Abe," Bryon said. His deep voice sounded sort of slippery.

"Good afternoon to you as well," Abe said in return. "I understand you've got a most stunning exhibit on display at your museum. You must have pulled many a string to convince Mr. Daunton's great-great-great-granddaughter to let you display such a priceless collection. After all, Mrs. Vera Glitter is known for being rather emotional and protective of her collection."

Without saying a word, Byron just gave him a smug smile. Then he turned and walked down the sidewalk.

But I hardly noticed. That's because I couldn't *stop*

noticing the plastic bag that Byron carried. It looked like he had bought something in our Mom's store. I could see the outline of the item pushing against the bottom of the bag.

And that item was exactly the same size as the package we'd hidden in my pet carrier.

Holy Mackerel!

CHAPTER 16

Holy Catnip! My breath kind of caught in my throat, and I'm sure my eyes went wider than they'd ever gone before. Because I couldn't stop staring at the beige plastic bag that Byron Bygones was carrying as he walked away.

Abe picked up his box, winked at us and left. I stood frozen on the hardwood floor as the door closed behind him.

I turned to my brother. "Bogey, did you see that? Did you see what Bryon had?"

Bogey took a deep breath. "I saw it, kid. The outline in the bag was about the right size. But there's only one way to know for sure."

"There is?" I sort of squeaked out.

He nodded in the direction of the back room. "Yup, kid. We'd better go check out your pet carrier. And see if our package is still there."

Well, let me tell you, he sure didn't have to tell me twice. He took off running and so did I! For once in my life, I ran even faster than Bogey did. We raced around dressers and tables and sofas and bookshelves. We jumped around lamps and past display cases.

I flew through the opening into the back room, with Bogey on my tail. The pads on my paws were pretty hot by the time I put on the brakes. I screeched to a stop right smack dab in front of my big pet carrier. It was an extra big carrier for an extra big guy like me.

Then I just sort of froze in place. For some reason, my muscles wouldn't work. Maybe it was because I knew I was about to find out whether our package was still there or not. If it was, I knew I'd be one happy cat. But if it wasn't, I knew I'd be so disappointed I would probably quit being a cat detective forever. And worst of all, Bogey and I would never, ever find out what was wrapped up in that brown paper.

And I sure didn't want that to happen.

Bogey caught up to me. "Moment of truth, kid. Let's see if it's in there or not."

I still seemed kind of stuck in place.

Bogey patted me on the shoulder. "Daylight's burning, kid."

He was right. This was something that couldn't wait any longer. So I took a deep breath and forced myself to go forward. I pulled the door open and slowly stepped inside my pet carrier. I headed for the back, where Bogey said he'd hidden that package. It took me a couple of seconds to walk all the way through.

But just as I was almost there, I couldn't stand it any more. I ran the rest of the way and pulled up the blanket and the mat.

And sure enough, right where Bogey said he'd hidden it, was our package.

Holy Mackerel! Talk about relief!

I flopped over on my side, right next to our package. I let out a really big sigh and closed my eyes for a second. Funny, I didn't even know what was wrapped up in this bundle. Maybe it was something important and maybe it wasn't. But I sure was glad to see it.

"Well, kid?" Bogey hollered from the outside.

"It's here, it's here!" I meowed to him.

Then I pulled the mat and the blanket back over the

package again. I made sure it was hidden really, really well. So no one would find it. Then I walked out of my pet carrier and crawled over to my cat bed. I flopped onto my side and tried to calm down.

Bogey grinned. "See, kid? No need to sweat it."

I raised my brow and tilted my ears his way. If you asked me, I got the feeling Bogey was a little nervous about our package being gone, too.

He grabbed the bag of cat treats he had stashed behind his bed. "Okay, kid, I'll admit it. I was sweating it a bit myself."

"I'm still a little shaky," I told him.

I tried to rub my head with my paw. But I only bonked myself in the nose instead. So then I tried again. This time my big paw went exactly where I wanted it to go.

Bogey handed me a cat treat. "Here you go, kid. This'll get you calmed down."

I took the treat from him. "I'll be so glad when we get our package home. Maybe then I won't worry about it so much."

Bogey took a cat treat for himself. "Don't be so sure, kid."

I munched on my treat. "Um . . . what do you mean?"

Bogey passed me another treat and took one for himself. "Two people were already here today looking for a package, kid. And I'll just bet our package is the one they're after. Nobody's said a word about what's in it, but I'll bet it's something pretty special. Just judging by the way these people are acting. And when they don't find it here, they might suspect we took it home."

I munched on my second treat. "They might?"

Bogey stashed the bag of cat treats behind his bed. "Yup, kid."

I gulped. "And they might try to find it at our house?"

Bogey nodded. "'Fraid so, kid."

That's when I'd had about all the danger and scary stuff I could take for the moment. My heart started to pound and my paws started to shake. Sure, I was trying hard to be a big, brave cat detective. But sometimes . . . well, sometimes a guy just needs his Mom.

And a really good hug.

I jumped out of my cat bed. "I'll be right back," I said to my brother.

Bogey tilted his head at me. "You okay, kid? You look a little rough."

But I didn't want to tell him what I was thinking. After all, a good cat detective wasn't supposed to go running to his Mom for a hug. Instead I just raced out of the back room without saying a word.

Once I got into the main part of the store, I listened for our Mom's voice. When I heard her talking to Millicent, I made a beeline in their direction. I found my Mom on the other side of the store. I starting rubbing around her legs and meowing to her.

She kneeled down and petted me. "Hello, Buckley. I haven't seen you in a while."

Boy, she could say that again. I climbed right into her arms and wrapped my own arms around her neck. She laughed and held me nice and tight. I tucked my head under her chin and started to purr.

Millicent said, "Ooooh. What a nice guy you are, Buckley."

"There's nothing like a good afternoon hug," our Mom murmured into my fur.

I closed my eyes and drifted off. Suddenly all the scary stuff of the day sort of melted away.

That was, until Officer Phoebe strolled into the store and joined us.

"Just thought you'd like an update on that man who went out in the ambulance," she told our Mom and Millicent.

"Is he all right?" Millicent asked.

Officer Phoebe shook her head. "Not yet. He's still out cold. He's in the hospital and will probably stay there for a few days at least.   It looks like someone drugged him."

Our Mom and Millicent gasped.   I turned my head and looked at Officer Phoebe.

So Bogey had been right!   Someone had given the sea captain something to knock him out.

Holy Catnip!

"I guess that's why he was weaving like he was," our Mom said.

Right about then, I noticed Bogey standing off to the side.   He must have followed me out of the back room.

He caught my eye and motioned for me to join him. Let me tell you, I had a pretty good idea what he wanted to talk about.

So I gave my Mom a kiss on the nose.   Then I jumped down out of her arms and off I went with Bogey. Seconds later, we were both sitting in our cat beds again.

"That was a good call, kid," Bogey told me. "Running off like you did.   Otherwise we might have missed that part of the puzzle.   We never would've known what happened to the sea captain.   That he's still in the hospital.   And he'll be in the hospital for a while. Somebody sure wanted that guy out of commission."

"B-b-but, Bogey," I started to say.   "I was really kind of running to our Mom to get a . . ."

Bogey held up his paw.   "No need to explain, kid. Every good cat detective has gut feelings.   Sometimes you just gotta act on 'em right away.   You did a great job."

I bit my lip.   "Gee, thanks, but the truth is . . ."

Bogey shook his head.   "Don't say another word, kid.   I've been in your paws a time or two myself.   Now, then . . . about this case.   Doesn't it seem strange to you that all these people shopped in our Mom's store in one day?   The sea captain, Delilah, and Byron?   And Delilah and Evaline and the sea captain all were looking for something in Abe's store, too?"

Well, Bogey sure had that one right. It *was* kind of strange.

I nodded. "I also noticed they weren't very nice. Even to each other. Maybe one of them drugged the sea captain."

Bogey stared off into space. "That'd be my guess, too, kid. Because I think these people are all connected somehow. They seem to know each other. Almost like they were friends once."

I shook my head. "Well, they sure aren't now. But one thing is for sure. This is our most complicated case ever."

Bogey reached over and gave me a paw bump. "You can say that again, kid."

Then he glanced up at the clock on the wall.

"It's almost time for our Mom to leave, kid," he said. "Gracie will be home from school pretty soon."

That meant we would be going home with our Mom. Holy Mackerel, this was one day that had just flown by.

"Best get into your pet carrier," Bogey said. "So our Mom doesn't notice it's got something extra in it."

"Aye, aye," I said to my brother.

I tried to salute him and this time I was only slightly off. I touched the top of my head, but not quite all the way down to my forehead. Boy, I sure hoped I could get my paws to go where I wanted them to go someday.

"Okay, kid," Bogey said. "Pull the package out and sit right on top of it. So it doesn't scoot around when our Mom picks up your pet carrier. And so the weight is in the middle."

"Got it," I told him.

And I did just that. I pulled our package into position. Then I laid down right on top of it. Smack dab in the middle of my pet carrier. It was a good thing I was an extra big cat with really long fur. Because I covered our package perfectly. It wasn't exactly comfortable, but sometimes being a cat detective isn't very comfortable.

Now Bogey jumped into his pet carrier, too.

And not a moment too soon.

Our Mom came strolling in and grabbed her purse from the cabinet.

She smiled at us. "My goodness, boys. It looks like you two are ready to go."

Normally I would have given her a kiss on the nose. But not this time.

She zipped up our pet carriers and then picked us up.

She groaned when she picked up mine. "My goodness, Buckley. Are you growing some more? I don't remember you being this heavy this morning."

I just meowed to her. A few minutes later, we were in the car and on our way home. Finally. I was so happy to know our package was with us.

That was, until our Mom drove out of the alley, turned the corner and drove past the front of the store. That's when I saw Delilah, Byron, Evaline and Murwood. They were all standing on the street and staring at our car. And let me tell you, they did not look happy! In fact, their heads all turned and they just kept on watching us as we drove by.

Holy Catnip!

CHAPTER 17

Holy Mackerel! I scrunched down lower into my pet carrier and tried to stop shaking. There was something about the way those four people had been staring at us that gave me the creeps! I sure hoped they didn't come looking for our package at our house, like Bogey had thought.

But as long as I'd known him, he'd almost never been wrong.

"Did you see those people?" I asked my brother.

He nodded toward the window. "Oh yeah, kid. I saw them all right."

I pushed my front paws against the sides of my carrier, to steady myself. "They sure were staring at us."

Bogey stood up and glanced toward the back of the car. "Yes, they were, kid. We might want to start running extra surveillance rounds tonight."

I gulped. The only times we ran extra surveillance was when we really needed it. When we thought there might be a threat to our house or to our family.

Bogey turned back to me. "Let's hide that package under the couch when we get home, kid. I'll let you know when the coast is clear. We'll move it upstairs tonight when our family is asleep."

"Aye, aye," I told him. I tried to salute him and this time I got even closer to my forehead.

Our Mom pulled into our driveway and then into our garage a few minutes later. After that, everything happened really fast. Our Mom brought us in, put us on the kitchen floor and then unzipped our pet carriers. Gracie got home from school and our Mom went to the front door to greet her.

"Quick, kid!" Bogey hollered to me. "Here's your chance! Move that package now!"

I didn't wait for him to tell me a second time. I jumped out of my pet carrier and turned around. Then I picked up our package and backed out of there. I had that bundle safely hidden under the family room couch before our Mom and Gracie came into the room.

Gracie kissed us cats hello before she went and changed her clothes. Then she didn't waste any time getting right to her piano practice. After all, her recital was coming up on Saturday night!

As always, Bogey and I scampered into the living room to listen to her play. We nodded to Lil and the Princess before we joined them on the floor behind the baby grand piano. Gracie was already practicing her recital song, and if you asked me, she played it even better than yesterday. She was almost through the whole song before she made a mistake.

And that's when she quit playing. "Ugh!" she cried out.

She put her hands over her eyes and hung her head. "I'll never get this right. Everyone is going to laugh at me at the recital."

That made my ears perk up. After all, I couldn't imagine anyone laughing at Gracie. I'd be pretty mad at them if they did!

Especially when we knew she could play her song really well.

Maybe all she needed was a little encouragement. I

remembered what had helped her yesterday. So I jumped up onto the piano bench beside her. Then I reached up and gave her a kiss on the nose. Below me, Bogey grinned and jumped up to the front ledge of the piano. He reached down and hit a few piano keys with his paws.

And though Bogey might be one of the greatest cat detectives ever, well . . . his piano playing was a different story.

Gracie giggled. "Okay, boys. I get the message."

I was sure glad she did. Because it was a really important message. I gave her one more kiss on the nose just to be sure. Then I sat back on the bench to let her play.

She put her fingers to the keyboard and started from the beginning again. This time she played her song perfectly.

She practiced clear through until dinnertime. While our family ate, Bogey and I had a bite to eat, too. Then I stretched out on the family room couch.

I was so tired from the day, that I just closed my eyes for a second. I must have dozed off at some point, because the next thing I knew, Bogey was shaking my shoulder.

"Look alive, kid," he said. "We may have company."

I rolled on my side and stretched. "Company? I like when our Mom and Dad have company."

"Not that kind of company, kid," Bogey told me. "This is the bad kind. You won't like this company."

"The bad kind?" I opened my eyes and glanced around.

The whole house was dark. Our family had gone to bed. I couldn't believe I'd slept through it all.

"Time to get our package upstairs," Bogey said to me.

"Um, okay," I told him while I stretched. "But what about the company? The bad kind?"

Bogey nodded toward the hallway. "I'll show you from the upstairs window, kid."

I tried to rub the sleep out of my eyes with my arm. That's when it dawned on me. If we were taking our package upstairs, that meant . . .

Suddenly I was wide awake. "Bogey, is it time to open our package?"

He grinned at me. "Yup, kid. We'll run surveillance right after that."

I could hardly believe it! Pretty soon I would finally get to see what was wrapped up in all that paper.

I pulled it out from under the couch and carried it in my teeth as I followed Bogey down the hallway. Funny, but that package seemed even heavier now than it had before. Especially when I took it up the stairs.

Bogey pointed to a spot on the landing. "Let's leave that thing here for a minute, kid. I've got something to show you outside first."

So I dropped the package and ran after Bogey to our favorite upstairs window. The one where we got a good view of the whole street. And a big part of the block in our neighborhood, too.

We jumped onto the seat cushion and looked outside.

"Over there, kid," he told me. "See her?" He pointed a paw toward a streetlamp.

I turned in the direction he had pointed. And sure enough, I saw someone standing under the streetlamp and leaning against the pole.

"Bogey, that looks like . . ." I started to say.

"Yup, kid," Bogey finished. "It looks like Delilah, all right."

"What's she doing out there?" I asked.

And just as soon as I said the words, I already knew the answer. Or at least, I had a pretty good idea what the answer was. I started to shake just a little bit. I was really glad we were on the inside and she was on the outside.

"Do you think she's watching our house?" I asked my brother. "Maybe in case she'd like to break in and well . . ."

Bogey nodded. "I'd say so, kid."

Holy Catnip. I gulped.

Bogey put his paw on my shoulder. "Maybe it's time we found out what's inside that package, kid. And the reason it's so important to these people. So take it in the sunroom and start opening it. I'll be along in a minute. First I need to do something in our Mom's office."

I felt my brow go up. "You do? What?"

Bogey grinned. "Let's just say the St. Gertrude Police are about to get a mysterious tip, kid. Something about a stranger lurking in our neighborhood."

I tilted my head. "O-o-o-h."

Without another word, Bogey took off for the first floor. And I went back and retrieved our package from the landing. Then I carried it into the sunroom.

As soon as I walked in, I spotted the Wise One on her purple velvet couch. The Princess was lounging on a chair across from her.

I tried to bow like Bogey had taught me to do. But it wasn't exactly easy to do while I was carrying that heavy bundle.

Miss Mokie waved her paw over me from above. "No need for formalities, young Detective. It appears you are carrying a heavy load. Please come in and unburden yourself. The good Princess Alexandra has told me of your recent case. She said you'd be bringing a package up to be unwrapped."

I dropped the package in the middle of the floor and turned to the Princess. "But how did you know?"

She smiled and stared at me with her big, green eyes. "I heard all about it while you were napping, Buckley. Bogey told Lil and me everything that happened today. We all agreed the sunroom would be the best place to put this package. Because we can hide it up here if we need to."

I'm sure the things the Princess was saying probably made a lot of sense. But at that moment, I could hardly make sense of anything. All I could see where those big, green eyes. I just sort of went gooey inside and my heart started to pound really loud.

Miss Mokie sat up very straight and very tall. "Shall we open it now, young Detective?"

"Um, okay," I managed to say.

And that's when it hit me. Finally, at long last, I was going to see what was inside. I had waited so long to find out. It felt like a year had gone by since I first found the package in that cabinet.

I only hoped it would be something worth waiting for.

I turned to see Lil join the party. She saluted me. Perfectly, without hitting her nose, her ears or even her whiskers.

"Thought you might need some help, Detective Buckley," she told me.

"Thanks," I said with a smile.

Then I ducked my head down and started yanking at the knot in the string. Someone had tied it pretty tight. But after a few tries, I was able to pull it loose and then pull it apart. I moved onto the next knot and did the same thing.

After that, Lil helped me pull the string out from around the whole bundle.

Next we started working on the brown paper. We used our claws to pull it off in shreds. Underneath, we found a layer of soft cloth. In fact, it looked like the whole object had been wrapped in this cloth. So Lil grabbed one end of the cloth and I rolled the object in the opposite direction. I pushed it over and over and over.

Until the thing that had been wrapped up finally appeared.

A little black cat statue.

Made from a shiny, sort of sticky black plastic. It had a tail that curved around in a half circle.

"It's a cat," I said. Though I figured everybody could

probably see that.

Right at that moment, I wasn't sure whether I should be happy or disappointed. Sure, as plastic cat statues go, this one was a nice one. Still, it probably wasn't worth a lot.

The Princess jumped down and moved closer to get a better look. "That plastic looks kind of rubbery. And stretchy. It's sort of funny looking."

I stared at the black cat. "I know."

That's when I realized something wasn't right.

I glanced at Lil. "But why would a plastic cat statue be so heavy? Plastic should be light."

The Wise One's voice floated down from above us. "Look deeper."

Look deeper? Huh? How was I supposed to do that?

Now Bogey trotted in and joined us. He walked right over to that cat statue, put a sharp claw into the plastic and ripped it wide open. Suddenly something sparkly popped out. Something that was a beautiful dark blue, with some shiny silver beside it. In fact, there was lots and lots of blue.

Blue gems.

The Princess and I both gasped. The cat statue had been covered in a black plastic coating. But just below that . . .

All of us cats jumped in to rip up the rest of the plastic coating. Before long, we had pulled all that plastic off in strips.

And revealed the cat statue underneath.

It was made from a silver-colored metal and mostly covered in blue stones. The nose had a red stone and the eyes had green stones.

The Princess sort of sighed. "Oh my goodness, those blue stones are sapphires. Kashmir sapphires. The best kind."

"Are you sure?" I asked her.

She nodded. "I'm sure, Buckley. I know my gems."

And then I remembered that she did. In her life

before she came to live with us, she had been around a lot of jewels.

"The green stones are emeralds," the Princess went on. "And the red ones are rubies. And the main part of the cat is made out of platinum."

"Wow," Lil and I sort of murmured.

The statue was so shiny and beautiful, I couldn't stop staring at it. None of us could stop staring at it.

Lil finally spoke. "So . . . is that what I think it is?"

Bogey grinned. "Yup, I'd say so."

Then he turned to me. "Why don't you be the one to say it, kid? You know what it is."

Well, I had to say, Bogey was right. I knew exactly what that cat statue was.

I took a deep breath before I spoke. "It's Tobias," I said. "One of Danby Daunton's cat statues that went missing."

"Looks like it's not missing any more," Bogey said.

Holy Catnip!

CHAPTER 18

Holy Mackerel! I could hardly believe it. I closed my eyes a couple of times and looked again, just to make sure it was real. But every time I opened my eyes, there it was. One of Danby Daunton's most favorite pieces. Not to mention, one of his most famous!

The Tobias half of his Best Friends statues.

A statue that had been missing for almost a hundred and fifty years!

All of us cats just stood there and stared at it for a few minutes. The blue stones sort of lit up like little blue lights. The whole thing was so shiny and sparkly that it even sort of glowed. It was one of the prettiest things I've ever seen in my whole life.

Mr. Daunton sure went to a lot of work when he made this cat statue. It was in the perfect shape of a cat. And it must have taken him a long, long time to put all those stones in. Plus the huge curved tail was designed to fit perfectly with another cat statue. I could tell it was meant to be part of a set.

But even by itself, it was too beautiful for words. It was so much prettier than the painting of the cat statues that we'd seen at the Museum. And then later on the Internet.

Suddenly I understood why all those people had come into our Mom's store. If they were looking for this statue, I could sure see why. It was so stunning and probably worth a lot of money.

But how did this statue even get into our Mom's store in the first place? Who put it there?

Above us, Miss Mokie purred. "Ah, such a remarkable piece, young ones. Of course a true artist would only use his cats as subjects for his greatest works. After all, what better subject could there possibly be?"

The Princess smiled up at Miss Mokie. Then she sat right next to the statue. The blue of the sapphires sort of reflected off her snowy, white fur. Funny, but to me, the Princess was just as pretty as any statue. In fact, when I looked back at the statue, I wasn't as dazzled as I was at first. Then I remembered what Miss Mokie had told me before. About not being dazzled by shiny things. And about looking deeper.

That's when I noticed the little symbol on the bottom of the statue. It was in the outline of a cat. Exactly like we'd seen in the picture of the painting on the Internet.

I pointed to the bottom of the statue. "Bogey, look! There's a symbol here."

Bogey patted me on the back. "Good job, kid."

"Um, thanks," I told him. "I still wonder why he put those symbols on his statues."

Bogey nodded. "Me, too, kid. I have a feeling they're connected to this case somehow. But I'll bet we find out *how* pretty soon."

For some reason, I kind of shuddered. Sure, I wanted to find out what those symbols had to do with our case. But then again, if it meant running into people like Delilah . . . well, let's just say I wasn't in a big hurry.

Still, a whole bunch of other questions raced through my mind.

"I wonder where the other cat is?" I asked out loud. "Where is Tessa?"

Bogey shook his head. "That's a good question, kid."

The Princess ran her paw over the front of the Tobias statue. "Before I came to live here, I used to hear a lot about the Daunton statues. It's said that Mr. Daunton never made any more after the Tobias and Tessa statues disappeared. He was so heartbroken. He put his heart and soul into those statues."

I shook my head. "Wow, that's really sad. Because I'll bet Mr. Daunton would have made a whole bunch more statues if he hadn't been so upset."

Bogey leaned against the Wise One's couch. "Makes you wonder, doesn't it, kid? If he quit making statues all of a sudden, he probably had lots of stuff left over. Stuff he would've used to make more statues."

Suddenly my heart skipped a beat. "You mean more gems and gold and silver? Stuff like that?"

Bogey grinned. "Yup, kid. That would be my guess."

Now Lil joined in. "So what happened to all his statue-making materials?"

Bogey raised his brow. "I don't know. But you can bet he put it in a safe place. He probably hid it."

Lil looked back to the hallway. "I believe you're right, Detective Bogart. Because, if his beloved cat statues were ever found, he would've been happy once more. And he would've started making new statues again."

Bogey grinned. "You got it, Lil. And wherever he hid his stuff, I'll bet it's still there today."

Lil looked at the statue. "Because there's never been any record of a treasure trove like that being found."

By now, my head had been going back and forth. Looking at Bogey then Lil then Bogey then Lil and on and on. When they finished talking, I had to shake my head to make all the pieces fall into place.

That's when it hit me. And let me tell you, it hit me hard. "You mean . . . hidden treasure?"

Bogey nodded. "Yup, kid, this case might just turn into a treasure hunt, too."

A treasure hunt?

Holy Mackerel!

"But first we'd better hide this Tobias statue," Bogey said. "So nobody finds it."

Up until now, the Wise One had been sitting quietly on her couch. Listening to every word. Maybe that was just one of the ways she'd gotten to be so wise. By listening to things a lot.

She waved her paw above us. "I believe you'll find a false bottom in the closet over there. It would make an ideal hiding place. No one would ever find it."

Wow. Lil and the Princess and Bogey and I all looked at each other with big eyes. I sure had to wonder how the Wise One knew that. Then again, she was the Wise One. She knew a lot of stuff that no one else knew about.

Bogey and the Princess ran off to look in the closet. Then Lil helped me roll the statue up in the cloth it had been wrapped in before.

Minutes later, us cats had dragged that statue across the floor. Together we carefully tucked it away into the empty hiding place in the closet. Then we covered it with the false bottom. No one would ever know it was there.

Bogey glanced at me. "I've got a few things to check out kid. Then we'd better get back to our surveillance rounds. Meet you in ten?"

I tilted my ears forward. "Ten?"

Bogey grinned. "Minutes, kid. Ten minutes."

I nodded. "Oh, okay. I'll be there."

Then one by one, all the other cats left the room. But I stayed behind. For some reason, I just wasn't ready to leave yet.

The Wise One looked down at me from her couch.

"Is something bothering you, young Detective? I sense that something is weighing on your mind."

Well, to tell you the truth, I didn't think anything was really bothering me. Except for the usual stuff. And, well . . . all the things going on with this case . . .

But before I could even think about it any more, a whole bunch of words just sort of came pouring out of me. It seemed like I started talking and I couldn't stop.

"I don't understand," I said. "The people that came into our Mom's store today . . . the ones who were probably looking for this statue . . . Bogey thinks they used to be friends. And boy, they sure don't act like they were ever friends. They're really pretty mean to each other. But how can they act like that? How can they be friends once and then not be friends? I'd be pretty upset for a long, long time if Bogey and I weren't friends any more. Having him as my best friend is the best thing ever. What would I do without the Princess or Lil or Ranger or Amelia? And . . . you. Having friends means more to me than anything."

Miss Mokie nodded her head and smiled. "Ah, yes, young one. You are wise for your years and you have a good heart."

I tilted my head. "Gee, thanks. But why do these people act like they do?"

Miss Mokie raised her paw and flexed her claws. "First, one must know something about human behavior. It can be quite difficult to understand, of course. Human behavior can be so far beneath that of feline behavior."

"It can?" I asked.

"Most certainly, young Detective," Miss Mokie said. "Humans are prone to such folly as greed."

I leaned in to listen closer. Maybe if the Wise One became wise from listening, maybe I could become wise by listening, too.

Now Miss Mokie sighed. "Humans, I fear, often have a strange desire to own shiny and sparkly things. Objects they believe to be valuable. And in some cases, the more they own, the better. They see such objects as great treasures, things to be prized above all else."

"Is that bad?" I asked her.

After all, I had a nice collection of cat toys. Some of them had sparkles on them. And some of them were shiny. Gracie had even made me some shiny cat collars. Plus I had a nice bed and a great food dish. And I sure did like all those things.

Miss Mokie leaned forward and stretched her front legs out before her. "It is certainly not wrong, unless one starts to value their possessions over anything else. And as long as one doesn't lie, cheat, or steal in order to possess such prized objects. And as long as one doesn't cause harm to their friends, or treat others badly. But so often, humans stop at nothing to own objects they consider to be valuable. They do so at the expense of the ones they care about the most."

"Wow," I sort of breathed. "So sometimes humans think the stuff they own is more important than their friends. And they do bad things just to get the stuff they want."

Miss Mokie nodded. "Ah, yes, you understand correctly. You have learned well, Grasshopper."

I smiled. And for a moment, I just sat there and thought about what she'd said. Even so, I never understood why she called me Grasshopper. She did the same thing to Bogey, and he didn't understand it either. Still, I sure understood what she was saying about friends and owning stuff and all that. So, as near as I could tell, the people we ran across today had all been friends once. But the Tobias statue was more important to them than their friendships.

I had to say, I thought that was very sad.

Miss Mokie waved her paw above me. "You must leave me now, young one. It is time for me to rest."

So I thanked her and bowed and backed out of the room. I noticed she'd already closed her eyes before I had gone through the door.

I ran straight for our favorite upstairs window. Bogey had a grin on his face as he stared out and down the street. I looked out, too, and saw Delilah standing under the streetlamp like before. Only this time, there was a police car right next to her. The officer inside looked like he was talking to her from his open window.

A few seconds later, Delilah got into the front passenger seat and the car drove away.

"Dames?" I said to my brother.

He nodded his head slowly. "Dames, kid. But that's one dame who's a pretty nasty piece of work."

Boy, he could say that again.

The rest of the night, we ran extra surveillance runs. We made sure all the doors and windows were locked. Plus we kept an eye outside for anything unusual.

We did the same thing the next night and the next night. On Tuesday night, we spotted a man underneath the streetlight outside. I wasn't sure, but I thought it might be Murwood, wearing a fedora hat and trench coat. The next night I thought I saw Byron. He looked like he might be in disguise, too. But neither one of them stayed very long. So we didn't have a chance to call the police.

Still, we kept our senses on full alert and kept our eyes wide open every night. Plus we decided to add extra surveillance runs during the day. While our family was out of the house. Thankfully, nobody tried to break in. And our statue stayed hidden up in the sunroom closet.

"What are we going to do with our statue?" I asked Bogey late Wednesday night.

He was busy typing on our Mom's computer. I stood on the desk and looked at the screen. There were a couple of articles about Danby Daunton that Bogey had been reading.

Bogey grabbed a bag of cat treats he had hidden in a vase on top of the desk. He handed one to me and took one for himself.

"We'll keep the statue hidden until we get this case

figured out, kid," he told me. "We still don't know who broke into our Mom's store. Or, who drugged the sea captain. And since he's still in the hospital, we probably won't find out much from him."

I munched on the fish-flavored treat. "And now we might be looking for treasure, too."

Bogey passed us both another round of treats. "Yup, kid. Not to mention, we've still got to keep our family safe from all these shady characters running around."

I finished my second treat. "But who does our statue really belong to? I don't think we can keep it. Can we?"

Bogey raised his brow. "Good question, kid. One that might take some sorting out. Probably someone in Daunton's family somewhere should legally own it. My money's on Mr. Daunton's great-great-great-granddaughter, Vera Glitter. I'll bet we'll find it belongs to her in the end."

"And we still don't know where the Tessa statue is," I added.

Now Bogey grinned. "Oh, I have a feeling it may not be so far away, kid."

That made me sit up straight. "You do?"

Bogey pointed to the computer screen. "Think about it, kid. The Tobias statue is stolen, and then the Tessa statue suddenly goes missing. But I've got a feeling the Tessa statue wasn't stolen. I'll bet Mr. Daunton hid it."

I felt my eyes go wide. "So nobody could steal it."

Bogey nodded. "Yup, kid. That would be my guess. It's probably with the rest of the stuff he hid."

All of a sudden, I had a hard time breathing. "The treasure!"

Bogey passed me another treat. "You got it, kid. If we find the Tessa statue, we'll find the treasure, too."

Holy Catnip.

I glanced around the room. "But where would he hide it? I'll bet his relatives already looked all over his house."

Bogey pointed a paw toward the ceiling. "Think about it, kid. How many times have you run surveillance on that sunroom? Did you know there was a false bottom in that closet?"

My mouth fell open wide. "Well . . . no."

"Me either, kid," Bogey said. "Could be lots of hidden spaces in buildings around town. Hidden places that no one even knows about."

"Wow," I just sort of breathed. "That treasure could be anywhere."

Bogey nodded. "You got it, kid. Daunton helped found St. Gertrude. He probably helped build some of the first buildings here. Maybe he put some secret spaces into some of them."

I flopped onto the desk. "This case is so complicated. I'm having a hard time keeping everything straight."

Bogey tilted his head. "You and me both, kid."

He passed us each another cat treat before he stuffed the bag back into the vase.

I shook my head. I sure wished I could make the pieces of this puzzle fall into place. But it seemed like the more I tried and the more I learned, the more confusing this case got. And it didn't help that I was pretty tired after running all those extra surveillance rounds. All hours of the day and night.

So by the time Thursday rolled around, I was exhausted. Bogey was, too. We both almost jumped a mile when the doorbell rang late that afternoon. Right after our Mom and Gracie had barely walked in the door.

Bogey signaled for me to get into position by the front door when our Mom opened it.

When she did, we saw a deliveryman standing on our porch, carrying a bunch of metal pans. He had long black hair pulled into a ponytail. Big, black glasses sat perched on his nose and his face was sort of hidden by his huge hat. He was also wearing an extra-large navy jacket and pants that looked way too big for him.

Funny, but even though I'd never seen the man before, he seemed kind of familiar.

"Good evening, madam," he said to our Mom. "I've been asked to deliver this delicious meal to you and your family. It seems you have a customer who wanted to give you a gift. She hired us to deliver this to you."

Our Mom's eyebrows went up. "She did? But who is 'she?'"

The deliveryman shook his head. "I'm afraid, dear lady, that she wanted her identity to be kept secret. But she was so pleased with the help you gave her, that she wanted to do something nice for you, too."

Our Mom blinked a few times. "Oh, that is so sweet."

The man smiled. "It certainly is. She sent over pans of mashed potatoes, green beans and salmon. And chocolate cake for dessert. Enough for your entire family."

Before our Mom could say another word, he passed the pans to her. Then he tipped the bill of his hat and practically ran down the sidewalk. He climbed into a white van and drove off.

Gracie joined us and took two of the pans from our Mom. "Wow, that was really nice, Mom. Now we have supper for tonight. And Dad likes salmon a lot. And you like chocolate cake."

"You've got that right," our Mom agreed with a laugh.

Our Mom closed the door. Then she and Gracie took the food into the kitchen.

I turned to Bogey. "That was nice. And we like salmon, too. Maybe our Dad will give us some."

Bogey squinted his eyes at the door. "Not so fast, kid. Did you notice something funny about that delivery man?"

I looked at the door, too, since Bogey was staring at it. "Um, no. Did you?"

Bogey ran to the window to look outside. "Yup, kid. His glasses were too big and I think he was wearing a wig."

I felt my eyes go wide. "He was?"

"That's right, kid," Bogey told me. "We'd better go check out that food."

So we did. We ran into the kitchen, and when our Mom and Gracie went upstairs, we jumped on the counter.

Bogey made a beeline for the salmon. "Something's fishy here, kid."

I crinkled my brow. "Um . . . is it the fish?"

Bogey pulled the aluminum foil from the top of the pan. "You got it, kid. Take a good whiff."

I did just as Bogey asked. That's when I smelled it. Something funny.

"What is it?" I asked my brother.

For once, Bogey turned serious. Really serious.

He moved closer to the fish. "Exactly what I smelled on the sea captain's breath, kid. Someone's put something in this salmon. Probably ground up sleeping pills."

They had?

Holy Catnip!

CHAPTER 19

Holy Catnip! I took another good sniff of the salmon, and I knew Bogey had been right. Someone had put something in the fish.

My chin practically hit the counter. "Who would do that to our family?"

Bogey moved to the other side of the pan. "Someone who wants our family to be sound asleep tonight, kid."

I blinked my eyes a few times. "But our family *always* sleeps at night."

Bogey glanced at the edge of the counter and then back to the pan again. "Whoever sent this fish, kid, wants to make sure our family doesn't wake up for a while."

I shook my head. "But why would they want that?"

Bogey put his paw on the edge of the pan. "They probably want to break in here tonight, kid. And they want to make sure our family doesn't wake up while they're searching our house."

My heart skipped a beat. The light was finally starting to dawn. "Because they want to look for our statue?"

Bogey turned the pan so it was lined up with the

edge of the counter. "You got it, kid. And by sending over salmon, they probably figured us cats would get a few bites, too."

Now I started to shake just a little bit. "Then we would be asleep, too."

Bogey pushed the pan forward an inch. "That's right, kid. And nobody would interrupt them while they searched away."

Just then we heard our Dad drive into the garage. He was home from work already. That meant our family would be eating this dinner really soon. And it wouldn't be good for them. For all I knew, they might end up in the hospital just like the sea captain.

But Bogey and I couldn't let that happen. We had to do something.

And fast.

I glanced at Bogey with wide eyes. "Bogey, how can we stop our family from eating this bad fish?"

Bogey pointed his ears toward the garage door. "Way ahead of you, kid. Turn around, and on the count of three, we'll shove this pan off the counter with our back feet. Give it all you've got. Right when our Dad is walking in. When it goes flying, drop down off the other side and hide."

"Aye, aye," I said. I saluted him and this time my paw went almost where I wanted it to go.

Then I turned around and got into position, just like Bogey had told me to. I wanted to ask a whole bunch of questions, but I knew I'd better not. We just didn't have the time. We had to act quick if we wanted to save our family.

What happened next all sort of happened in a blur. Bogey turned around, too, and put his back feet against the pan. Then our Dad turned the doorknob and Bogey started to count to three. On "two," our Dad began to open the door. When Bogey said "three," we both pushed that pan of fish just as hard as we could.

And let me tell you, we must have kicked it pretty hard. I glanced back to see that pan go soaring through the air like an airplane taking off.

At the exact moment when our Dad stepped inside and yelled "Hello!"

Holy Mackerel!   Or maybe I should say, Holy Salmon!

Bogey and I didn't wait around to see what happened next.   Instead we jumped right off that counter and flattened ourselves against the cabinets. Just as we heard that pan go crashing onto the hardwood floor.   Then we heard kind of a *splat* and a bunch of *ssszzzzz* noises.   I figured that was probably the fish hitting the floor and sliding into pieces.

Our Dad yelled, "Aaaaaaaahh!!"

Bogey motioned for me to follow him and we ran straight into the dining room.   Only seconds before our Mom and Gracie went running into the kitchen.

"What happened?" our Mom gasped.

"I don't know," our Dad said.   "I just walked in the door and this pan of fish came flying right at me."

"That's really strange," our Mom told him.

"Tell me about it," he said.

"Maybe it was the air suction from opening the door that did it?" our Mom wondered out loud.   "Or maybe we left the pan too close to the edge of the counter?"

"I don't know," our Dad said.   "All I know is that I walked in and that pan was airborne.   The fish broke into a million pieces when it hit the ground.   It went sliding everywhere!   We'll be cleaning up fish for a month!"

For some reason, Gracie started to giggle and couldn't stop.

Our Mom started to laugh, too.   "Looks like we're ordering pizza for dinner now."

Beside me, Bogey grinned and gave me a paw bump. And that's when I kind of grinned, too.   We'd saved our family from eating any of that bad fish.   Even if they didn't know it.

Bogey pointed to the front entry.   "We're not out of

the woods yet, kid. Someone's probably planning to break into our house tonight. To search for our statue. We'd better be ready."

I gulped and nodded. "Maybe we should get Lil to help out. And the Princess, too."

"Good plan, kid," Bogey said. "We could use some extra paws on the job. Let's go chat with them."

So we did just that. We ran into the living room when Gracie started to practice the piano. Lil and the Princess were already there. Then while Gracie played, us cats huddled together and came up with a plan. Of course, we wanted to stop any burglars from *even* getting into our house. But just in case they did, we came up with a backup plan. And either way, we wanted to get a good look at anyone who tried to break in. To help figure out who was behind all this.

But just talking about burglars made my paws start to shake. I noticed the Princess was shaking a little bit, too. And that's when I started to get mad. The idea of anyone trying to hurt my family always made me feel like that. Especially when it came to a really small cat like the Princess. At least a big guy like me had a chance to defend himself. But a little one, like the Princess, didn't have a chance at all.

I turned to listen to Gracie's music and tried to calm down. She had just started to play her recital song. The music was so pretty, and I kind of floated away.

She was almost all the way through the song when she made a mistake. A big mistake. She quit playing and tears instantly rolled down her cheeks. I knew she was extra nervous, since the recital was only a few days away.

And well, if anyone understood what it was like to be nervous, it was me! But I also knew how to help Gracie so she didn't feel so nervous any more.

I nodded to Bogey and he grinned back.

"We know the drill, kid," he said.

We sure did. I jumped up on the piano bench and Bogey jumped onto the front ledge of the piano. I gave

Gracie a kiss on the nose while Bogey leaned over and hit some piano keys.

She giggled and gave me a hug. "Oh, Buckley. I love you so much. I love all you cats. If only you could be at my recital. I wish I could sneak you all in. Then I'd be fine."

I gave her another kiss on the nose to let her know I loved her, too. She giggled again and started to play. She went all the way through her song and played it perfectly. I was so proud of her.

Later that night, after our family had gone to bed, we ran our surveillance rounds. Only tonight, we ran extra rounds. We checked doors and windows and looked outside, too. Lil and the Princess took one route and Bogey and I took another. Then we switched. It was around midnight when we heard someone fiddling with the lock on the back door.

But we were ready for them. And all of us cats knew exactly what we were supposed to do. Thanks to the plans we'd made that afternoon.

Bogey hollered, "Get into positions! They're picking the lock!"

Without a peep, the Princess jumped onto the kitchen counter. She flipped the switches and turned on the kitchen lights. In a split second, she bounced down from the counter, raced from the kitchen and flew upstairs to wake up our Mom and Dad. Bogey pulled the curtains open on the window next to the door and tried to get a good look at the burglar.

In the meantime, I pulled the cupboard open where our Mom and Dad kept the pots and pans. Then Lil and I started pulling them out one by one. We made as much racket as we possibly could. Those pots and pans fell on the floor with a whole bunch of loud *clangs!* Especially when one pot fell on top of another pot.

It was enough to wake up our Mom and Dad, just like we'd planned. They sort of came stumbling down the stairs, turning on lights as they went.

And that was enough to scare our prowler away.

Especially since they'd probably been expecting our family to be sound asleep for the night!

When our Mom and Dad came downstairs, Bogey and I raced upstairs. We saw the Princess wave at us before she ducked into the sunroom. And downstairs, we knew Lil would now be hiding under the dining room table.

Bogey and I made a beeline for our favorite upstairs window. We were just in time to spot a figure in black dodging from house to house. Whoever it was, they looked like they were trying to hide in the shadows.

And even though us cats can see really well in the dark, we still couldn't tell who it was.

"Did you get a good look at them?" I asked my brother. "From the back window?"

He nodded. "I did, kid. There was only one of 'em, and I couldn't see their face. They were wearing a mask, and a big black sweatshirt and pants. And gloves. It could have been anyone."

I let out a long sigh. The burglar that Bogey had seen sure knew what they were doing when it came to breaking in. They'd been all ready to do the job. And if we hadn't been ready like we were, they might've even gotten into our house. I knew I probably should've been upset about it all. But for the moment, I was just happy our family was safe.

Even if our Mom and Dad were kind of grumbling by the time they came back upstairs. Luckily, they were too tired to say anything to us. Instead they just went straight back to bed.

But we kept up our surveillance rounds the rest of the night. And the next day, too, while our family was out of the house. By then, it was Friday afternoon and I was so tired I just wanted to sleep.

When Gracie and our Mom got home, I figured we were probably safe for a few hours. So I padded right over to my cat bed and flopped down. After all, a growing boy like me needed lots of sleep. And with someone out there wanting to break into our house, I wasn't exactly getting a lot of sleep.

I was about to drift off when I heard Gracie bring three pet carriers into the kitchen.

"Are you ready, Buckley?" she asked.

Ready? Ready for what? If she meant sleep, I was more than ready. I was almost there.

She picked me up and gave me a kiss on my head. "We're going to the Blessing of the Animals this afternoon. At church."

We were? I'd forgotten all about that.

Gracie put me in my pet carrier and shut the door. And our Mom put the Princess and Bogey in their pet carriers, too. I tried to catch Bogey's eye. But it looked like he'd settled down for a snooze in his carrier already. Then the next thing I knew, we were all being loaded up in our car. If nothing else, I figured I'd get a little nap in along the way.

That was, until our Mom pulled up in front of Hector's house. His Mom was waiting for us with Hector in her arms. They got into the car, too, and Hector started to talk right away.

So much for my plans to take a nap.

As usual, Hector talked and talked and talked. He talked the whole way to the church. I tried to cover my ears, but it didn't work. I could still hear him.

"Do you know about the Blessing of the Animals, Buckley?" he asked.

But Hector didn't even give me a chance to answer. Instead he just kept going on and on and on.

"Oh yeah, I know all about the Blessing of the Animals," he bragged. "It's in honor of a guy named St. Francis of Assisi. He loved animals a lot and he really took care of them. All kinds of animals. He saw animals as his brothers and sisters because they were God's creatures, too. Did you know that, Buckley? Did you?"

I was about to tell Hector that I didn't know that.

But he didn't even wait for me to speak.

"I read what St. Francis said about animals," Hector said without taking a breath. "I memorized it exactly. He said, 'Not to hurt our humble brethren is our first duty to them, but to stop there is not enough. We have a higher mission — to be of service to them wherever they require it.' Bet you didn't know that, did you, Buckley?"

By now, I noticed the Princess and Bogey were sound asleep. I sure wished I was sound asleep, too. Then again, I really liked learning about this St. Francis guy. He sounded like a nice guy.

Thankfully, the church wasn't very far away. In fact, it was only a few blocks from our house. The building was made from really old stone blocks and had big spires on the front. It had pretty stained glass windows in arch shapes. It was the first church ever built in St. Gertrude, and one of the oldest buildings in town.

Our Mom parked the car, and Gracie carried me in my pet carrier, while Hector's Mom carried him. Our Mom carried Bogey and the Princess in their pet carriers.

A lady held the huge wooden front door open for us. Then we went into a room with lots of old wooden pews. In fact, I saw lots of old woodwork all over the place. There were wooden ceiling beams and carved pillars. There was a little wooden balcony near the front. And the whole place was filled with shiny silver and gold candleholders and crosses. Plus I spotted a big, tall golden goblet right up at the front.

I noticed all the metal pieces were also decorated with some gems arranged in different designs. Kind of like the statues in the Daunton Exhibit.

Everything inside that church looked like it was very, very old. Probably because the church was so old. And to tell you the truth, I thought it was pretty in there. I liked being inside that old stone building.

"We're in church now, Buckley," Gracie whispered down to me. "You're supposed to be really good and quiet in church.   Especially when we're sitting in the pews."

I meowed up to her.   To let her know that I'd be really good.

I sure wished Hector would have gotten that message.   Because he just wouldn't be quiet at all.

"Did you know, Buckley?   They use Holy Water for the Blessing of the Animals," Hector went on.

Holy Water?

Holy Catnip!

That got my attention.

"Oh yeah," Hector went on.   "They do something called total immersion."

"Total immersion?" I managed to squeak.

"Yeah, that's right," Hector said.   "I read all about it. That's where they dunk you in the Holy Water."

And that's when I tried to scramble right on out of my pet carrier.   In fact, Gracie almost dropped it when I tried to get out the back.

Nobody said anything about getting dunked in any water!   And I really didn't like that idea one bit.   I didn't even like getting a bath at home.   And our Mom sure didn't dunk me all the way under when she gave me a bath!

"Buckley!" Gracie said in a loud whisper.   "You're supposed to behave!"

She scooted into a pew with me in my carrier.   And our Mom came in beside her with Bogey and the Princess in their carriers.   Hector's Mom scooted in next to them.

I was all for behaving.   Most of the time.   But not when water or dunking was involved.

Bogey stretched and started to wake up.

"Bogey," I meowed.   "Bogey!   Do you know what's going to happen?   Quick!   We need to escape.   You get the Princess and I'll figure a way out of here!"

Bogey just tilted his head and looked at me cock-eyed.   "What's got you so shook up, kid?   Maybe you've been working too hard."

Gracie turned to our Mom. "I don't know why Buckley's so upset. He was fine until a few minutes ago."

Our Mom crinkled her brow. "That is odd for Buckley. He's usually so good. Maybe if you just take him out and hold him. Give him a nice hug. Maybe he'll be okay then."

Let me tell you, that was all the chance I needed. Gracie had barely opened the door when I practically flew out of that pet carrier. I jumped onto the stone floor and tried to take off. I started sliding all over the place, until I remembered how I learned to run on the marble floor at the Museum.

Then I took off and ran for all I was worth. I ran out of that room and down a long stone hallway. I could hear people running after me and Gracie yelling for me to come back.

But I kept on going. I ran through an open door and down another stone hallway. And another stone hallway.

Until I saw something that made me stop dead in my tracks. That's when I skidded to a halt. I'd been running so fast that I almost didn't notice them.

For there, carved into the very bottom of the stone wall that lined the hallway, were little symbols. Tiny little symbols. Symbols I'd seen before. One was a pointy sun peeking out from a cloud. There was also a flower, a pine tree, and a moon peeking out from a mountain.

And last but not least, I saw the little outline of a cat.

They were the same symbols we had seen on the Daunton statues!

Holy Catnip!

CHAPTER 20

Holy Catnip! I blinked my eyes a few times, just to make sure I'd seen them right. But no matter how many times I opened my eyes, those little symbols were right there. In exactly the same spot in that long hallway.

I sniffed at them and felt some cold air ruffle my whiskers. Almost like a little breeze was blowing through there.

I wanted to look more, but I didn't get the chance. Hands circled my ribs and grabbed me tight. I looked up to see Gracie.

And well, she looked a little mad.

Okay, she looked really mad.

"I can't believe it, Buckley," she said. "I just finished telling you to be good. Then you took off running."

Beside her was the minister. He had a nametag on that read, "Pastor Tom." He was wearing a long white robe with green trim. But I could see a black shirt with a round white collar poking out at the top of the robe.

"Hello, Buckley," he laughed. "You're not the first cat to take off running when he was about to be blessed."

Gracie picked me up and held me tight. "Usually Buckley is a very good cat. I don't know what got into him."

Pastor Tom laughed. "Well, don't be too hard on Buckley, Gracie. Maybe I just need to use some *extra* Holy Water on him."

Holy Mackerel! They were going to use extra Holy Water? Wasn't getting dunked enough?

I tucked my head under Gracie's chin and wrapped my arms around her neck. Then I just held on for dear life. I started to shake really hard.

Gracie whispered into my ear. "Buckley, there's nothing to be scared of. You'll be fine."

I would? This sure didn't sound fine to me. As far as I was concerned, there was a whole lot to be scared of!

"Are you ready, Buckley?" the Pastor asked.

"N-o-o-o-o!" I howled.

"Yes, he's ready," Gracie said.

I turned my head in time to see Pastor Tom pull out a little flask of water. Then he sprinkled a few drops on my forehead and said, "In the name of the Father, Son, and Holy Spirit, I bless Your beautiful creation, this beloved cat, Buckley."

Gracie smiled and kissed me on the head. "See, Buckley! Now you're done. You're all blessed."

I was? That was it? Right about then, I think my chin practically dropped to Gracie's shoulder. What happened to the dunking in Holy Water that Hector had told me about? What happened to that "total immersion" thing? It turned out there was no dunking at all. In fact, getting blessed wasn't so bad. It was really kind of nice.

And well, now I felt kind of embarrassed that I'd gotten so shook up.

I gave Gracie a kiss on the nose, just to say I was sorry.

She giggled. "Okay, Buckley, I forgive you."

And then, just for good measure, I reached over and

climbed up to Pastor Tom. He laughed and took me in his arms. I gave him a kiss on the nose, too.

"You're some kind of cat, Buckley," he said.

He handed me back to Gracie. "I think the Holy Water did the trick," he told her with a big smile.

"I sure hope so," Gracie said. "Otherwise we might have to bring him back."

After that, Gracie carried me back into the main part of the church. Where all the other animals were with their humans. I saw a few big dogs and some little dogs. I saw some hamsters and guinea pigs and ferrets. Plus there were lots of cats. All waiting to get blessed. Just like I got blessed.

We were almost to our pew when I heard someone meowing out to me. "Buckley, over here!"

I turned to see our friend Amelia. She was there with her Mom. Boy, Bogey was sure going to be happy when he found that out. Especially when I told him she was only a few pews away.

"Hello, Amelia!" I meowed back. "Are you getting blessed, too?"

"I am, Buckley," she said sweetly. "Even though my Mom says I'm already a blessing."

"Don't worry," I told her. "You won't get dunked under the water. It isn't bad at all."

She kind of crinkled her nose at me. "Huh?"

But I didn't get a chance to say any more. By then Gracie had already taken me to sit back in our pew.

Our Mom smiled at Gracie and petted me on the head. "I wonder what got into Buckley."

"I don't know," Gracie said. "But Pastor Tom blessed him in the hallway. After that he's been fine."

And just to prove that she was right, I gave her another kiss on the nose.

Bogey stretched and sat up in his pet carrier. "What happened to you, kid?"

"I didn't want to get dunked in the Holy Water," I told him. "And I sort of freaked out and ran off."

Bogey yawned. "Dunked in the water, kid? Where'd you get an idea like that?"

"From Hector," I told him.

Bogey shook his head. "That explains it. Don't believe everything you hear, kid. Especially stuff that Hector says."

Boy, he could say that again.

I leaned closer to Bogey's pet carrier. "But it turned out to be a good thing that I ran off. Because you'll never believe what I found!"

"What was it, kid?" Bogey asked just before our Mom opened his pet carrier.

But I didn't get a chance to tell him. Not before our Mom took him out of his carrier and then scooted out of the pew with him. That's when I noticed lots of people taking their animals out of the pews, too. One by one, they went up to the front of the church. And Pastor Tom sprinkled Holy Water over them, too, and blessed them. Just like he had blessed me.

Now I watched Hector's Mom take him up and, of course, Hector talked the whole way. A few minutes later, our Mom brought Bogey back and put him in his pet carrier. Then she took the Princess up. I saw Amelia's Mom take her up to be blessed, too. The Princess and Amelia smiled at each other on the way back.

Then Bogey spotted Amelia and he kind of went all goo-goo eyed. I figured now might not be a good time to tell him about the little symbols I had seen carved into the stone wall.

Once all the animals had been blessed, we were taken into another room for a reception. The dogs had to stay on one side and the cats on another. The rest of the animals were kind of kept in one corner.

The people had punch and cookies, while the animals got treats. The cat treats were fish-flavored, and I had to say, they were excellent.

Gracie sat with us, while our Mom and Hector's Mom chatted with the other cat Moms.

I had just finished my second treat when another black cat approached Bogey and me. He was wearing a white collar.

"Good afternoon, fellow felines," the cat said. "I'm Luke, the church cat. I trust you're having a grand time at our little party."

The Princess perked up her ears and leaned forward. "Why, thank you, Luke. It's lovely to meet you. And yes, we've had a most wonderful time. Thank you for your hospitality."

Then she introduced us all.   She spoke very smoothly and with such grace. We could always count on the Princess when it came to good manners.

It just made my heart start to pound like a big drum. Especially when she turned her big, green eyes on me. But I helped myself to another cat treat and I felt a little bit better. Then I noticed Bogey was having a hard time concentrating with Amelia around. I decided I'd better help him get his mind back on things.

So I turned to Luke. "Everything sure looked nice inside the church. I really liked the candlestick holders and the crosses and the big goblet."

Luke smiled. "Thanks, that's very nice of you to say. We call the goblet a chalice. And all those things were made for our church by one of the people who founded it. A long, long time ago."

Suddenly the Princess glanced behind me. I looked to see what had gotten her attention. That's when I saw a couple of cats huddled together not too far away. They didn't seem to be mixing with the rest of the cats at all. One was a fuzzy, tan-colored kitten who had her eyes shut. The other was a pure white cat who looked like a Turkish Angora, just like the Princess.   Only he had blue eyes.

They seemed sort of lost in their own world.

"Do you know those cats over there?" I asked Luke.

"They're our special needs cats. Annie and Henry," he told us. "The people at the church are trying to find homes for them. But it's quite difficult to find homes for special needs animals."

I tilted my head. "What exactly is 'special' about them?"

"Well, Annie is blind and Henry is deaf," Luke told us.

Amelia stood up nice and tall and kind of frowned. "They look like perfectly wonderful cats to me."

The next thing I knew, she walked right over to Annie and introduced herself. Annie started to purr right away. She lifted her nose to Amelia's nose and Amelia wrapped an arm around her. Then she and Annie started chatting away. If you asked me, it looked like they were practically best friends already.

Kind of like me and Bogey!

Then Bogey grabbed a couple of cat treats and he and I walked over to Henry. Henry didn't notice us at first. And when he did, he kind of jumped.

But Bogey grinned and Henry grinned back.   I waved at Henry. Henry waved back.

I put my paw to my mouth and then pointed to a treat. Henry nodded at me and I gave him a treat.

"There you go, kid," Bogey said. "The international language of cat treats."

"The what?" I asked him.

Bogey handed Henry another treat. "Nothing, kid. I'll just let the treats do the talking. I think they kind of speak for themselves."

"Oh, okay," I said.

Henry made kind of a motion with his paw.

Luke came over and joined us. "Henry knows some sign language," he said. "He just said 'thank you' with his paw."

He did? Holy Mackerel!

Luke showed us what Henry had said and then he showed us some sign language, too. Before long, we were using our paws to talk to Henry. That was, until Hector came over and joined us.

Let me tell you, Hector sure didn't understand the

meaning of sign language. Instead he just talked and talked and talked. His mouth kept moving nonstop. Henry helped himself to a few treats and Hector did, too. And for some reason, Henry kept on looking at Hector and smiling. He even started to purr.

"Well, I'll be . . ." Bogey kind of murmured.

"You'll be what?" I asked him.

Bogey grinned again. "Nothing, kid. Just an idea that came to my mind. I'll tell you about it later."

Before long, all of us cats were gathered around with Annie and Henry. Gracie came over and took turns holding each cat. It turned into a pretty nice party before our Moms told us it was time to go home.

We waved goodbye to all our friends as our Mom and Gracie took us away in our pet carriers.

But not before we saw Pastor Tom put down food and water for Luke and Henry and Annie. He said goodnight to the cats and punched in the alarm code on the keypad. Then he locked the door and headed for his own car.

Bogey watched Pastor Tom the whole time. "Did you see that, kid? The church has an alarm system."

I looked over at my brother. "Um . . . yes, I saw it."

Bogey squinted his eyes. "Churches didn't used to have alarms, kid. Not when I first got started in this business."

I glanced backward in my carrier as Gracie took me to the car. "Well, there was lots of pretty stuff in there. Things someone might want to steal. So they probably have an alarm, just like our Mom's store. And just like the Museum."

"Yup, kid," Bogey sort of murmured. "Just like the Museum. Just like all museums. All over the world."

Seconds later, we were in our Mom's car and headed home. Gracie got in the front and put my pet carrier on her lap with me inside. Our Mom put Bogey and the Princess in the back in their pet carriers. And Hector's Mom sat in the back and held onto Hector.

By now, I'd hoped that Hector would be all talked out. But no such luck. He meowed and meowed and carried on the whole way home. But instead of gossiping like he usually did, he talked mostly about Henry. I guess his new friend had made a pretty big impression on him.

Our Dad was already home when we got there, and things were pretty busy from the moment we arrived. Gracie went to practice her piano and us cats all gathered around. Then there was supper and lots more activity with Gracie getting ready for her recital the next day.

I didn't really get a chance to talk to Bogey until that night. Not until after our family had gone to bed and we'd run our first surveillance round. That's when Bogey and I sat on our Mom's desk. And that's when I finally told Bogey about the little symbols I'd seen at the church. I described how I found them carved into the bottom of the stone wall in that hallway.

Bogey booted up our Mom's computer and pulled out a bag of cat treats. "That's brilliant, kid. Absolutely brilliant. Someday you'll be a *great* cat detective."

I would?

Holy Mackerel! I sat there sort of stunned for a moment. Funny, but I didn't feel any more brilliant today than I did yesterday. Or the day before. I tried to say thank you, but instead I just kind of stammered.

Even so, it really made me feel happy to hear Bogey say what he did. Especially since I'd been working so hard to become the best cat detective I could be. And Bogey's words made me want to work even harder. I suddenly felt a little taller than I did before.

Bogey passed me a cat treat and then took one for himself. "Here you go, kid. This'll get you going again."

I munched on my treat and watched while my brother typed onto the computer keyboard. An article from the *St. Gertrude Times* popped onto the screen.

He nodded at the article. "Something you said earlier, kid, made me think about museums. Not just here, but around the world. Then I remembered something I read in the paper about a month ago. Take a look at this."

I scooted closer so I could read it. The title said, "Volunteers Travel to Turkey to Help Museum." It had a big picture right underneath.

"That's nice," I told my brother. "Volunteers can really help a lot."

"Yup, kid," he said. "But I don't think these volunteers were there to help."

"They weren't?" I asked.

He handed me another treat and took one, too. "Nope, kid. Take a closer look. Who do you see in the picture?"

I put my treat in my mouth and scooted right next to the computer screen. That's when I noticed Byron Bygones and Evaline Esterbrook in the picture. They were standing with some other people under a big sign that read "Istanbul Museum."

I'm sure my eyes went really wide when I turned back to my brother.

He nodded before I could even say a word. "Do you remember where the sea captain sailed from, kid? In the La Paloma?"

I had to think for a moment. I remembered it was a bird name. Then it finally hit me.

"Turkey?" I managed to squeak out.

"You got it, kid," Bogey went on. "And where did Delilah fly in from?"

I thought of the airline schedule we had taken from her purse. "Istanbul?"

"And where is Istanbul?" Bogey asked.

"In Turkey?" I sort of half-said and half-guessed.

Bogey nodded. "Yup, kid, that's right. And I'll bet that's where our Tobias statue was found after all these years. One of the articles we read before said it was the last place it had been spotted. So I'll bet one of the people running around here found it and brought it back to St. Gertrude."

Now I was starting to catch on to things. "And the other people figured it out. Then they chased the one who had the statue. Because they wanted the statue for themselves."

Bogey gave me a paw bump. "Good job, kid. You got it. I told you you're going to be a great cat detective some day."

There they were again. Those same words about me being a great cat detective. I didn't know why Bogey kept saying that. Or, for that matter, why he believed it. But if that's what he thought, I figured maybe I could try acting more like it. The best I could. And maybe it was time I tried to think on my own a little more.

So I stood up and paced back and forth across our Mom's desk. "But who had the statue? And why did they bring it to St. Gertrude? And who put it in our Mom's store?"

Bogey grinned and passed me another treat. "Don't know, kid. But keep it up. You're on a roll now. You're thinking like a real cat detective."

"Um, okay," I told him. I paced some more and said the first thing that came to my mind. "So if those people were after the Tobias statue before, they're probably still after it. Because none of them have found it. That's because we have it."

Bogey nodded. "Good job, kid. Keep it up."

I took a deep breath. "Um, okay. They probably suspect that we have it, but they don't know for sure. And maybe they figured out that none of the others have the statue, since they're all still acting like they're after it. Because, they probably figured if one of them had it, that person wouldn't act like they were searching for it any more."

Bogey grinned and passed us another round of cat treats. "Like I said, kid. Brilliant. Keep going."

I paced back and forth some more. "And maybe they're all on the hunt for the Tessa statue, too."

Bogey stashed the cat treats back in the vase. "As

well as the rest of the treasure."

Now I stopped pacing and stared at my brother. "And as long as we have the Tobias statue, someone might try to break into our house again. To search for the statue."

Bogey nodded. "That's the size of it, kid. And our family could still be in danger."

I gulped. "But how do we stop these people?"

Bogey flexed a front paw. "Easy, kid. We find the Tessa statue and the treasure, too. Then we turn everything over to the police. So these people have nothing left to hunt down."

Easy? Did he say easy?

I paced a little more. "Um, okay . . . but where do we find the Tessa statue and the treasure?"

Bogey grinned. "We'll start by looking right where you found those symbols, kid."

I stopped and stared at my brother again. "In the church?"

Bogey nodded. "That's right, kid."

"But how will we get there?" I asked him. "And how will we get in? That place is locked up when nobody's there. Plus they have an alarm."

Now Bogey grinned again. "Let's put it this way, kid. No matter what, we've gotta go to Gracie's recital tomorrow night. At the church."

We did?

But our Mom already told Gracie that we couldn't go. And well, I didn't think cats were exactly invited. So how would we get there?

Holy Catnip!

CHAPTER 21

Holy Mackerel! I could hardly believe it. There we were, about to sneak into our Dad's truck all over again. Just like we did the on night when our Mom's store was broken into.

But this time we weren't going to our Mom's store. This time we were going to the church for Gracie's piano recital. We only hoped our Mom and Dad and Gracie would be too distracted to notice us going along for a ride.

Especially since poor Gracie had been a nervous wreck all day. She'd practiced her recital piece several times this afternoon. And no matter how hard she tried, she just kept having trouble with it. But when I gave her a kiss on the nose and Bogey tapped on the keys, she always did just fine.

Unfortunately, she seemed to have a lot of tears in between.

At one point she hugged me tight and cried into my fur. "Oh, Buckley, if only you and Bogey could go tonight. I know I could play really well if you boys were at the piano with me."

I reached up and licked the tears off her face. To let

her know I loved her. And that Bogey and I *would* be going to the church tonight.

I hoped.

Finally, after a long day, the moment came when our family was about to leave for the recital. Bogey and I were ready to zoom out the instant they opened the door to the garage. And Lil was standing by to hold the door for us. Exactly like she did the night we snuck out to our Mom's store.

Gracie dragged her feet toward the door and looked like she was fighting back tears. She was wearing her prettiest dress and hugging her sheet music to her chest. I had never seen her look so sad before. Our Mom and Dad followed her.

"I just know I'm going to mess up," Gracie said to our Mom.

Our Mom put her arm around her shoulder. "Now, honey, you don't know that. You've played that song before without messing up. I have a lot of confidence in you."

Our Dad held the garage door open for them. "Just do your best, Gracie. It's more important to try than to give up."

But no matter what our Mom and Dad said to her, it didn't seem to make her feel any better.

After that, everything happened so fast I could barely keep track of it all.

Once our Dad had the door wide open, Lil got into position to hold it for us. She kept it open long enough for Bogey and me to slip through. Thankfully, our Mom and Dad were so busy taking care of Gracie that they didn't even notice us. And they didn't see us when we slinked up into our Dad's truck, the second they opened the doors. We went straight to the backseat and hid on the floorboard. Right where no one would ever spot us. It was a good thing we'd already done this once before. Because it sure helped to have some practice.

To tell you the truth, I was pretty happy with the

way things had gone so far. That was, until I glanced out under an open door. That's when I saw something that made my heart start to race.

The Princess!

She must have decided to join us! The only problem was, we didn't know she was coming. And, she'd never had to sneak into a truck before with only a few seconds to spare. If she didn't time it right, the doors could be slammed shut and she could get caught in between!

Now there she was, scrunched down in the middle of the garage floor. She acted like she wasn't sure what to do.

I waved frantically to her. "Hurry!" I sort of mouthed.

She saw me and her eyes went wide. Then she scurried for all she was worth and leaped inside. Just seconds before Gracie finished climbing in and shut the door.

I helped the Princess slip over to hide with Bogey and me. Unfortunately, our hiding place was just big enough for two. Not for three.

So Bogey and I scooted over and let the Princess hide behind us. We watched quietly as Gracie fastened her seat belt. She seemed lost in her own world, and I could tell she was trying so hard not to cry. But a tear slipped down her cheek anyway, and she looked down to wipe it away.

And spotted us.

At first her mouth fell open and her eyes almost popped out of her head. Then Bogey put a paw to his mouth, signaling for her to keep quiet.

She smiled and put her hand to her mouth. I could tell she was holding back a giggle. It was the happiest I'd seen her all day.

Minutes later, when we arrived at the church, she leaned over and whispered, "Now you cats be sure to walk in right behind me. I don't want you running around outside. I don't want you to get lost."

Bogey and the Princess beamed up at her and I

reached up and gave her a quick kiss on the nose.

"What was that, honey?" our Mom asked from the front seat.

"Oh, nothing," Gracie said.

Gracie held the door open long enough for us to get outside and hide under the truck. Then she lagged behind our Mom and Dad while they all went into the church. She watched while we quickly followed her and then let us inside the building.

"Make sure you find me when it's time to come home," she whispered to the three of us.

I gave her a quick rub around the legs to let her know I understood. Then all three of us took off running down a hallway of the old stone church. I led the way, since I knew where the symbols were. We had barely turned the first corner when we saw Luke the church cat. He was sitting on a bench next to Henry and Annie.

That's when the three of us paused to say hello to the three of them.

Music echoed out to us from inside the church hall. And we knew the piano recital was starting. I sure hoped we'd be done checking out those symbols before Gracie started playing her song. Because I really wanted to be sitting beside her on the piano bench when she started.

Bogey leaned into my ear. "I have an idea, kid. On how we can find a home for Annie and Henry."

I turned to look at my brother. "You do?"

"Yup, kid," Bogey said. "Let me chat with Luke for a minute. I'll bet he knows how to work the church computer."

"Um, okay," I said.

And while he did, I sneaked back up toward the front door again. I glanced into the main part of the church to see where the kids in the recital were playing. So I could find Gracie when it was her turn to play.

I saw a piano had been set up on a little stage in the

front of the room. The rest of the people were sitting in the audience while the kids took turns playing their songs.

I knew exactly where I'd be going right after we checked out those little symbols.

I turned to race back to Bogey and the Princess. But not before I glanced up and saw the alarm keypad. I remembered what Bogey had said about it yesterday. Right when Pastor Tom had punched in the six numbers on the keypad.

Six numbers.

Just like our Mom used for her own alarm code.

And just like the clue Bogey had found in the sea captain's pocket. There were six numbers on that sheet of paper, too.

I blinked a couple of times. Could it be the numbers on that sheet of paper were supposed to be an alarm code? Did someone write down Abigail's Antiques and the alarm code to our store? But the numbers on that sheet weren't even close to the numbers our Mom used for her alarm code. And why would someone have our Mom's alarm code anyway?

I ran back toward my brother. But I could barely see where I was going. Instead I just kept seeing that clue in my mind. I kept remembering what it said . . .

Bogey just grinned at me when I reached him. "Let me guess, kid. You've cracked this case wide open."

I nodded really, really fast. "Maybe . . . Um, yes . . . I think so."

I noticed Luke was gone now, so we said our goodbyes to Henry and Annie. Then the Princess and Bogey and I ran down the rest of the hallway. I told him my idea about an alarm code while we made a beeline to the spot where I'd seen the symbols.

"Good job, kid!" Bogey said with a slap on the back. "I'm proud of you."

Now I grinned, too. That was, until I started to think about things some more. Bogey had said we needed to find all the pieces to this puzzle before we could put it together. But my brain was busy trying to put everything together right now. Could it be we'd found all the pieces already? Could it be we just needed to fit them together?

Holy Mackerel!

Up ahead, I spotted the place in the hallway where those little symbols had been carved. I pointed them out to Bogey and the Princess. We stopped right in front of them and took a good look.

Bogey gave me a paw bump. "Good eye, kid. A lot of cat detectives would've never seen these. And you can bet the humans never spotted them either."

"They're so small," the Princess said. "I never would have found them either. You're such a great cat detective, Buckley."

She stared at me with her big, green eyes. And suddenly the room started to spin.

Luckily, a little breeze ruffled our whiskers, just like the first time I'd been there. It was enough to bring me back to my senses.

I leaned in closer to the symbols. "I wonder where that breeze is coming from?"

Bogey sniffed the air and pointed at the wall. "From in there, kid."

"In there?" I asked.

Bogey nodded. "Yup, kid. It's an old church. I'll bet there's a secret passage in there."

A secret passage? Let me tell you, I didn't like the sound of that one bit. After all, weren't secret passages supposed to be dark and dank? And full of scary stuff? I sure hoped we weren't going into any secret passages.

But I should have known better. After all, I knew my brother. And well, Bogey sure wouldn't hesitate to go into any secret passages. No matter how much scary stuff was in there.

The Princess leaned closer to the wall. "I've seen something like this before. There's probably a lever here."

"A lever?" I asked.

"Uh-huh," the Princess answered. "Push on the cat symbol, Buckley."

So I did. I pushed with all my strength. And as I did, I noticed something kind of strange happened. Instead of stopping when I pushed it against the stone, my paw just kept on going forward. Farther and farther and farther. Beside me, Bogey cheered me on and the Princess gasped.

"It's a secret door," the Princess said, looking up.

Bogey and I looked up, too. That's when we saw a stone-covered door in the wall start to creak open. Funny, but I sure hadn't noticed that door before.

Now the breeze was a little bit stronger. It came out in a big whoosh and then it sort of stopped. That's when the door stopped opening, too.

And sure enough, there was a secret passage. Right smack dab in front of us. Judging by all the cobwebs and dust, I figured that door hadn't been opened in a long, long time.

The three of us stood and stared at each other with wide eyes. Before we could say another word, Bogey turned and stepped right into that secret passage. Then he trotted down that dark, dusty hallway. The Princess and I followed him.

The floor stones were much cooler here, and the whole place smelled kind of musty. The walls were made of stone just like the rest of the church. In a weird way, I felt like I had just stepped back in time. Because obviously no one had set foot or paw into this place in a while.

We ran on and on, until we were quite a way from the entrance. And that's when we saw it. A little wooden chest. A very, very old chest. Covered in dust and sitting close to a wall.

But we could still make out the initials D.D. on the front.

"Danby Daunton," the Princess whispered as she touched it.

Let me tell you, my heart was racing as Bogey and I paused for a moment in front of that little chest.

"Daylight's burning," Bogey said quietly.

I wiped the dust off with my paw and he pulled the latch open. Then he nodded to me and I knew exactly what he was telling me to do. I jumped over to one side of the chest while he jumped to the other. Together we lifted the lid.

But it didn't exactly open up easily. The hinges squeaked and stuck as we tried to pull it up. It was so stiff that it felt like nobody had moved that lid in about a million years. It took all the strength we had to get it open. The Princess even helped out by pushing from the front.

Finally, we had that lid up and resting back against the stone wall.

What we found inside amazed us all. And it took my breath away. Brilliant colors of blue, red, green, gold, and silver sparkled and blinked up at us. Together we stood back and stared with wide eyes.

"Could this be . . .?" I sort of choked out.

"Yup, kid. I think it is," Bogey whispered.

"I think so, too," the Princess said in her soft voice.

"It's the treasure," I managed to say. "Danby Daunton's treasure."

Holy Catnip!

CHAPTER 22

Holy Mackerel! When I decided to become a cat detective, I sure never dreamed I'd have a day like today! I never, ever thought I'd be staring at a treasure chest full of treasure.

Now the three of us couldn't *stop* staring at all the stuff inside that little chest. Everything sparkled and shined like nothing I'd ever seen before. It practically glowed with a life of its own, even in the dim light of the secret passage.

There were little containers of diamonds and emeralds and sapphires and rubies. On the sides were little bars of gold and silver, too. All stuff that Mr. Daunton would've used to make more statues.

The only thing was, he quit making those statues after the Tobias statue was stolen and the Tessa statue went missing. He loved those two statues the most, since he modeled them after his own cats. And he was so upset about the theft, that he never made another statue again.

As I thought about it, I felt sad all over again. If he hadn't been robbed, Mr. Daunton probably would've made a lot more statues. He sure had enough stuff to make them with. And I guessed any new statues would've been just as pretty as all the other ones he'd made.

Now I wondered how all his statue-making stuff ended up right here. Hidden in the church. In a passageway that nobody knew about.

But somebody must have known about this secret passage. The people who built the church would have known.

That's when something sort of dawned on me.

"Didn't Mr. Daunton help found St. Gertrude?" I asked Bogey.

He nodded. "Yup, kid. You're on the right track. From what we read about the guy, we know he helped to settle this town. I'll bet he even designed this church. Probably because he was a member here. Did you see that chalice and those crosses yesterday? And those candlestick holders?"

I'm sure my eyes went really wide. "Uh-huh. They looked just like the kind of stuff Mr. Daunton made. And Luke told us they'd been made by one of the founders of this church."

Now the Princess jumped in. "And this church was built when St. Gertrude was founded."

I glanced up at the ceiling of the stone passageway. "So maybe Mr. Daunton built this secret passage. And when he decided to hide his stuff, he put it right here. Where nobody would find it."

Bogey grinned at us both. "That'd be my guess. This stuff probably hasn't seen daylight in almost a hundred and fifty years."

"Wow," the Princess and I both whispered.

It was kind of weird to think that we were the first ones looking at it, since the time when Mr. Daunton decided to hide it.

The Princess scooted closer to the chest and ran her paw over the jewels. They were so dazzling they were almost blinding. It reminded me of the day when Bogey and I saw the Daunton Exhibit at the Museum.

And suddenly the words of the Wise One came back to me.

Always look deeper.

So I did. I dug my big paw into the chest and through all those jewels and other stuff. Once I hit bottom, I kind of poked around a little. That's when I felt something wrapped up in cloth. I latched my claws onto it and pulled. It took me a few seconds to drag that object to the top. But sure enough, out came something about the same size as the Tobias statue we had at home.

Let me tell you, I already had a pretty good idea what was wrapped up in that cloth. My jaw practically fell to the stone floor.

The Princess gasped. "Is that what I think it is?"

Bogey grinned. "Yup, I'd say so."

Then together we unwrapped it just enough to make sure. And we were right. Under that cloth was the second missing statue.

The Tessa statue.

It was covered with lots and lots of little white diamonds. It had eyes made out of emeralds and a ruby for a nose. And I could tell the tail was curved so it would connect perfectly with the Tobias statue.

It was the other half of the Best Friends set.

Now the Princess laughed. "Danby Daunton had it all the time."

I just kept staring at that statue. "So he did hide it. That way the people who stole the Tobias statue couldn't steal Tessa, too."

Bogey nodded. "You got it, kid."

The Princess sighed. "Tessa has been without her best friend all these years."

All of a sudden, I really wanted to see the two jeweled cats together again. Just like Danby Daunton had wanted them to be.

Bogey seemed to be reading my mind. "A hundred and fifty years is too long for these best friends to be apart. What do you say we get them back together?"

I turned to my brother. "But how?"

Bogey tugged the cloth back around the statue. "At the end of the piano recital, kid. We'll get some of the humans back here and show them what we found. Then we'll show our Mom the Tobias statue when we get home. We've gotta get this stuff into the right hands."

I helped him pull the cloth tight, and we scooted the statue to the side of the chest.

"Before Delilah and Byron and Evaline and Murwood get their hands on it?" I asked him.

Bogey glanced at me. "That's right, kid. As well as the mastermind behind all the stuff that's been going on."

I sort of gasped. "Um . . . mastermind? What do you mean?"

Bogey put his paw on my shoulder. "Think about it, kid. You already started to put the pieces of this puzzle together. When you figured out the part about the alarm code."

I'm sure my eyes went extra wide right about then. "I did?"

Bogey nodded. "Yup, kid. You've almost got this case cracked."

"I do?" I choked out.

Bogey squinted his eyes and sniffed the air. "Something's fishy here, kid."

He tiptoed toward the back of the chest.

I pointed my ears in his direction. "Is it the mastermind?"

Bogey shook his head. "Nope, kid."

He leaned on his side and reached one of his long, slim arms behind the chest. The next thing I knew, he was pulling out a little burlap bag.

Now what had he found? More treasure?

Before I could say a word, Bogey used his sharp claws to tear open the bag. Out fell some really old feather cat toys and a few . . . really old cat treats?

They looked and smelled like hard little squares of fish. I could hardly believe my eyes. Or my nose, for that matter.

Bogey sniffed them over. "These seem to be okay, kid. Well preserved. Salt cured fish."

He passed one to me and the Princess before he took one for himself. The treats were a little hard and a little salty. But other than that, they tasted pretty good.

"This'll help you think, kid," he told me.

The Princess smiled at me. "You can do it, Buckley. I just know you can figure it out."

I was careful not to look into her beautiful green eyes. Because one thing I knew for sure — if I looked into her eyes, I wouldn't be able to think at all! So I just stared at the stone wall of the secret passage instead. Then I munched on the treat and tried to think as hard as I could. But no matter how hard I tried, the answers wouldn't come into my mind.

Thankfully, Bogey jumped in to help. "Remember the note from the sea captain's pocket, kid? It had the name of a store on it. We thought it was our Mom's store."

I nodded my head. "Uh-huh."

Bogey passed us all another treat. "Plus that paper had some numbers on it. And thanks to your good detective work, kid, we now believe those numbers were an alarm code. But if they were, they weren't even close to the numbers our Mom uses for her alarm code."

"Um, right. They weren't," I said before I ate my next treat.

Bogey finished his second treat. "So maybe the name and the alarm code weren't for our Mom's store, kid. Maybe they were for a different store. Don't forget, that paper had gotten wet. The ink ran and it smeared the writing."

I crinkled my forehead. "But why would someone have the name of a store and the alarm code on a paper? Our Mom never gives out her alarm code."

The Princess raised her paw. "I know this one, boys.

It's so someone can go into a store and drop off some things that were stolen. Without anyone ever seeing them. The person making the drop goes in late at night. The store owner usually hides a key outside for them somewhere. Then the delivery person uses the key, goes in, and turns off the alarm with the alarm code. They stash the stuff in the place where they were told. When they're done, they set the alarm again and leave. And they lock the door and replace the key on the way out. No one ever knows it happened. The store owner finds the stolen things the next day."

I turned and sort of stared at the Princess. Sometimes I forgot about the life she'd been forced to live before we rescued her. And right about then, I sure was glad we had rescued her.

But I had to say, the stuff she told us was really helping to solve this case!

I put my paw to my head. "So if the sea captain had that note, was he the one delivering something? To a store that sounds a lot like our Mom's store?"

Bogey grinned at me. "You got it, kid. I'd say someone made arrangements for the sea captain to deliver the Tobias statue. He's the one who hid it in our Mom's store."

Now I was the one nodding. "But that was the wrong store."

Bogey passed out another round of treats. "You nailed it, kid. Because he'd already been to the right store."

I blinked a couple of times. "The right store?"

"Yup, kid," Bogey said. "He'd already been to the store he was supposed to go to. The store that was really written down on that piece of paper."

I munched on my cat treat. "But the alarm code didn't work at the right store. Because the paper was wet and the numbers ran. And he got the wrong numbers."

Bogey nodded. "Exactly, kid. And because he didn't

have the right numbers for the code, the alarm went off. So that's when he locked the door and went to our Mom's store. He must have thought he'd just gotten the wrong store in the first place."

I shook my head. "But he didn't have a key for our Mom's store. So he had to break in. He probably looked for a key, but just thought he couldn't find it. Since it was so foggy that night."

"So he broke in instead, kid," Bogey went on. "And that set off the alarm. Then he punched in the numbers from the paper, trying to turn off the alarm. But it didn't work. By then he was probably so confused he didn't know what store he was supposed to be in. So he just stashed the package with the statue and ran."

I raised my paw. "Later, he figured out that he'd been to the wrong store. Especially when the person who was supposed to get the package didn't get it. And wanted to know where it was. So he showed up at our Mom's store first thing Monday morning. Looking for the package."

Bogey gave me a paw bump. "Bingo, kid."

Holy Catnip. This really was our most confusing case ever!

"Then what was the right store?" the Princess asked.

And that's when the answer practically hit me like a thunderbolt.

All of a sudden, I had a hard time speaking. I just sort of sputtered, "Uh, uh, uh . . ."

Bogey grinned at me. And I knew that he knew that I knew the answer. And I knew that he knew, too.

Finally, we both blurted out together, "Abascal's Antiquities!"

"The store owned by Abe Abascal," Bogey added.

"That means Abe . . ." I started to say.

And Bogey finished with, ". . . set it up to bring Tobias over from Istanbul."

I'm sure my eyes practically popped out of my head right about then. "So Abe is the mastermind. He's the one behind it all!"

Bogey nodded. "You got it, kid."

"Wow," the Princess kind of breathed. "So who does the Tobias statue really belong to now? Since it was stolen all those years ago?"

Bogey passed out the last of the treats. "Probably the Daunton family. But one thing's for sure, it doesn't belong to Abe. Or any of the rest of the crooks who've been after it."

I munched on my last cat treat and shook my head. I could hardly believe it. Abe Abascal. He'd been so nice to Bogey and me when we'd seen him at our Mom's store. And even after he'd found us at his store.

We were all silent for a few seconds, and that's when we heard piano music. It sounded like it was far, far away. Gracie would be playing her piano piece pretty soon. Hers was at the end of the show, and I wanted to be there when she played it.

But what would we do about the treasure?

I was about to say something to Bogey when we heard sort of a scuffling sound. It was coming from the entrance to the secret passage. We all turned to look. Just in time to hear a click and see a bright light shined right into our eyes.

"Well, hello there, kitties," a man said in a musical voice. "My, but I do like a good treasure hunt. And I can see that you do, too. Though I must say, for your part, it is rather a shame. Because this is one treasure hunt that will prove to be your undoing. Perhaps you've heard the expression, 'curiosity killed the cat?' If not, you'll soon find out what it means."

The man switched off his flashlight, and we could now see his face.

Abe Abascal.

The mastermind behind our most complicated case ever. Standing right in front of the entrance to the secret passage.

Suddenly my whole body started to shake.

Holy Catnip!

CHAPTER 23

Holy Mackerel! There we were. Face to face with the man behind all the shady dealings going on in St. Gertrude lately. And I had to say, I sure didn't like what he said about curiosity killing any cats. Then again, I didn't really like the way he was talking to us either. He sounded kind of nice, and at the same time, he sounded pretty scary.

Though to tell you the truth, I could barely hear him. That's because my heart was pounding really, really hard. And loud.

I gulped and glanced at my brother. I tried my best to figure out what he was thinking. Without moving his head, he looked up and down the secret passage. So I figured he probably wanted us cats to zoom out. Before Abe had a chance to catch us.

But if we did that, I knew Abe would take off with the treasure. And the Tessa statue. Then no one would ever know we'd found it, and it would probably disappear for good. I wasn't really crazy about that idea.

The Princess scooted over next to me. I could tell she was scared, too. She was shaking even more than I was.

But I didn't want the Princess to be scared. That's when I decided to try to be a little more brave. Like Bogey. So she wouldn't be so afraid.

A few inches away, Bogey sat up nice and tall. He stared at Abe beneath eyelids that were half-closed.

Abe took a few steps toward us. "I must offer you my thanks for finding this wonderful secret passage. You two black cats are quite the excellent detectives. Though I suspect very few humans are aware of your skills. I recognized them at once when I found you in my store. Of course, it was only one of many reasons why I've been keeping my eyes on you and your family. I trust you have the Tobias statue in your possession."

Bogey and I didn't even meow. Instead I took a deep breath and stared at Abe just like Bogey did. Then I secretly nudged the Princess a little with my back foot. Just to let her know it would be time to run pretty soon.

Abe moved ever closer. "Ah, yes, the strong silent types. I do love those who face the end with such courage. But who is the little white cat with you today? Another feline member of your family? I must say, it's a shame your family didn't eat the dinner I delivered the other night. Though I would suspect you boys had a paw in it. You probably wouldn't let your family go near the fish I had laced with sleeping pills."

Again, Bogey and I didn't say a thing. We just kept staring at him.

And he kept on talking. "I must say, I certainly didn't have any problem getting the sea captain to eat some similar fish. Those pills put him under for days. And it was a good thing, too. I could hardly have him running around telling everyone where he'd left the package he was supposed to deliver to me. No, I figured out where he'd left it. And I knew it most likely went home with you. I'll be retrieving it from your house later. Even if I have to drug your family correctly this time. Without you around, they won't have anyone to warn them."

Right about then, I quit being scared and just started being mad. I didn't like it when people tried to harm my family. Or even talked about it.

I slid my eyes over to get a peek at my brother. He nodded his head ever so slightly toward the door. That's when I knew he wanted us to run. So I put my paw around the Princess, ready to push her forward. Just as soon as Bogey gave the signal.

Abe took a few more steps toward us. I think it was the first time he got a really good look at the treasure.

He kind of gasped and hiccupped at the same time. "My, oh my, but what a fantastic treasure trove you've uncovered. Never have I seen so many jewels in one place. If I thought you'd go along with me, I'd employ you kitties in my criminal ventures. But alas, I fear you're what might be considered to be the 'good guys.'"

Boy, he sure had that right. We were the good guys! That's why his words were making me madder by the minute. I edged the Princess just a little farther forward. I could feel her resist when I pushed her. Sometimes when the Princess got really scared, she just sort of froze up.

Just like I used to do. Back when I was a new cat detective.

But I wasn't a new cat detective any more.

"Don't even imagine you'll survive your little adventure," Abe went on. "Because I certainly can't risk having you open up this secret passage again. And set someone on my trail. No, I'm afraid you cats won't come out of this one. I'll be locking you in here forever. No one will ever find you. Though I will see that a statue is made in your honor. I do like a good statue, and I'm sure you do, too!"

Then he laughed. A really loud, creepy kind of laugh.

Suddenly I realized just how chilly it was in that secret passage. Somewhere behind me, I heard a drop of water hit the stone floor. And that's when it dawned on me — if Abe locked us in here, we might never be found. Because we were the only ones who knew about this secret passage.

Abe leaned over to run his fingers through the jewels in the treasure chest. Just as he did, Bogey gave the signal.

It was time for us to zoom out of there!

Bogey and I leaped forward, and I pushed the Princess along with me. Once she got going, that cat was ready to run. We were halfway to the entrance when I thought we were home free. That was, until we smelled a smell that made Bogey and me freeze in our tracks. The Princess held back when we did.

To tell you the truth, we actually smelled two smells. But one was a lot stronger than the other. And that scent made shivers run up and down my spine.

It was perfume.

And it was coming from the woman now standing in the entrance to the secret passage.

Delilah.

Holy Catnip!

And parked right next to her was the sea captain. They both seemed like they were out of breath. Like they had been running or something.

"Well, well, well," Delilah drawled. "Isn't this just cozy? We've got Abe and the two cats I'm going to turn into a collar and a hat."

Now she spotted the Princess and pointed at her. "And oh, look. There's a third one. A little white one. She'll make a lovely pair of mittens."

Without thinking, I scooted right in front of the Princess. So Delilah couldn't get her. Out of the corner of my eye, I saw Bogey sizing up the opening to the secret passage. But I knew there wasn't enough room for the three of us to get out. Delilah and the sea captain blocked it pretty well.

"Arrr," the sea captain said. "Those are the kitties from that store. The one where I left my bundle. I'll bet they stole it."

Delilah and the sea captain started moving forward.

Bogey and the Princess and I started backing up.

Behind us, Abe sighed. "Hello, Delilah. I see you've turned up once again. While I generally do like a person who is as determined as yourself, I'm afraid in this case I simply find you annoying. Frankly, I've had head colds that were easier to shake than you are."

Delilah squinted her eyes at Abe. "Give me what is mine and I'll be out of your life forever. Then we'll all be happy."

Abe laughed. "What is yours? As I recall, I owe you nothing. Unlike your double-crossing companion beside you."

"Arrr," the sea captain hollered. "I got confused. That's all. 'Twas an easy thing to do."

"Zip it, Ralph," Delilah shouted.

I jumped and so did the Princess.

"Now, Abe," Delilah said sweetly again. "You know I was the one who found the Tobias statue in Istanbul. Hidden away in the far corner of that nobleman's home. I found it when I was having dinner with him one evening, after I had excused myself to powder my nose. Of course, I wasn't able to steal the statue that night. Though I most certainly stole some of his lesser jewels. In any case, you know I planned to steal that statue later."

Delilah and the sea captain inched closer, and us cats kept on scooting back.

Abe stood with his hands on his hips. "Ah, yes, dear lady. I fear your downfall is that you simply talk too much. You shouldn't have been bragging about it all over town. My people found out about it, and I arranged to have it stolen first. Then I had it shipped to St. Gertrude via our mutual friend here — Ralph the captain of the La Paloma."

Delilah smiled. "That may be, Abe, but I contacted Ralph shortly after he set sail. I convinced him to work with me instead. He was to meet me here in St. Gertrude at the Museum. He was supposed to give me the statue instead of dropping it off at your store. Our signal was a foghorn."

Abe snickered. "My, but you have a flair for the dramatic! There was never a foghorn. It was simply a recording on your cell phone. A good one at that. Not that it mattered. Because Ralph decided to stick with *our* original agreement. Unfortunately, when it came to the actual delivery, I fear Ralph failed miserably."

"Arrr," the sea captain said. "I couldn't get my land legs. Not in that blasted fog, I tell you. It was a wet one. It made the ink run on the note you gave me. I couldn't tell what store I was supposed to leave your package in. And I couldn't tell what numbers I was supposed to use."

Then Delilah did something that really scared me. She smacked the sea captain across the face.

"Stupid, stupid, stupid," she said. "You were supposed to meet me inside the Museum and bring me the statue. I thought you were there that night, so I tried to get in. I thought you had shut off the alarm, but when it went off, I knew you had double-crossed me. And I knew you had gone downtown to Abe's store instead. So I raced over there in that awful fog. But then I saw police cars at that other store, and I knew you had messed up your delivery. So I kept trying to find you, and I even looked for you at the Museum the next day. Thanks to you, I was blasting my foghorn sound everywhere."

"But you didn't need to do that," said a man's deep voice. "You knew I loved you, Delilah. I've always loved you. I was so close to getting that statue. And once I had it, I would have shared it with you. I knew you would have loved me then, too."

Now we all turned to see Byron Bygones standing at the entrance to the secret passage.

Delilah sneered. "Byron, you fool. You weren't even close to getting either of those statues. And besides, I could never love you. I only used you so I could steal more antiquities."

I glanced at my brother and the Princess. Not only
was this even more confusing than ever, but now I
wondered how we would ever escape. Bogey looked at
me and then nodded toward the entrance.

With the humans arguing away, us cats started to
slowly tiptoe out. We saw openings on either side of
Byron's legs. And we were pretty sure we had just
enough space to escape.

Bogey whispered to me, "On the count of three, kid.
You bring the Princess along like before."

I nodded back. Then I watched while he tapped his
paw on the floor once. Then twice. I put my arm
around the Princess, ready to get her moving. I was just
waiting for Bogey to tap on the floor one more time.

And that's when two more people showed up at the
entrance to the secret passage.

Evaline and Murwood.

Once again, we stopped in our tracks.

Holy Mackerel!

How many more people were going to show up? If
only the people from the recital would appear. Then we
would be saved.

Now Evaline started yelling at Byron. "That statue
belongs to me, Byron. Once you got it, you were
supposed to give it to me. You told me you would."

"Yeah," Murwood said. "And once she sold it, she
was going to split the money with me."

"I told you nothing, Evaline," Byron shouted. "You
made that up in your mind."

Then all the people started talking at once.
Suddenly I wished the walls weren't made of stone.
Otherwise, the people in the piano recital hall would
have heard all the noise. Then someone might have
come in and saved us.

Murwood and Evaline and Byron started walking
into the secret passage. And us cats scooted back
again. All the while, Bogey and I kept an eye out for an
opening between the people. Something big enough for

the three of us to zoom through and escape.

But no matter how hard we tried, we couldn't find an opening. We were boxed in.

Soon all the people noticed the treasure. Then they started arguing about who should get to keep what. Thankfully, no one noticed the Tessa statue that was wrapped up in the cloth. That's because it was next to the chest and sort of out of sight. But I figured the people would spot it any minute now, since I heard someone mention it. Seconds later, they all started arguing about it, too. And they accused each other of having it.

Strange, but I remembered what Bogey and I had talked about. How all these people knew each other and probably had been friends once. But when I looked at them now, they sure didn't act like friends. And just like the Wise One had told me, sometimes humans stop at nothing to own something. Things like the Tobias and Tessa statues. Even if it meant losing their friends. They just didn't understand what was really important.

But *I* knew what was important. Starting with the two other cats who were here with me now.

I only hoped the humans might be so busy arguing that they'd forget about us. But I couldn't have been more wrong about that.

Because Murwood raised his hand and asked, "By the way, who has the first statue? That Tobias statue."

Abe pointed to us. Then suddenly all the people went quiet and stared right at us.

"Those cats!" Delilah shouted. "Get them!"

And before we knew it, Delilah grabbed the Princess. Murwood grabbed Bogey and the sea captain grabbed me.

Well, let me tell you, if I thought I was scared before, it was nothing compared to how I felt right now. A cold chill passed over my whole body and my fur stood on end. I didn't know what they planned to do with us, but I didn't care to find out either. I tried to catch Bogey's eye, but he was busy trying to fight off Murwood.

That's when I decided to take things into my own paws. After all, I'd been a cat detective for a while now. And everyone kept telling me I was going to be a great cat detective someday. So maybe it was time I started to act like it. Maybe it was time for me to come up with a plan of my own. A plan to save us and keep the treasure out of the hands of these crooks.

I knew I needed to get the people from the recital back here. So they could rescue my friends. And in order to do that, I needed to get their attention. I needed to do exactly what Bogey and I had done when we were at our Mom's store. And when we were at the Museum.

I had to create a distraction. In fact, I had to create the biggest distraction a guy like me could create. I had to distract all the humans away from the piano recital and onto me.

In a split second, I figured out how to do just that.

Right then and there, it sure paid to be an extra big cat. And an extra strong cat. Especially when all that fear and anger seemed to make me even stronger than before.

I wrestled around in the sea captain's arms. Just enough to reach over and sink my teeth into his hand. I bit him so hard that he screamed louder than I've ever heard anyone scream. He dropped me, grabbed his hand and bent over.

The humans turned their eyes to him.

"Run, kid! Run!" Bogey shouted.

And I did just that. But first I grabbed the Tessa statue by the cloth that covered it. Then I picked that statue up and took off. As fast as I could go. I dodged around legs and between people. Carrying that heavy statue the whole way.

"What's that cat taking?" Delilah shouted.

"It's the other statue," Evaline said. "He's got the Tessa!"

"Get him!" yelled Murwood.

Now I heard the Princess' sweet voice.   "Hurry, Buckley! Save us!"

That was exactly what I intended to do. I didn't even look back. Instead I weaved around a few more legs and ran for all I was worth. I zoomed through the entrance of the secret passage. I turned right into the hallway of the church. And I just kept on going.

It took every bit of strength I had to run and carry that statue at the same time.

Behind me, I heard footsteps thumping on the floor and echoing in the hallway. I knew the people were trying to catch me.

But I had to make it into that recital without getting caught. The lives of my friends depended on it.

The only question was, could I do it, without those crooks catching me?

Holy Catnip!

CHAPTER 24

Holy Mackerel! I pushed my legs just as hard as I could and kept on running. The statue I was carrying felt like it weighed more and more and more. With every step I took.

It was strange, but I'd already run those hallways a few times before. And they didn't seem all that long to me then. And it didn't seem like it took much time to run them.

But now it was different. Now it seemed like those hallways were a million miles long. I wasn't sure they would ever end. Especially with all those people chasing me.

Right after I'd turned the corner out of the secret passage, I'd heard another person scream. I really, really hoped that scream came from Murwood. More than anything, I wanted to believe that Bogey had bitten him and gotten away, too. And I sure hoped he would be flying up to join me as I ran. Because right about now, teamwork sure would have been nice.

More than ever in the last week, I had learned just how important friends are. They made all the difference. And this was one time when having my best friend with me would have made a difference.   A really big difference.

I would have given anything to see Bogey grin at me. And to hear him say, "Don't sweat it, kid."

Because let me tell you, I was sweating it all right. A lot. I couldn't remember ever feeling so scared. And well, so tired. My legs were already getting worn out as I raced along. It wasn't easy carrying that statue, let alone running with it. Behind me, I could hear the shouts of the people chasing me. I didn't even look back to see how many were there. I was afraid it would slow me down.

And if I slowed down, I might get caught.

Now my legs started to ache. And for just a second, I thought about dropping the statue and running straight to our Mom and Dad.

But that wasn't part of the plan I came up with. If I dropped the statue, the crooks behind me would take it and disappear. They would take the treasure, too. And they would probably close up the secret passage so no one would ever know it was there.

Worst of all, who knew what they would do to the Princess? And Bogey, if they still had their hands on him? Plus, our Mom and Dad wouldn't know what was really going on. After all, we weren't supposed to even be here right now. Our Mom and Dad would never know the Princess and Bogey were with me. They would never know about the secret passage or how we'd been captured or anything.

Sure, I knew Gracie would tell them us cats had been in the truck when our family went to the recital. And people might even search for Bogey and the Princess. But they'd never let me go running around the church again. So I'd never be able to open up the secret passage. Not that my friends would be in there by then anyway.

After all, Delilah kept talking about turning them into things she could wear.

So my friends would probably never, ever be found. Not in time to save them.

And I wasn't about to let someone hurt Bogey and the Princess.

But there was only one way I could figure out to save them. I had to bring the Tessa statue to the recital and show it to the people. It would get their attention, and then they'd wonder where I got that statue. Then I could get them to follow me to the secret passage. To save my friends. Before it was too late.

That meant I couldn't stop running. And I couldn't get caught. I had to outrun all the crooks who were chasing me. No matter how tired my legs were getting. And no matter how heavy that statue felt.

I gritted my teeth even harder around the fabric covering the statue. And I pushed my legs to keep running, running, running. As fast as I could go.

More than anything, I wanted to stop and take a really nice deep breath.

But I tried not to think about it. Instead I tried to think about things that made me happy. My Mom and Dad. And Gracie. And my home. And my brother and the Princess.

All of a sudden, I got a sick feeling in my stomach when I thought about Delilah grabbing the little Princess. I remembered how Delilah had tried to hurt Bogey. Would she do the same thing to the Princess now?

I couldn't let that happen. I had to get the people from the recital back to the Princess. Before Delilah could hurt her.

So I kept on running. The people behind me sounded like they were getting closer. Or maybe I was just starting to slow down.

I crinkled my forehead and pushed myself even harder. By now the statue dangling from my mouth felt like it weighed a million pounds. When Mr. Daunton made the Tessa statue, he used the best stuff he could find. But he must have also used the heaviest stuff he could find.

Seconds later, I felt someone on my tail. Was this it? Had my plan failed? Would we be goners?

The next thing I knew, a black streak flew up and joined me.

It was my brother!

Just seeing him gave me an extra boost of energy.

"Good job, kid," Bogey said as he ran next to me. "This is one for the record books." He grinned at me like he always did.

I don't think I'd ever been so happy to see Bogey before in my life. Except for the day when I got adopted from the cat shelter. And I found out I was going to have a big brother.

There was so much I wanted to tell him, but I knew I couldn't. I didn't dare stop and put that statue down. I just had to keep running as hard and fast as I could.

Bogey glanced behind him. "Here's the situation, kid. We've got four behind us. Byron, Abe, Evaline, and Murwood. Murwood's pretty sore because I took a page out of your book. I bit down on him pretty good. That arm of his will probably never be the same. So he wants to pay me back as much as he wants the statue."

I nodded a little bit. Just to let Bogey know I understood.

"Byron is our big worry, kid," he went on. "He wants to get the statue to show off to Delilah. And Delilah, by the way, had a good hold on the Princess. I don't think the Princess will be getting away from her anytime soon."

I sure didn't like the sound of that!

Now Bogey kept pace with me as I ran. And let me tell you, it sure helped a lot. For some reason, I could focus on his running and not mine.

"I'm guessing you're going to drop that statue in the middle of the recital, kid," Bogey said. "It's a good plan and it might just work. As long as we can get the recital people to follow us back to the secret passage."

I sort of grunted through my teeth, to let him know I'd heard him.

"Okay, kid," Bogey said. "You just do your part and don't sweat it. I've got your back. Now it's time for me to run a little interference."

With those words, Bogey loped off to the side. That's when I saw Murwood jump ahead of me and try to grab me with his hands. Before he could get me, Bogey came flying through the air and landed on his back. He sunk his claws into Murwood's skin and Murwood threw his arms up and screamed. He fell to the floor on all fours.

I jumped around him and Bogey dropped down and ran beside me again.

Just as we turned the corner. I had one last hallway to run and then I was home free.

Up ahead, we saw Luke the church cat sitting with Henry and Annie. Luke's eyes went wide and so did Henry's. They probably didn't understand what was going on, but they sure knew Bogey and I were in trouble.

They dropped down from the bench they'd been sitting on. Ready to help us out.

Bogey hollered out to Luke. "You take the one on the left and get Henry to take the one beside him. I'll get the one on the right."

"Anything we can do to help," Luke meowed back.

He signaled to Henry and Henry nodded. Henry might not be able to hear, but he was as good a guy as you could ever find. And he picked up on what Luke was saying.

He charged like a tiger right past me. I glanced back to see him go straight for Evaline. When he was just a few feet away, he made a flying leap right at her head. He had his arms out and claws fully extended. Evaline screamed and skidded to a stop. She fell backwards and hit the floor. Henry landed on her stomach and knocked the wind out of her. She screamed and rolled over as Henry jumped away. He made a quick U-turn and loped on back.

By now I was starting to slow down. No matter how hard I tried to keep going, my legs started to wobble. They felt kind of rubbery, and they just wouldn't go where I wanted them to go.

But I pushed on through until I finally reached the bench where Annie was sitting. That's when it seemed like I couldn't take even one more step. In fact, I could barely stand up. I stopped beside the bench and put the statue on the floor. Then I stood there and gasped for air.

I turned back in time to see Bogey and Luke take on Abe. Abe tried to kick Bogey, and the second he lifted his leg, Luke bit the other leg from behind. Abe fell forward and Bogey jumped on his back. He sunk his claws into him as the man went down. Abe hit the floor. Hard.

Then Bogey, Luke and Henry all went after Byron.

Music from the piano recital floated out into the hallway. And I heard the song I knew by heart. Gracie's song.

That meant it was the end of the recital and it was her turn to play.

Above me on the bench, Annie said. "Here, Buckley. Take a drink of my water. That will help."

She pushed a little water dish my way. I jumped up on the bench and took a few slurps. Out of the corner of my eye, I saw my friends take down Byron. It took a little more to get him to the ground, but my three friends managed to get the job done. They gave each other paw bumps when they were finished.

"Thanks," I gasped to Annie.

"I wanted to help, too," she said.

Well, she had helped a bunch. Because that water was exactly what I needed. I was ready to roll again.

And not a moment too soon. Murwood was heading my way like an angry buffalo. And the other people were slowly getting to their feet, too.

So I jumped off the bench and picked up my statue.

Then I ran for all I was worth. Straight for the open door.

The other cats quickly caught up to me. Bogey ran beside me and Luke and Henry ran behind me. We zoomed as fast as we could go while the crooks now chased after us again. Together we all went barreling down that last hallway.

Gracie was still playing her music, and so far she'd been playing it perfectly. That was, until just a few seconds before we reached the doorway. Then she played a few wrong notes and stopped playing altogether. The crowd kind of gasped and I was afraid Gracie was going to start crying.

But maybe not after she saw what was headed her way.

Us cats were running so fast that we skidded around the corner and ran right into the room. Seconds later, the crooks ran in behind us.

"Go, kid, go!" Bogey hollered to me.

And I did just that. I ran like I've never run before. My paws barely touched the floor as I made a beeline for that little stage with the piano. I heard Gracie cry out as I leaped on the stage.

Then I turned around and dropped my statue on the floor. I held onto one edge of the cloth with my teeth and pushed the statue with one of my big paws. The statue started to roll, and kept going until it was completely out of the cloth.

That's when the overhead lights caught the diamonds on the statue and sent sparkles of light flashing all over the place.

Now the crowd really gasped.

Bogey and Luke and Henry ran to the edge the stage and moved over to the side. So everyone could see the statue.

The people chasing us stopped right in the middle of the aisle. Kind of like they just realized they had run smack dab into a crowd.

The people in the audience started murmuring and

talking and making more gasping noises.

Someone shouted, "What is that?"

And another person said, "Isn't that one of the missing Daunton statues? The Tessa statue?"

"It is!" someone else screamed. "That's the missing Tessa statue!"

I sat up nice and tall and showed my full size. Then I stared straight into the eyes of Abe Abascal.

Holy Catnip!

CHAPTER 25

Holy Mackerel!

I just stretched up even taller and straighter and kept on staring at Abe. I didn't even blink.

Neither did he. In fact, he and Murwood and Evaline and Byron stood frozen in place.

But the people in the audience were sure active and excited. Everyone was talking and some people stood up. Others pointed and murmured. Gracie wiped away her tears and she stared at me with wide eyes.

Officer Phoebe stood up from her seat close to the front. "That *is* the missing Tessa statue! Now *I'd* like to know why these people were chasing Buckley and the other cats. I don't like the looks of this."

She scooted out from her row and took three big steps toward the crooks.

All four of them took a few steps back.

"Not so fast," Officer Phoebe commanded them. "Stay right where you are. I'd like to know what's going on here."

That's when Abe pointed at Evaline. And Evaline pointed at Byron. And Bryon pointed at Murwood. And Murwood pointed at Abe.

Then every single one of them spoke at the same time. They all said, "He did it."

Except for Abe, who was pointing at Evaline. And he said, "Here's your culprit, Officer."

"Uh-huh," Officer Phoebe said. "I think you'd all better have a seat. Apart from each other. It looks like you've got some explaining to do."

She pointed to some chairs off to the side. All four of the crooks grumbled and did as they were told. Then Officer Phoebe used her radio mic on her shoulder and called for backup.

Right about then, I quit staring at them. It was time to save the Princess.

Bogey looked up at me. "Have you got this covered, kid? I'm gonna head to the church office with Luke. We've got an email we need to send."

And I knew exactly who he would be sending that email to.

I nodded. "I've got this."

Bogey took off with Luke. Then Pastor Tom stepped onto the stage. He carefully picked up the Tessa statue with his handkerchief.

I heard Gracie hollering to me. "Buckley! You came!"

And she was right. But now I needed her to come with me. Along with our Mom and our Dad and any other humans I could get.

So I ran over to Gracie. I jumped up on the piano bench beside her and gave her a kiss on the nose. She tried to give me a hug but I jumped back.

Her eyes went even wider. "Buckley, what's wrong?"

I grabbed her sleeve with my teeth and started to pull.

"Buckley," she kind of laughed. "What are you doing?"

Now I grabbed her bracelet in my teeth. This time I tugged so hard that I almost pulled her over.

"Buckley! Why are you acting like this?" Gracie

cried out.

Just like I'd hoped, our Mom and Dad joined us by the piano.

Gracie looked at our Mom. "What's wrong with Buckley?"

Our Mom shook her head. "I don't know. How did he even get here? How did Bogey get here?"

That's when Gracie sort of gulped. "Um, Mom. They came with us. But they're not the only ones. Lexie was with them."

Our Dad's eyebrows shot up. "They did? Then where is Lexie?"

I let go of Gracie's bracelet and latched onto my Dad's sleeve. Then I tugged as hard as I could.

"I think Buckley's trying to tell us something," our Mom said. "Lexie must be hurt. Or trapped."

Gracie jumped to her feet. "We've got to find her!"

I bounced down from the piano bench and ran to the edge of the stage. Then I turned my head and looked back at them. I let out a really loud and really long, "Meeee-oooow!"

Our Dad looked at our Mom. "Does Buckley want us to follow him?"

Our Mom nodded. "Looks like it to me."

Gracie was the first to run after me. "Take us to Lexie, Buckley. We've got to rescue her!"

Holy Catnip! She had that right! I only hoped we weren't too late. My heart was pounding like a big drum as I led my family out of the room and down the hallway. Another Mom and Dad joined us. Then some of the piano recital kids came along, too.

Before long, it seemed like I was sort of leading a parade. The hard part was, I was ready to run for all I was worth. But the people behind me were just walking fast and not running. And I didn't want to lose them. Especially when I turned into the secret passage.

The closer we got to that secret passage, the more chills raced up my spine. I started to wonder, was I too late? Would the Princess still be there when we got

there? Or had Delilah cat-napped her once and for all?
More than anything, I wanted to stare into those big,
beautiful green eyes again. Even if they did make me go
all goey inside.

I turned down another hallway and waited for all the
humans to catch up to me. Then I trotted along, hoping
I might get them to move a little faster. Finally, after
what felt like forever, I was just inches from the opening
to the secret passage. I stopped to let the humans catch
up again.

And, so I could listen for any sounds coming from
the secret passage. I wanted to hear the Princess meow,
to know she was okay. And, to know that she was still
there.

But instead, I heard Delilah and the sea captain.
Even though it wasn't the Princess, at least it meant
Delilah hadn't cat-napped her.

"I think I like this ruby the best, don't you, Ralph?"
Delilah drawled.

"Arrr . . . she's a beauty, all right," the sea captain
agreed.

"Well, you big, strong, handsome man," Delilah said
sweetly. "Why don't you just take this chest full of
treasure right out of here for me? Maybe we should get
going. Before the others get back."

"Anything for you, my lady," said the sea captain.

Right about then, our Mom and Gracie caught up to
me.

"How come you stopped, Buckley?" Gracie asked.

I rubbed Gracie around the legs, and then I led them
straight into that secret passage.

"Wow," our Mom said. "I didn't know this was here."

"Neither did I," our Dad agreed.

I zoomed on ahead as fast as I could. Right to where
Delilah was sitting on the floor in a pile of gems she'd
taken out of the treasure chest.

I instantly spotted her holding the Princess by the
back of the neck. The poor Princess looked absolutely

terrified and almost like she was going to faint. At least her eyes lit up the second she saw me.

But seeing Delilah hold the Princess like that made me so mad I could hardly stand it. I lunged right at Delilah, without even thinking.

That's when the sea captain saw me. He jumped up and tried to grab me. I ducked out of his way.

"Arrr," the sea captain said. "It's that cat that nearly took my hand off. He'll be a dead cat now!"

"Oooh, get him!" Delilah hollered. "That's the cat I'm going to turn into a hat. And I'm going to use this little white one for mittens. Especially since I don't think she'll make it through the day. This pathetic little creature is fading fast!"

She held her up and the Princess hung kind of limply.

Then suddenly everything went dead silent. Delilah and the sea captain stared up and froze. Delilah dropped the Princess and the Princess ran right to me. I put my arm around her and she tucked her head into my shoulder.

"I knew you'd come back for me, Buckley," she whimpered. "I just knew you would."

I looked up to see what had made Delilah and the sea captain freeze up like they did.

That's when I saw our Mom. And I have to say, I don't think I've ever seen her so mad. The only word I could use to describe her was "furious." Her dark eyes burned with anger and her jaw was clenched really tight. So were her fists.

Our Dad stood behind her. He looked really mad, too.

Right about then, I think our Mom could have taken on twenty Delilahs and come out on top.

She pointed to Delilah. "You again! You tried to hurt my cats once and now you've tried again. I will see to it that you go to jail."

Delilah and the sea captain scooted back and moved closer together.

"They're just a bunch of dumb cats," Delilah squeaked out.

"Nobody calls my cats dumb," our Mom yelled. "And nobody, but nobody, tries to hurt them and gets away with it."

Behind her, our Dad smiled.

Then our Mom pushed her arm out toward Delilah. I thought she might slap her. Delilah cringed and ducked.

"Let's see how you like the same treatment you gave little Lexie," our Mom said.

With those words, she grabbed Delilah and pulled her up by the back of her collar. She practically lifted her off the ground. Then she pretty much marched Delilah out of the secret passage.

"Please get Lexie and Buckley," our Mom said to Gracie.

Gracie smiled. "With pleasure!"

Our Dad grabbed the sea captain's arm and walked him out behind our Mom. Gracie leaned down, and the Princess and I climbed into her arms. We both wrapped our arms around Gracie's neck and tucked our heads under her chin.

Then we all went back to the recital room. I climbed down from Gracie's arms but the Princess stayed cuddled up. I figured she probably would for a while.

Our Dad looked at Officer Phoebe. "Here's a couple more for you. They were trying to harm Buckley and Lexie."

Officer Phoebe raised her cell phone. "I know all about it. I just got an email with the whole story and enough evidence to put this whole bunch behind bars. And this looks like Delilah Wunderfully. She's wanted in fourteen countries and fifteen states here. Looks like there's a lot of reward money attached to her."

"Good," our Mom said before she pushed Delilah into a chair. "That means she'll be going away for a long time. So who sent you the email? I'd like to thank them."

Officer Phoebe shook her head. "That's the strange thing. It was only signed with 'BBCDA.'"

Just then Bogey and Luke ran up to join me. Henry brought Annie in, too. We had paw bumps all around.

"BB . . ." our Dad started to say.

Then he and our Mom and Officer Phoebe looked at Bogey and me.

"Nooooo . . ." Officer Phoebe said.

"It couldn't be . . ." our Mom kind of murmured.

Our Dad smiled. "Oh, I don't know. This week I've seen fish fly off the counter, 'Take Your Cat to the Museum Day,' and Buckley uncover a priceless missing statue. So, right about now, I think just about *anything* is possible."

Seconds later, Officer Phoebe and the other police officers had carted the crooks away. The rest of the people were all laughing and talking loudly.

Then Gracie's piano teacher, Ms. Knotes, clapped her hands. "Excuse me, everyone! But we have one student who didn't get to finish playing her song. If everyone would please take your seats, Gracie can now play "Rondo Espressivo." Are you ready, Gracie?"

Gracie tried to smile, but I could tell she was nervous all over again. While she passed the Princess to our Mom, Bogey and I made a beeline for the piano. I jumped on the seat and Bogey jumped on the ledge above the keys. Then he reached his paw over and hit a few keys.

The whole audience laughed and Gracie giggled, too. She walked back up to the stage and sat down.

That's when I gave her a big kiss on the nose.

Now she really giggled. Then she started to play.

Perfectly. Right there in that hall, her song sounded the prettiest I had ever heard it. I just closed my eyes and purred and floated away.

When she hit the last note, I reached up and gave her another kiss on the nose.

She hugged me tight. "I love you, Buckley and

Bogey. I am so glad you were here. I couldn't have done it without you."

Boy, I sure knew that feeling. I couldn't have done anything without all my friends either.

I gave her another kiss to let her know that I loved her, too.

That's when Bogey reached down and added one more note to the song.

First the whole audience laughed. And then they started to clap so loud it almost made my ears hurt. Everyone stood up and clapped and cheered and clapped some more.

Gracie giggled and went to stand at the front of the stage. She bowed a couple of times and people clapped even harder.

Bogey and I went to stand beside her, and I'm not sure, but I think they clapped for us, too.

Holy Mackerel!

CHAPTER 26

Holy Catnip!

Right after the recital, lots of people wanted to chat with our Mom and Dad. And everyone wanted to congratulate Gracie. Finally, we were just about ready to go when Pastor Tom showed up with a piece of paper in his hands.

He spoke directly to our Mom and Dad. "Well, good news. Luke, our church cat, just brought this paper to me. It looks like Henry and Annie have been adopted. Though I don't remember getting a phone call or anything on this. Anyway, it says you'll be dropping them off at their new homes. Do you mind? I'm not sure where this paper came from. And I wasn't sure if you even knew about this."

Our Dad rolled his eyes and dropped his head into his hands.

And our Mom just laughed. "We seem to get a lot of these mysterious notes around our house. But yes, we'd be happy to take them with us. Just give us the addresses where they are supposed to go."

Pastor Tom handed them the paper he was holding.

A few minutes later, we were all loaded up in our

Dad's truck. Us cats were all in the back with Gracie. Bogey and Henry were on the floor, and the Princess and Annie sat on the seat. I sat on the backseat, too, right next to Gracie. I stayed next to her until she fell asleep. That was a few seconds after our Dad drove out of the parking lot. Then I jumped down with the boys.

But at least Gracie had fallen asleep with a smile on her face. I was so proud of her for playing her song so well. It was a lot of hard work for her. But our Mom was right. All that practice had paid off!

I glanced at my friends. I could tell Annie and Henry were a little nervous. The Princess put her paw over Annie's.

"Are you sure they're going to want me?" Annie sighed. "I guess I'm not like other cats."

The Princess patted her paw. "I know they want you. Very, very much. And no cat is like another cat. We're all different and special and wonderful in our own ways."

That made me smile. If there was anyone who knew something about being wonderful, it was the Princess. She was as wonderful as they got. And I thought she was especially wonderful for saying what she did to Annie. After all, that little Princess had been facing death right in the face just a little while ago. She'd been scared out of her wits.

Now here she was, thinking of someone else who might be scared instead.

A few minutes later, we pulled up to Amelia's house.

"Annie, are you ready to go?" our Mom said gently. "This is your new home."

She reached back and picked up that fuzzy little tan kitten.

"Good luck," we all said to Annie. "We'll bump into you again!"

"Goodbye," Annie said with a shaky voice.

I could tell she was pretty nervous. But our Mom cuddled her close and Annie started to purr.

Bogey and I jumped up to the window to get a good view. We watched closely as our Mom took Annie up the front steps.

Amelia and her Mom both answered the door. Our Mom and Amelia's Mom chatted for a moment. And I heard Amelia's Mom say, "I figured we'd be getting Annie. Amelia loved her so much when she met her. And Amelia's tired of being an only cat."

The next thing I knew, Amelia was standing in the doorway, and cuddling right up to Annie. Annie looked happier than I've ever seen her. Amelia gave her new sister a hug and took her inside the house.

Beside me, I noticed Bogey had gone all goo-goo eyed.

"Dames," I murmured to him.

"Dames, kid," he said. "And that dame is one in a million."

I glanced down at Henry and he crinkled his brow. I could tell he was wondering what was wrong with Bogey. So I just put my paw to my chest and bounced it a few times.

Henry grinned.

Our Dad drove us away from Amelia's house, and I went in search of the bag of cat treats Bogey had stashed under the seat. I passed treats to Henry and the Princess. After that, I gave one to Bogey.

"Here you go," I told him. "This'll get you going."

And it did. Bogey seemed to recover and he joined us again.

"Thanks, kid," he said. "I needed that."

Now he passed me a treat. Just as we pulled up in Hector's driveway.

Bogey and I used our paws to talk to Henry. We explained the situation to him. And we showed him that we lived practically right across the street. He nodded and grinned really big.

That's when I noticed something. Something was different when I used my paws to talk to Henry. For once my huge paws went exactly where I wanted them to go!

Now I smiled, too. It was pretty nice to have my paws working the way I wanted them to. Could it be I was growing into them a little?

I passed us all another round of treats before Henry had to go.

Our Mom leaned back and petted Henry on the head. He smiled up at her. Then she picked him up, all ready for delivery.

We waved goodbye to Henry and let him know we'd see him later. Then we stood at the window and watched when Hector's Mom came to the door. Hector walked out to the front porch. As usual, he talked and talked and talked and talked. And talked some more. I wasn't even close to him and I was about to go crazy from all his talking.

Our Mom put Henry down with Hector. Henry just smiled up at him.

Hector's Mom sounded a little confused at first. But then our Mom seemed to explain things to her.

All the while, Hector kept on gabbing away to Henry. Then he made a few motions with his paws. That's when Henry nodded and made some motions back. Now Hector smiled and gave his new brother a paw bump.

I crinkled my brow at my own brother. "Do you think that's going to work? Henry can't hear a word Hector is saying."

Bogey grinned. "I know it, kid. That's the beauty of it. He's the only cat alive who could stand to be around Hector all the time."

I tilted my head and watched Henry as he smiled up again at his new big brother. "And they sure seem to like each other. Henry needs a home, and Hector . . . well, he's probably kind of a lonely guy. So he needs a brother."

Bogey nodded. "Yup, kid. It's perfect. I think it's the beginning of a beautiful friendship."

A few minutes later, we finally got home. We had a

special dinner that night, to celebrate everything that had happened. Us cats got tuna fish and our humans had fried chicken. While they ate, Bogey and the Princess and I told Lil the whole story. She laughed and shook her head and seemed to enjoy it all.

Later that night, after Gracie had gone to bed, we led our Mom and Dad to the sunroom. The Wise One sat like a queen on her purple couch. Bogey and I helped her down, and we let her do the honors. She watched over everything as Lil and the Princess managed to open the false bottom in the closet. Then Bogey and I pulled the cloth away from what we had hidden there.

As soon as we did, the Tobias statue sparkled up at us. It was so pretty it even made me feel dazzled for a few seconds.

Holy Mackerel!

Our Mom gasped and our Dad just shook his head.

"How did that get there?" our Dad laughed.

Our Mom picked up the statue and stared at it with wide eyes. "I don't know. I didn't even know this closet had a false bottom. But this house is around a hundred years old. Someone must have hidden it there long before we bought the house."

"And it's just been sitting there. All those years," our Dad murmured.

But us cats looked at each other and smiled. Little did he know, that Tobias statue had been traveling for a long, long time.

Maybe even as much as the Wise One had traveled.

But soon that Tobias statue would be going home. And joined up with his best friend, the Tessa statue.

Our Mom was still staring at it. "I wonder if we have any false bottoms in any other closets. Or a secret passage like the church. And I still wonder who found that secret passage. Was it the crooks?"

Our Dad put his arm around our Mom. "I don't know. But maybe we could hold off on looking for any more secret places and hidden treasure and things.

Just for a week or two. I wouldn't mind if things got back to normal for a while."

Boy, he sure could say that again.

And he did, when we were all back at the Museum a week later. That's when Mr. Daunton's great-great-great-granddaughter, Vera Glitter, held a special banquet in our honor. She wanted to thank all of us cats for finding the Best Friends statues again.

And let me tell you, it was funny how it all worked out. It turned out the Tobias statue legally belonged to her. And so did the Tessa statue. But the treasure chest and all the treasure ended up belonging to the church. Don't ask me how. All that legal mumbo jumbo was way too complicated for me.

But our Mom got the reward money for capturing Delilah. And she and our Dad put it away for Gracie's college fund.

When Gracie found out, she picked me up and started spinning. Around and around and around we went! I just wrapped my arms around her neck and hung on for dear life. Somewhere in there she announced she was going to be a veterinarian. And while I wasn't exactly crazy about ever going to the vet's office, I knew Gracie would make a good one.

If she ever outgrew her spinning phase.

Anyway, Vera was really happy to see her great-great-great-grandfather's favorite statues on display. And the church was sure happy, since they needed some money for repairs. Especially since the place was so old. Plus, they decided to build a shelter for homeless cats. To give them a place to live and help them find homes.

They decided to call it the Buckley and Bogey Cat Care Center. Luke was going to be the cat in charge. Though, of course, there would be some humans running the place, too.

Now I glanced over at my brother as we both sat at the cat table in the middle of the Museum banquet hall.

We were wearing red satin bow ties that Gracie had made for us. Just for this special occasion. And I had to say, we looked pretty handsome. Gracie had on a matching red satin dress. And she was sitting at another table with our Mom and Dad and Hector's Mom and Dad. Amelia's Mom and Dad were there, too.

The Princess sat beside me, wearing the diamond collar she had from her life before she'd joined us. Amelia sat beside Bogey, and then Lil sat beside her. I was so happy that the Wise One had even decided to come with us. Though our Mom and Dad had a nice cat bed all ready for her, just in case she got a little tired. All the rest of our friends made it, too. Luke, Annie, Hector, and Henry.

I sure had to say, Henry had been a really good influence on Hector. Because now Hector talked to his brother with his paws, instead of out loud all the time. It sure made things a lot quieter for the rest of us.

But last to join the party was Ranger. He strolled into the room with his Mom and Dad. Ranger had his tail held high and a big grin on his face.

"Hi, everyone! So great to be here," he said with a wave as he found his place at our table.

"Congratulations," the Princess said to him. "We're so happy to hear your Mom is going to be the new curator here at the Museum."

Ranger couldn't stop grinning. "Thanks. Me, too. Now I'll be working here every day. It'll be one of the best adventures of my life. And you can count on more 'Take Your Cat to the Museum Days.' Though I've been told the Dinosaur Hall will be off-limits to us cats."

Well, let me tell you, that was just fine by me. Even though I knew those dinosaurs were only skeletons, I still didn't like to think about them. As far as I was concerned, dinosaurs were scary things, and I'd had enough scary things for a while.

"Not a problem," Bogey said to Ranger as he gave him a paw bump. "We'll be happy to see the Daunton Exhibit whenever we want."

Then we all talked more about visiting the Museum. And I have to say, it turned into quite a party. The cats and the humans all talked and laughed a bunch.

Finally, the dinner was served.

Bogey took a sniff at his plate.

"Something's fishy here, kid," he told me.

I rolled my eyes.

Holy Catnip! Not again. Now what was going on? Then I looked my own plate. "Is it the fish?"

He grinned at me. "Yup, kid. You got it."

We both laughed and gave each other paw bumps.

Later, after dinner, we strolled around and enjoyed all the beautiful Daunton statues. Our Mom carried Miss Mokie so she could see them, too. The Wise One nodded and smiled with each statue she saw.

"Lovely," she meowed to us. "Simply lovely. This is such a treat, young Detectives. I've seen many a wondrous sight in my day, but this is one of the most beautiful."

"Glad you're enjoying it, Miss Mokie," I meowed back.

The Wise One had helped us out so many times. Now it made me feel good to see her happy, too.

Of course, we all paused at the Best Friends display. At long last, the Tessa and Tobias statues were together again. Right where they belonged. The curved tails made the statues fit together perfectly.

That's when I smiled like never before.

Seeing those two statues united made me feel really happy inside. Sure, they were sparkly and shiny and beautiful. But they were about so much more. They were about friendship. And in the end, that was what really mattered. Friendship was the real treasure. Especially best friends. Without friends, we'd never really be happy.

And speaking of best friends, mine jumped up onto the little counter beside me. "I gotta hand it to you, kid. You did a great job on this case. It's nice to see those two statues back together again."

I nodded. "They sure are pretty."

He grinned back at me. "Yup, kid. Like the man said, 'they're the stuff that dreams are made of.'"

I tilted my ears toward my brother. "They're what? What man?"

But Bogey didn't answer. Instead he just kept on grinning and jumped down.

I followed him and leaped down, too. That's when the Princess spotted me and ran right over. She looked up at me with her big, green eyes. My heart started doing that funny, jumpy thing that it always did whenever she looked at me like that.

She moved a little closer. "I wanted to thank you, Buckley, for saving me. You were so smart. And so brave."

Then she reached up and gave me a kiss on the nose.

Right about then, the room started to spin and I flopped over onto the floor. I could barely see her scamper off. Bogey came to stand beside me.

He waved a fish-flavored cat treat in front of my nose. "Here you go, kid. This'll get you going."

I took the treat and munched away.

He helped himself to one from a foil pouch. Then he stashed the bag behind the display case.

"Dames," he murmured.

"Dames," I repeated.

He nodded toward a small group of people. "Better pull yourself together, kid. I just overheard some people talking. Looks like we might have another case for the Buckley and Bogey Cat Detective Agency."

"Another one?" I kind of gasped.

Bogey grinned at me. "Yup, you got it, kid."

Holy Catnip!

THE END

About the Author

Cindy Vincent was born in Calgary, Alberta, Canada, and has lived all around the US and Canada. She is the creator of the Mysteries by Vincent murder mystery party games and the Daisy Diamond Detective Series games for girls. She is also the award-winning author of the Buckley and Bogey Cat Detective Caper books, and the Daisy Diamond Detective book series. She lives with her husband and an assortment of fantastic felines.